THE WITCH HUNTER

THE WITCH HUNTER SAGA - BOOK ONE

NICOLE R. TAYLOR

The Witch Hunter (Book One in The Witch Hunter Saga)

Copyright © 2013-20 by Nicole R. Taylor

Newly revised and edited - November 2020.

First Published March 20th, 2013.

This book is written in British/AU English.

www.nicolertaylorwrites.com

Cover Design: MoorBooks Design

Edited by: Silvia Curry

CHAPTER 1

Zac was twenty-three when he died. Problem was, he didn't stay that way.

He was a captain in the Confederate army until a Union soldier shot him. Captain Zachary Degaud. That was one hundred and forty-seven years ago, in 1865, circa the American Civil War. It was cold comfort the fight had ended shortly thereafter.

Actually, it was like a punch in the face.

Today was his one-hundred and seventieth birthday and he sat at the bar, in a dive posing as a respectable restaurant, in the small southern town of Ashburton, Louisiana—the hole in the swamp where he was born a puny human being.

But at least the sun wasn't burning him alive, the liquor was flowing, and he was undead. Zac Degaud was just another binge drinking vampire with an unremarkable story, languishing in the midst of the murky swampland of the South. Edward, Louis,

Armand, Lestat... if these vampires existed, he hadn't met them.

"Happy birthday, brother." A man slapped him on the shoulder and sat on the neighbouring stool.

Zac's younger brother Sam was just as dead as he was. Stuck together for eternity.

They were both dark-haired and green-eyed, but Zac took after their mother. He was tall and wiry, while Sam was shorter by a head and heavily built like their father. Their parents had died shortly after the Civil War had ended, and neither talked about that time anymore. It didn't do well to dwell on things they couldn't change.

"How does it feel to be a year older, old man?" Sam joked.

"I don't feel a day over twenty-three." He rolled his eyes. Like time mattered anymore.

They drank a few rounds before Sam stood and said, "That's my lunch break done. Gotta go back to the grind."

"I'll never understand why you got a job. It's not like we need the money." Their family had been extremely well off, owning a large plantation before they'd died. One-hundred and forty-seven years of interest made them wealthy vampires.

"No, but you know it helps with the whole human thing," Sam whispered in his ear, conscious of the busy restaurant around them.

"Assimilation." Zac rolled his eyes. *Yeah, assimilating as a gardener.*

"You got it, brother."

The bothers had returned to the town they had grown up in just over a year ago. Their nomadic life had done nothing but serve as a constant reminder of what they'd become. It had done Sam good blending in with the humans and reconnecting with his old human life, but for Zac, it wasn't quite the same. Something was still missing, though he could never work out what. He ended up spending more time in the local bar than anywhere else. The alcohol helped curb the cravings typical for a creature who fed on human blood.

Sam lingered. "You'll be okay?"

"As long as I've got my dear old friend scotch whisky, I'll be just fine."

"Okay, well, just make sure you pay your tab this time."

"I've got a down payment all ready," he muttered, slapping a fifty-dollar bill down on the bar. "Don't let the sun bite, Samuel."

The sun hadn't been a problem ever since they'd found a bruja in the south of Mexico willing to help them with a little anti-uv spell...in exchange for a grisly favour, of course.

Looking over his shoulder as Sam left, he caught sight of Liz embracing his brother outside.

Liz was tall and lithe with long, golden blonde hair

and blue eyes. All American. Twenty-one years old and almost a year since she had died. Sam had found her dead in the forest...until she'd woken up.

She kissed Sam on the lips and lifted her pale hand, smoothing her fingers through his hair. They looked perfect together, which felt like pouring salt on the open wound that was Zac's entire vampire life.

Zac couldn't tear his eyes from her. He and Sam had fought the way only brothers could over a pretty girl while she was still human. When she became... Well, now it was different. She was his brother's girl, but it didn't stop the fact that he cared for her more than he ought to.

Zac's line of sight was broken as a dark figure passed in front of him. Shaking his head, he turned back to his drink, aware of an ominous shadow that loomed as if waiting for him to acknowledge its presence. Zac knew a man stood there, and he knew he was a vampire—they both did.

The stranger sat beside him, his black leather jacket creaking as he leaned forward. He rested his elbows on the bar and waited.

Zac didn't look at him straight away; instead, he downed the last of his glass of scotch before sliding the empty glass toward the bartender, who caught it and began to refill the contents. He knew all too well that Zac wanted another. His reputation, and his down payment, proceeded him.

Finally turning, he nonchalantly looked at the stranger and made his assessment.

On first glance, the man was a typical vampire. He had a similar stature to Zac and a grace in his actions that betrayed what he was. There was a hardness in his eyes that suggested he'd seen more than his years, exaggerated by the sharpness of his close-cropped blond hair. With his black clothing and leather jacket, he looked out of place with the typical lunch crowd. That, and it was a humid cesspool outside.

"What do you want?" Zac asked with a sigh. In his short stint as one of the undead, he knew vampires didn't bother to speak to one another unless they wanted something, and that something was often bad news.

"I'm looking for a woman vampire. Black of hair, blue of eye," the stranger said like he was from another time.

Zac snorted, stifling a laugh. "Are you serious? Are we at a renaissance fair? Shakespeare's Globe?"

The stranger didn't blink. "I am deadly serious."

"Look buddy, if you want to blend in, maybe you should change up your language a little. Get with the times and all."

The vampire's eyebrows rose. "And who are you to speak to your elders in this way?"

He was old then. Ancient, maybe. Zac could never tell exactly how many years they had on him until they were trying to beat the crap out of him. The older vampire, the stronger they became, but that didn't mean they got any smarter.

"I'm the one who has claimed this town," he said with a sneer.

The vampire looked him up and down like he didn't believe a word he was saying. "Then you will be able to answer my question. It would be better if you do, then we could avoid any trouble."

Zac knew a threat when he heard one—he'd given them out often enough. "Tell me who you are, and I'll think about it."

The vampire laughed. "Either you're idiotic or very brave. I am Alistair Payne, and who are you?"

"Zachary Degaud, vampire extraordinaire." He inclined his head.

"And the answer to my question, Zachary? Have you seen this woman? It would be unadvisable to withhold her whereabouts."

"I'm the only vampire in these parts, so your answer would be no," he said with a shrug. "Did your girlfriend hurt your big bad vampire feelings?"

"Oh, come now, Zachary. I saw two outside not a moment ago. Do you really think I'm that stupid? She's wanted for crimes against her own kind."

He couldn't help it. "What are you, the vampire police?"

"Keep prodding, vampire, and we will see how stupid you truly are."

Zac had no idea who this woman was and didn't

really care. There were no other vampires in this town. "I have no idea who this woman is. She's not here, unless she's turned up in the past day and even then, *I haven't seen anyone.*"

Alistair stared at him as if he were trying to gauge the truth in his words.

Zac didn't dare look away from the vampire's hard gaze. Even though he was telling the truth, it would be taken as an admission of guilt if he backed down. Except, he couldn't help himself and turned back to his drink a little too soon. Rattling cages ought to be in his job description.

Alistair's lips curved into a malicious smile. "One thing I have plenty of, is time. I'll be seeing you again, Zachary Degaud. And it will be sooner than you think."

Zac watched Alistair's receding form and grimaced. He was in trouble...*again.*

"Game on," he muttered, turning back to his scotch. *Better get out another fifty.*

Afternoon light filtered through the tops of the tall, moss-ensnarled trees as Liz made her way through the forest bordering Ashburton.

She'd grown up here, spending her entire human life exploring the streets, woods, and bayou. *Human life...*it was still an alien description to her.

Sam had found her not far from here the day she'd died. They'd been friends for months before, but it wasn't until she'd woken up that she found out that Sam and his brother Zac were vampires and that she was becoming one, too.

She never knew who'd turned her and left her for dead. It wasn't like they hadn't tried to find out, but they never had found any insight.

Liz never doubted the brothers when they swore they had nothing to do with it. They had a friendly rivalry over her when they had first moved to town, but they'd never take it that far. Especially since they'd both been turned against their will, too.

Liz stood in the dappled sunlight. She smiled when she saw Sam's dark form flash through the trees. He was fast, and before she could dodge him, he grabbed her around the waist and swung her around, laughing.

"Hello, beautiful." He grinned, kissing her lightly on the mouth. "Are you ready?"

She ran her tongue over her bottom lip, tasting him. "Uh-huh. Let's go."

Despite her last human memories, the forest was their special place. They'd spent hours hunting together; Sam teaching her how to use her vampire strength to her advantage. They only fed on the blood of animals, both in agreement that they didn't like being predators. There were other ways to survive.

Besides, human blood messed with their attempts to remain a peaceful part of society.

Zac didn't agree with their choice and left them to wander the forest eating 'baby bunnies and fluffy kittens', but Zac was the one who'd taught her control when it came to being around humans—something that was much more difficult than she'd thought it would be.

Catching the scent of deer, Liz tapped Sam on the arm, motioning to her right. He nodded and darted off silently to circle around, leaving her to stalk them head on. Just as he'd taught her.

She crouched behind a tall cypress, watching the deer. She stilled herself completely, slowing her breathing and becoming frozen. The deer's head lifted; its nose twitched as it caught a scent on the air. If it bolted, she'd be too quick for it to shake.

Before she could pounce, she was pushed roughly against the tree, the bark grazing the skin of her cheek.

The deer bounded away, startled by the sudden laughter behind her.

Liz was pulled to her feet and shoved back against the trunk of the cypress, and she cursed. She'd been too fixated on the deer to notice anyone approach.

A group of five men stood around her in a semi-circle, eyeing her in a way that made her feel dirty. They could only be described as rednecks—unkempt beards, dirty jeans, and plaid shirts—except they had more muscle than anyone had a right to. Catching their scent on the air, she recognised the rank odour of werewolves.

Liz had only encountered the local pack once, not long after she'd turned. They'd harassed her at work, calling her names that any woman would find offensive. She wasn't a piece of meat and told them as much, but now she was afraid. There were five of them and she knew she couldn't hold her own against that many. She prayed that Sam hadn't gone too far and had heard them yelling.

"Well, looky here, boys. A little vampire chasing deer in our forest," the largest man drawled. "It's a true shame that she be one of them blood-sucking leeches. She's a looker." He raked his gaze over her and sucked his teeth. "Yeah, a real looker."

He walked toward Liz, gracing her with a waft of alcohol and sweat, but stopped in his tracks as Sam appeared. His approach had been so silent, not even the wolves noticed until he was there.

Liz sank back against the tree, not knowing how to defuse the situation. She might be a vampire, but she was still only twenty-one...and with the life experience to prove it.

Sam stood eye to eye with the hulking man, who seemed to be the alpha, his expression cold. Neither moved nor backed down.

Finally, the alpha laughed. "You're bold for a vamper. Be warned. If you come back onto our land, you and your little girlfriend will pay." He spat on the ground by Sam's feet and backed away, his wolves following. "This is your final warning, *leech*."

Their hooting and hollering grew fainter as they worked their way back through the forest.

It wasn't until they were far enough away that Sam turned and took her in his arms. "Are you okay? Did they hurt you?"

"No," she said, grasping him tight. "They just scared me, is all." The slight scratch from the tree had already healed itself.

He ran a hand through her hair. "Good."

Drawing back, Liz rested her forehead against Sam's. "I have to warn Gabby. Did you smell them? They were on a tear. If they're going to town, they might try something."

"Moonshine," Sam grimaced. "The wolf kind." It was so potent, not even Zac dared drink the stuff.

Liz took out her cell and dialled. Gabby was one of her oldest and best friends, and one of the three people who knew she was more than human. If she didn't warn her before she crossed paths with the wolves, she'd never forgive herself.

But if Liz knew Gabby, if it came to it, she'd more than give those dogs what they deserved.

Gabby sat at her desk at the *Ashburton Real Estate* office, tapping her pen against the tabletop, eyes focused on a faraway point across the room.

The buzz of her cell phone snapped her out of

her daydream, and she glanced around. When she was sure no one had noticed her slacking off, she sighed in relief. Luckily, her boss's office door was closed.

Picking up her cell, she saw it was her best friend Liz and picked up on the third ring, ducking behind the partition around her desk for good measure.

"Gabby, I need to warn you," Liz's panicked voice rushed out without greeting. "The werewolf pack is causing trouble again. I think they're headed for town."

"Are you okay?" she asked quietly, trying not to draw attention to herself.

"They just harassed us a little. Sam scared them off, but just be careful, okay?"

"Sure, Liz. I'll be on the lookout."

"Okay. I'm going home, but the boys will be at the bar later."

"Sure. Do you want me to come over?"

"No, it's fine. I just don't want to run into them, not today."

"Okay. Well, take care. Call me if you need anything."

Gabby put her cell back in her pocket and tucked her unruly brown hair behind her ear.

As if werewolves and vampires weren't enough, Gabby Cohen was a witch.

Liz and the brothers were the only ones who knew her secret, and she liked it that way. If anyone ever found out, she'd probably become a science experiment in a military installation in Nevada. At least, that's how it went in the movies, anyway.

As far as she knew, out of all her family, only her grandmother seemed to have had magic. Too bad she'd disappeared years ago after her husband tried to have her committed—all the more reason for Gabby to keep her uniqueness under wraps.

Soon after she'd stumbled upon her witch heritage, Gabby had found her grimoire, a book of spells and incantations, amongst some of Grams' things in the attic. It was only then that she began to understand her affinity with magic.

She started visiting the cemetery near the old Degaud Manor, conducting her 'experiments', trying different spells and rituals that were written in the grimoire. Silly things like lighting candles, making things levitate, and communing with the earth. The last was her favourite.

Every witch had an earth sense of varying strengths. She didn't quite understand what it meant, but when she concentrated, she could feel living things around her—plants, trees, insects...even the stars if she focused hard enough.

That's why she was surprised when she'd first met the brothers.

She was sitting cross-legged in the old cemetery early last winter, feeling the shift of the seasons in the surrounding plants, when she began to feel uneasy. She understood later that it was her latent power warning her that she was being watched. When she opened her eyes, a man was standing in front of her.

For a moment, she almost believed he was a statue until he grinned at her.

"Well, well, well..." he said. "What do we have here?"

Gabby panicked. She hadn't sensed the man at all, and she could always feel people when she had her earth sense focused. That would mean that the man was... dead? That couldn't be right. She scrambled to her feet and took a few steps back.

"Leave her alone, Zac." Another man appeared out of thin air to stand beside the first.

The first man, Zac, rolled his eyes. "I wasn't going to eat her, brother, if that's what you're thinking. I don't want her to point her witchy juju at me."

"Y-you're both d-dead," she stammered.

"As a doornail," Zac said with a lopsided grin.

"Forgive my brother," the other man said, stepping forward. "I think you know what we are. We can't hide from you, but we mean you no harm."

"Vampires," Gabby said, finally realising. The only undead creature that she was aware existed.

Zac started clapping. "Ten points to Glinda."

"Glinda?"

"From *The Wizard of OZ*," he replied. "I'm trying to be *nice*, but it gives me heartburn."

"Ignore him," the other man said. "I'm Sam. The moron is my brother, Zac."

Zac smirked. "Stupid is as stupid does."

It took her a while to trust the vampire brothers—being their mortal enemy and all—but she quickly came to realise that they were different despite all their faults. Zac was always an asshole and Sam was always kindhearted, but they never hurt anyone.

They'd ingrained themselves into the town as normal young men. Sam had even gotten a job as a gardener with help from her childhood friend, Alex. Zac...well, he became a professional boozehound.

So when Gabby walked into *Max's*, the bar they frequented after work, she smiled when she saw them sitting in a booth along the far wall.

She elbowed Zac as she sat down. "Happy birthday, you musty old man."

"Please, don't remind me." His eyes rolled in exasperation.

"Can I get you a drink?"

"Go for it, Glinda." They watched her retreating form. "I've been looking for you all afternoon," Zac hissed once Gabby was out of earshot.

Sam fidgeted. "I was out with Liz."

Zac didn't notice the gesture, he was too busy eyeballing Alistair, who'd just walked in. "Uh oh." He gritted his teeth.

Sam frowned. He knew all too well from his tone that Zac had gotten himself in trouble again. "What did you do?"

"I didn't start it, just so you know."

Like they needed more trouble. "Start what?"

"Big, bad, super creepy vampire over yonder is out to get us." He gestured toward Alistair, who was now over at the bar. "He's looking for some black-haired, blue-eyed woman who pissed him off, and he seems to think we know something about it."

"Obviously, we don't."

"I told him as much, but I don't think it matters anymore."

"You couldn't help but talk back, could you?"

Zac raised his hands in defence. "Hey, he came in talking like he was out of *Lord of the Rings*, even you couldn't pass on the opportunity. And it's my birthday. I deserve a potshot." Looking over at Alistair, he noticed Gabby standing beside him. They were talking and he was buying her a drink. Damnit, did she know he was a vampire? What kind of witch was she?

Sam snorted his disagreement, and before he could speak, Zac interrupted, "Yeah, yeah. Don't say it, bro. I get it. We can't afford to be exposed as blood-sucking parasites. Believe me, I get it."

"We have another issue to deal with."

Zac raised his eyebrows. "Oh, this ought to be good."

"Liz and I had a run in with the werewolves," Sam said, not looking at his brother.

He grunted and thumped his fist on the table. "Oh, so you want to have a go at me when you've been out riling up the puppy dogs? Did you cross into their imaginary territory?"

Sam nodded. "Seems like they want to claim the land bordering the manor."

"Sounds like they already have."

"They warned us off, but given any opportunity, they will attack us anyway," he said through gritted teeth. "They're getting bolder."

Zac felt anger rising inside him. He knew the only thing that had stopped the wolves from attacking was the fact that the moon wasn't even half full yet. Even juiced up on that rank moonshine they liked to drown themselves in, they couldn't take on vampires as old as he and Sam were.

He was thinking about the many ways he'd like to eviscerate the werewolf pack when Gabby sat back down at the table.

"I see Sam told you about the pack," she said when she noticed the scowl etched on his face.

"Wait until you hear who Zac pissed off today," Sam said, changing the subject.

"Who?"

"Your boyfriend over at the bar." Zac nodded toward Alistair.

"H-he's a..." Gabby stammered.

"You stammer a lot. It's unbecoming." Zac rolled his eyes.

"I didn't know," she hissed.

"What kind of witch are you that your witchy compass doesn't work?"

Gabby fidgeted and pushed away her glass as if she were suddenly wary of drinking it.

"What, do you think he put a vampire roofie in there?" Zac snorted and took the glass from her. Waste not, want not.

"Shut up," she snapped.

Zac stood, promptly ignoring her. "I'm going to have a word. You better leave, Sam. I don't want you more involved than you already are. You better split too, Tabitha."

"I like it better when you call me Glinda," Gabby muttered.

"Just don't go doing anything stupid," Sam warned, more out of habit than anything. Sam never expected him to act anything other than reckless...especially when he called Gabby Tabitha from *Bewitched*.

"Too late for that."

Zac sat next to Alistair at the bar. Gesturing at the bartender for a drink, he caught the glass that slid down to meet him.

"You don't know what's good for you, friend," Alistair said, lifting his glass to meet Zac's.

"What can I say? I have a knack for trouble," he replied with a note of irony.

"Are you ready to tell me what I want to know?"

"Well, gosh darn it, Alistair, I can't tell you what you want to know because I know nothing about it." Zac downed a mouthful of scotch.

Alistair sipped his drink. "I see the werewolves aren't too pleased about your little brother and his mate running about their forest."

"It's not their forest or their town," Zac snarled, not wanting to play games anymore.

"I believe they would beg to differ." Alistair swirled his drink around the bottom of his glass, the ice clinking. "And I believe they would like to do something about it, given the right persuasion."

"Be careful what you say." He stood abruptly, the stool scraping against the floor.

Alistair rose gracefully and stared at his adversary with disdain. "Do you know how old I am, vampire? I am over five-hundred years. I could squash you like the pathetic ant you are."

Zac stood eye to eye with the vampire and snarled, "Maybe you shouldn't come to *my town* and threaten the people I care about."

"This is your town? We'll see about that." Grabbing Zac by the scruff of the neck, Alistair dragged him through the kitchen, no one paying them any attention, and out the back door to the service lane. Before he could try to wrench himself free, he was thrown clear across into the fence opposite, the chain-link rattling.

Zac groaned, rolling onto his front. "I see you pre-compelled the staff so they wouldn't piss in your soup." Compulsion, otherwise known as the vampire party trick of mind-control, was nearly the only fun thing about being able to live forever. Until moments like these.

Ignoring him, Alistair walked over to the fence and pulled free the iron cross bar. Weighing it in his hands, he nodded in appreciation before approaching Zac, who was trying to drag himself to his feet. The vampire swung once, an audible crack as the pole broke both of Zac's legs, and swung again, this time breaking his spine.

"Consider this a warning," Alistair said as Zac groaned in pain. "Piss me off again and I will put this through your heart."

The iron bar clattered to the ground and Alistair disappeared, leaving Zac on the ground with nothing to do but wait until his bones healed.

The back door of the bar opened, and a grease-stained cook walked out, his eyes glazing over the vampire on the ground, and lit a cigarette.

Great, Zac thought, staring up at the starry sky. *Best birthday ever.*

CHAPTER 2

The half-moon had risen high in the sky by the time Zac reached the gates of the Degaud Manor.

It had taken a full hour before he could drag himself to his feet, his spine healing enough to restore feeling to his broken legs. Limping all the way from town to the house on the outskirts was a seven-mile journey, and he fumed all the way, anger filling each step. He could've run, but he wanted time to think about the revenge he would have on Alistair before Sam could talk him out of it.

His thoughts traveled to memories of the many fights he'd gotten into when he was in the army. He'd given his fair share of black eyes and bloody noses and received just as many, but fighting as a vampire was a unique experience. His ability for healing made for more painful injuries—gashes, broken bones, pulverised flesh, internal bleeding—painful, but irrelevant. His body would heal all but a severed head and a torn-out heart...pretty much.

He trudged up the driveway to the manor, feet dragging in the dirt. The same house they'd once lived in as children and as young men and had been the location of so much death. They'd reclaimed it from disrepair and despair alike, spending a great deal of time and money renovating and restoring the interior.

Sam held the deed, as he was more responsible with those things, and with little effort, they reclaimed the legal title. Despite all of this, the grounds and house were of historical significance, so as they wanted to do things by the book, they couldn't do much to the exterior. Two vampires who never locked their door couldn't argue with the fact that the house didn't look lived in because of the heritage overlay. It kept visitors away, along with the giant padlock on the gate.

Zac slammed the front door closed and barged into the parlour, throwing down his jacket, glaring at his brother who gave him a familiar look of disapproval.

The parlour was where the action was. It was also where Zac kept the booze, so they gravitated here because of it. Right now, he needed alcohol...lots of alcohol. His clothing was covered in dirt and mud was caked into the knees of his jeans, all glaring signs pointing to what he'd been up to all night.

Sam eyed him up and down. "What happened to you?"

"What do you think happened?" he sneered,

pacing back and forth in front of the fireplace, seething. The walk had done nothing but fuel his anger until it was a burning inferno.

Sam sighed and placed his head in his hands, his resignation crystal clear.

"I'm not going to let that bastard get away with it," Zac raged, waving a finger wildly at Sam. Getting into trouble was part of being a vampire; it was a rite of passage they went through at least once a decade.

"We can't afford any trouble, Zac. If anyone found out who we really are..."

"Yeah, yeah." Zac waved him off. "He broke both my legs and my spine. I'm trying not to give into my urges, but you know how it is. All I want to do right now is beat the crap out of the bastard and stake him to a tree."

"Did you even try to talk reasonably with him?"

"He came there looking for a fight, I didn't have to do anything. It's down to him or us. And I'd rather it be us," he said. Zac couldn't understand himself most days, let alone vampire politics. He supposed he'd become a little mad as well once he hit five hundred. *Couldn't wait for that.*

"What do you suggest?" Sam asked.

"The only option there is," Zac replied, deadly serious. "We kill him."

He scoffed, "What's this *we* business?"

"Family sticks together, Samuel."

"So, we kill him and then what happens when his friends come looking?"

Zac stared his brother down. "Next time I won't look away."

Liz wiped her brow, grimacing. That was the billionth time she'd dropped coffee grounds all over the floor. Distracted wasn't the right word for it. Off the planet was closer to the truth.

She'd been skittish ever since the encounter with the werewolves.

Sam had dropped her off at work that morning before going to work at the gardens across the street with Alex. Gabby was coming to get her soon, so she wouldn't be alone if there was trouble.

It was so silly. As a vampire, she should be able to take care of herself, but it was something she'd struggled with since day one. She was too kind-hearted, which contradicted everything she'd become.

Sighing, she knelt behind the counter and swept up the coffee grounds, dumping them into the trash.

Working at the coffeehouse wasn't the most glamorous job in the world, but it was something to take her mind off the fact that she was A: a vampire and B: a vampire who was undecided if she was going to college or not in the spring. At twenty-one, it was later than most, but she'd had to defer last year because she was busy learning how to control her bloodlust. The year before was spent working full-time at the same job making coffee, earning money for tuition.

She was cleaning the coffee machine when Gabby opened the front door, the bell ringing merrily. They'd closed for the day already, but everyone knew her friend, so they didn't mind that she ignored the closed sign and barged right in.

"Are you ready yet?" she asked, grinning. "I'm starving."

"It's only five o'clock!"

"Yeah, but I had to skip lunch today. I'm so hungry my stomach is eating itself."

Giving the bench a final wipe, Liz waved to her boss, Mrs. Greene, and they made their way along the three blocks to *Max's*, laughing about her uncoordinated day.

It was great to catch up with her friend. It'd been weeks since they'd had the time for a girls' night.

They'd just sat down in a booth when Gabby said, "Aw, crap."

"What's wrong?" Liz asked, turning toward the door. Catching sight of a rather refined and handsome blond man, she frowned. Was he...?

"That's Alistair," Gabby told her. "He's the one who threatened Zac."

"Oh." Liz bit her lip, frowning. Sam had warned her about him that morning when he'd picked her up.

The fact that he was lurking about must have been the reason the werewolves were absent. The thought made her blood run cold. *The wolves were trouble enough on their own.*

The vampire caught her eye and she quickly looked away, glancing at Gabby, wondering if she should text Sam. Before she could decide, the vampire slid into the booth beside Liz, trapping her against the wall. Gabby eyed him uncomfortably, steeling herself for whatever stunt he was about to pull.

"Ladies," he said. "I believe you know who I am."

"Alistair." Gabby grimaced. She was not in the mood for games, especially the games of vampires.

"You're the witch." He pointed at her before turning to Liz. "And you must be the newborn."

Liz couldn't help shuddering as his cold eyes raked over her body.

"What do you want, Alistair?" Gabby asked firmly, her strong brown eyes staring down the five-hundred-year-old vampire.

"I'm just coming to examine my prize." He put his arm around Liz's shoulder, grinning at her. "When I'm finished with that annoying Zachary and his brother, you and I will have some fun."

"Unlikely," Liz spat at him, trying to shrug his arm away.

"I can show you things you've never dreamed of."

"Back off, Alistair." Gabby's eyes narrowed in warning as Liz slid away from him as far as she could get, which wasn't very far at all. The wall was hard on her back, trapping her against him.

"Oh, my dear," he said silkily, leaning closer to Liz, "I will have you at least once before I'm through." He slid his hand up her leg, his palm lingering on her upper thigh. Her body stiffened at his touch, making her shudder in revulsion.

She glared at the vampire and snarled, "Get your hand off me, or I'll—"

"Or you'll what?" Alistair's grip hardened on her thigh, his fingers beginning to bruise the thin skin.

Liz stared him down, refusing to betray her fear at the sudden malicious gesture. She wouldn't be the damsel in distress. Suddenly, Alistair grasped his head, grimacing in pain, his fist banging against the tabletop in frustration. Gabby was scowling at him, deep in concentration, eyes narrowed.

"*Argh*," he growled, his voice betraying the pain that was exploding in his head. "All right, all right. You've got this round, witch."

Gabby relaxed and Alistair gripped the table, his knuckles white, glaring at her. "Leave," she said. "You have no claim here, vampire. Leave before it's too late for you."

Alistair laughed then, as if he knew Gabby was bluffing. Her expression was darkness, but Liz knew that her power was limited and no match for an ancient vampire. What she'd just done? That was the extent of what she'd learned to protect herself.

Alistair rose from the booth and bowed to them mockingly. "Next time we meet, I'll make sure the tables are turned."

They didn't tear their eyes from him until he'd exited the bar.

Shit, shit, shit, thought Liz. Old ass vampires who wanted in her pants and werewolves hell bent on harassing her out of town? How much more complicated could life get?

Reluctantly, she said, "Maybe you should call Zac and let him know…"

Gabby shook her head. "Not right away, let's just enjoy our food first. He won't be back tonight. We need this, and I won't let that jerk ruin our night."

Liz smiled, understanding her friend's sentiment. "Let's do it."

Zac thought about the many ways he could kill Alistair throughout the next day.

He was thankful Sam had gone to work. The constant badgering about his intentions would've pushed him over the edge. This was one thing he wouldn't be talked out of.

His train of thought was broken as his cell vibrated across the coffee table.

"Gabby," he said sharply as he answered it.

"Zac? Liz and I were just confronted by Alistair."

He sat up. "Where are you?"

"We're outside *Max's*."

"Go home," he snapped. "I will deal with Alistair."

"*Zac*." Gabby sounded worried.

"Just go home, Gabby." He hung up on her. Alistair had gone too far.

Soon enough, he found the offending vampire leaning up against the façade of *Max's*, arms crossed, waiting for him.

Zac strode up to Alistair and grabbed the front of his shirt. "That was a low blow, Al."

Pushing Zac off him, he sneered, "I can go lower, if that's what you really want."

"I don't know why you insist on all this when none of us know anything about your girlfriend."

"Oh, I'm well aware you know nothing. Making your life difficult is much more entertaining." The older vampire smirked, satisfied with the over the top reaction he'd received in greeting. "I could go for full exposure. Not everyone in this town has forgotten the true reason behind the massacre at the Degaud Manor. How would you like that?"

Zac grabbed the front of Alistair's shirt again, wrenching him close. "This ends here."

"Are you challenging me to a duel?" Alastair laughed, assured that he would be the victor no matter what.

Zac stifled his mocking laughter. "It's the twenty-first century, Al, you old bastard. I had more of a 'fight to the death' in mind, not pistols at twenty paces."

As he saw it, the only option he had was to kill the vampire, and that was going to be problematic. Alistair wouldn't let his guard down for an instant or stray from populated areas. He knew Zac would attempt bodily harm given the slightest opportunity. A fight to the death was the only option he would consider and was banking that the other vampire's arrogance would be his downfall. There was no way he would win on strength alone—there was close to four hundred years between them. If he were to actually kill him, a challenge of this magnitude outside of town was the only way.

Alistair's eyes brightened. "A fight to the death. No rules, only death for the loser."

Zac pushed him back, dropping his grip from his shirt. He wouldn't play mind games with this guy, no matter what he threatened to do. If he won, then Alistair would be gone for good and if he lost... well, he'd be dead. He could think of worse things.

"In the woods by the manor," Zac said. "Two hours. Come alone."

He knew he couldn't rely on Sam. His brother didn't agree with his tactics almost one hundred percent of the time. And a death match? Well, that one took the cake. This he had to do on his own.

The two hours had passed, and he hoped he was going to his victory, not his death.

Tucking a wooden stake in the back of his jeans, Zac made his way through the dark forest. Moonlight filtered through the trees, casting long, eerie shadows that distorted the ground ahead.

When he reached the clearing, he found the older vampire standing so still, he almost mistook him for another shadow.

Alistair's soft chuckle cut through the silence. "Are you ready to die, Zachary?"

"Quit the small talk, Al. Let's get on with it," he said, eager to draw first blood.

Alistair pulled a gun from behind his back, which had been hidden under his jacket. Pointing at Zac's thigh, he squeezed the trigger, the bullet tearing through flesh and splattering blood as it made contact.

The force of the close-range impact knocked Zac from his feet and he landed heavily on his back. He grimaced in pain, clutching his leg.

"Wow," he hissed through clenched teeth. "Talk about bringing a sword to a gunfight. You're a piece of work, Al. Where'd you get the wooden bullets? From ye olde carpenter shoppe? How long did it take you to whittle those, you old bastard?"

Alistair laughed, not put off by his sarcastic observations. "I'm not one for these devices." He tucked the gun into the back of his pants. "Call me old-fashioned, but I like to use my hands. That way I can feel the life bleed from you when I tear your heart from your chest."

Zac grimaced as he dug his fingers into his torn flesh and pulled the bullet out. Throwing it aside, his eyes darkened to black as he lunged for Alistair, knocking him to the ground with a roar. The stake was in his hand, but the older vampire grabbed his wrist before he could bring it down into his heart. There was a crack as his bone broke under the pressure.

Grimacing in pain, he dropped the stake as Alistair threw him to the side with enough force to crash him into a tree.

Landing with a thud, Zac was back on his feet in a flash, ignoring the pain in his broken wrist. He'd had worse. Alistair was on him before he could react, the older vampire's strength overpowering as he shoved him back against the tree trunk, a forearm crushing his neck, almost cutting off his airway. Twisting to the side, Zac freed himself, and Alistair's arm crashed into the tree, splintering the bark.

"Stop playing with your food, Al." He darted behind him, grasping his left arm, wrenching backward until it broke.

Alistair roared in anger, as much as he did on pain, and grabbed Zac around the neck again before he could escape. Zac tried to struggle out of the headlock, but this time, the other vampire's grip didn't budge.

"Oh, I like it when they struggle," he chortled as he

tightened his grip around Zac's neck, landing punch after punch onto his unprotected face.

Zac's nose broke with a crack and his lip split open, blood pouring out of the multiple gashes that were opening with every impact.

Gasping for breath, Zac eyed the gun that'd fallen onto the ground a mere four feet to the right. If he could loosen Alistair's grip and free himself, he might slow him down with a few bullets. Then he might have a chance at staking him.

Struggling, he kicked sideways, his shin connecting with Alistair's leg, the blow buckling the vampire's knee, causing him stumble.

As the grip slackened from around his neck, Zac lunged to the right and snatched up the gun before Alistair could kick it out of reach. Without hesitation, Zac fired, a bullet imbedding itself into the older vampire's stomach. It wasn't enough to knock him to the ground, but Alistair doubled over, clutching his bleeding abdomen in surprise.

It was the millionth of a second that Zac needed to stab upward, the stake hitting its mark with a sickening thud as it tore through flesh and sinew until it finally rammed home, deep into Alistair's heart.

"You were stronger, Alistair, but not smarter," Zac said with a sneer as the life drained from the vampire's eyes.

Alistair choked, gasping for air as his body began to desiccate and turn a sickly shade of grey. When he was finally still, Zac pushed him backward onto the ground.

Grimacing, he held his broken wrist and spat the blood that had pooled in his cut mouth. "Good riddance."

Turning away from the body, he paused as he saw a woman emerge from the surrounding forest.

She approached calmly, her hands clasped in front of her, but her expression was cold. Zac frowned as he took in her dress. Long white folds of silk hung low over her shoulders, draping to the ground, cinched at the hips by a golden belt—it was something like ancient Roman women would've worn. Her long auburn hair was pinned up in elaborate braids, a few curls left out to frame her frosty face.

"And who the hell are you?" he asked when she came to rest a few paces away.

The woman tilted her head and glared. "I am the founding witch Katrin, and you've just murdered one of my most beloved creations."

Just what he needed, a witch in fancy dress. "And what are you going to do? Cast some witchy juju spell on me?"

Before she could answer, Zac threw the stake at her with alarming speed, but as it made contact, she vanished. The stake imbedded itself in the tree behind the spot she'd been standing, the thud echoing through the empty forest.

"You will suffer, vampire, for the murder of your

own kind." He jumped as Katrin's voice came from behind. "I will enjoy hunting you and all those you love, inflicting pain the likes of which you cannot imagine."

Zac whirled around to face the witch who'd materialised behind him. "If you could kill me, you would've already done it." He waved his hand through her form, making it shimmer. *An illusion.* "You're transparent, so I'd like to see you try."

She laughed, filling the surrounding forest with her musical voice. "I'm going to enjoy watching you writhe in agony."

Gasping, he clutched his chest at the sudden pain that tore through his heart. Falling to his knees, he tried to take even breaths, but couldn't draw any oxygen as his airway closed in on itself. Just as suddenly as the pain overtook him, it was gone.

"That," Katrin crooned, "was a precursor, vampire. We will meet again, you and I."

When he looked up, he was alone, except for Alistair's cold, dead corpse.

Wiping the blood from his nose with the back of his hand, Zac groaned as he dragged what was left of the vampire away. The witch had disappeared but had left the heavy promise of retribution behind.

If Zac thought he was in trouble before, he was well and truly screwed now.

CHAPTER 3

I t was the second time in as many days that Zac walked home after a fight, his clothes torn and bloodied. He'd killed Alistair but had dug himself into a deeper hole. An ancient dead witch who had claimed to be the creator of all vampires had marked him for a slow, painful death.

How was he going to explain it to Sam? It wasn't exactly the kind of thing he could keep under wraps.

It was well after midnight when he finally came home, wandering up the driveway. Opening the front door with a little less force than last time, he shuffled into the parlour and headed straight for the scotch. He thought it was best to get a few drinks in his brother before telling him the grave news. Zac poured Sam a glass as he heard his brother sit on the sofa behind him.

"Do I even want to know what you've been doing all night?" Sam asked, exasperated. "I have a good idea, considering Liz came over and told me what happened with Alistair."

"I killed the bastard," Zac said, getting right to the point and handed the glass to him.

"And?" Sam took a large mouthful of the liquor as if to prepare for what was coming next.

"And his dead witchy overlord is out for my blood. Refill?" he asked sarcastically, waving the bottle of scotch at his brother.

"Wait," Sam said. "Start from the beginning. You killed Alistair? How?"

"I challenged him to a duel," Zac replied sarcastically. "Slapped him with a leather riding glove and everything. Very authentic. Then I staked him."

"Zac..."

"That, brother, was the truth. I challenged him to a fight to the death. Book smarts won over brute strength." He tapped his temple.

Sam closed his eyes and held his head in his hands. "And what if he'd killed you? Did you stop to think about us?"

Zac took a long draught of scotch straight from the bottle. "Yes, I thought about it. This was my issue to deal with, Sam. I did this to protect everyone. I did what I had to do."

"You could've warned me."

"And you would have stopped me."

"Well, that's just great." Sam shook his head. "Murderous vampires and now dead witches? Shit."

"Can you see into the future, Sam, because I sure can't," he seethed, the now empty bottle smashing into the fireplace, alcohol flaring in the flames. "He wouldn't have stopped until we were dead or exposed. Killing him was my only option."

"And this witch?"

"She claimed to be a founding witch named Katrin, but she was transparent. Very much dead and ghostly... dripping with ectoplasm."

"You could have come to me, Zac. We could have found another way. One without killing."

"Well, I'm so sorry I can't be the kind-hearted human-wannabe-vampire you so desperately want me to be," Zac drawled. "Guess what, brother. We're *vampires*. We fight, we hunt, and we kill. It's what we are."

"There's always an alternative, Zac. You just have to be open to hearing it."

"You might be content in fighting your true nature, but I've made my peace. I understand what I am, even if you don't." He walked across the room before turning around. "I'll speak to Gabby in the morning. You can stay out of it if that's what you want." He left the room, leaving Sam to make his decision, his mind already well and truly made up.

Gabby wasn't too pleased about being woken up at eight a.m. on a Sunday morning and even less pleased to hear Zac's voice. Pleading wasn't his thing, so he suggested it might be a good idea to help him to be guilty by association. She'd reluctantly agreed to come over to the manor once she was ready.

Zac was already into the alcohol by the time his brother woke. He was riled up already and had a feeling it was going to be a trying day, which meant he needed all the calming down he could get. Besides, he was getting hungry.

He sat heavily on the sofa. Leaning his head back, he stared at the ceiling. Dead witches took the cake so far. They'd never encountered so many supernaturals in one place before—witches, vampires, werewolves, and now ghosts. Next it would be voodoo spirit lords and Aztec witch doctors.

"I'm surprised to see you here, brother." Zac glanced up as Sam sat across from him.

"We're brothers, Zac. Your shit is my shit," he replied.

"And so eloquently put."

Sam snorted as they heard the front door close and footsteps approach down the hall. Gabby strode in, carrying her grimoire in her arms. The tattered book was over five hundred years old, protected from deteriorating and falling apart by magic.

She flopped down on the leather armchair and

said with a hint of sarcasm, "This better be worth giving up my Sunday for."

"Long story short," Zac announced, "I killed Alistair, his dead witchy overlord appeared out of thin air proclaiming that she was the founding witch Katrin, whatever that means, and that I will die a long and horrible death." He smiled. "Thoughts?"

Gabby stared at him in surprise, not expecting a tirade of that magnitude. At least not one that included the words 'founding witch'. She slowly glanced to Sam, who nodded. Well, at least it was a truthful tirade.

"Well..." she began as she carefully opened the grimoire.

Zac swirled his drink around in his glass. "Is there anything in your diary about this Katrin?"

Gabby glared and glanced back to the grimoire, turning the pages. "There's a passage about the founding witches and the one who broke her covenant with them," she stated. "Katrin betrayed her sisters for power and created a creature who could do her bidding long after she'd passed—vampires. She bound them to herself so they would follow her for eternity."

"She seemed to believe that she had created Alistair," Zac said.

"Then maybe she was telling the truth. Maybe she is one of the founding witches," Sam said. "She was an apparition, so maybe her spirit is still connected to the living, that's why Alistair was bound to her."

"And how she knew he was dead," Zac added.

"If she is, then she would be strong enough to do it. The founders were the beginning, the most powerful of us, ever. But why would she create vampires?"

"To do her dirty work," Zac said.

Gabby shook her head. "Probably, but I don't think that was the only reason. Why create a predator who needs blood to survive, who can only walk in the night, when all you need is someone to do your bidding after you're dead?"

"You're right, it makes little sense, but all we need to know is how to get rid of her," Zac pointed out, exasperated. "I'd rather be the one doing the hunting, not the other way around."

"You don't want to know anything about the first vampires? Why we are what we are?" Sam asked surprised.

"Why? We've been doing okay. The more we meet, the more trouble we get into."

Sam snorted. "Don't you mean, the more you piss off, the more trouble I get into?"

"You're the one who came along for the ride. Don't have a cry now."

Gabby sighed loudly. "If you two are finished bickering like children, I have more."

Zac rolled his eyes. "Please enlighten us, Tabitha."

"Right." Gabby stood and gathered her things. "If you don't want my help, you just have to say so. I have better things to do than take that attitude from you."

Sam rose. "Gabby, I'm sorry. We do need your help. Please stay." He turned and glared at Zac.

"What?" he asked, annoyed.

Gabby sat back down with an exasperated sigh. "There's a summoning spell in the grimoire that might be something."

"And what does it summon?" Zac asked.

"The Witch Hunter." Gabby flipped to the page and read aloud, "The one betrayed by their own. The one who punishes the ones turned evil, the hunter of witches who would do harm. Cast this call and perchance the hunter will deign to speak."

"You want us to summon a witch hunter?" Zac laughed at the notion. "How convenient!"

"It's all I've got," she replied. "But there's a warning that goes along with it... The Witch Hunter is a very old and powerful vampire, unpredictable and only serves their own end."

"And there's the catch." Zac snorted. "They sound like a *riot*."

"I don't think it's a good idea," Sam said. "It could do more harm than good."

"From what I can tell, the Witch Hunter helped one of my ancestors... the one who wrote the spell. It's kind of a big deal for a vampire to help a witch." She looked pointedly at Zac, who glared at her in return.

"Is there anything else about this Witch Hunter?" Sam asked.

"Not much, but this spell was written in 1542. It's

one of the first in the book and one of the few I can read," she explained, but didn't mention that she thought it was an omen. "The story goes that the Church and Crown in Wales passed through a law naming witchcraft a felony and those found practicing would face punishment of death. The first law of its kind. They accused the witch who wrote the spell, having been framed by another witch, who was using her powers for evil—exploiting the townspeople and summoning devils. That's what drew the Witch Hunter to the village. They formed a tentative alliance and under the cover of darkness, the Hunter tore the devils to pieces and stole the evil witch's light."

"Stole her light?" Sam murmured, intrigued by the story. "What does that mean?"

"By the sounds of it, they probably took her power. Anyway, the Hunter left a trail of mutilated bodies in their wake, horrifying the good witch. The next morning some angry townsfolk, who'd been spying on them, tore the witch from her bed. She had no trial and was tied to a wooden pole at the centre of the village. They intended to burn her for the crime of witchcraft and murder because they believed it was her who had summoned the devils. As the flames grew around her, the Witch Hunter came back and saved her from the fire and took her far away from the angry mob to live out her days in anonymity. She married and had a family and passed the grimoire to her daughter. It had a good ending. Bittersweet, but the best of a bad situation."

"The Hunter has a heart, at least," Sam said absently.

"If you call tearing apart devils, mutilating their bodies, and stealing a witch's power having a heart, then we have a serious problem," Gabby exclaimed, snapping the grimoire shut. "That kind of stuff won't fly in the modern world."

"Pfft, it's just a story," Zac scoffed.

"It's meant to serve as a warning," Gabby scolded. "One you would do well to pay attention to. Whoever this vampire is, they won't discriminate. If they think you deserve what's coming you, they'll probably do Katrin's work for her."

"So what?" Zac said. "Do the spell. Damn the consequences."

"No," Sam said, shaking his head. "Rushing headlong into situations is was what got us into this mess in the first place."

"Can you banish a founding witch's spirit for eternity, let alone find her?" he asked both of them. When they remained silent, Zac said, "Thought so."

"I'll do it," Gabby said with a sigh. "Just know that I don't want to, but I'm helping you anyway. You owe me, Zac."

"And we thank you for that," Sam said, understanding what Gabby was sacrificing to help them. Witches and vampires had been at war for hundreds of years—that they had become friends in the first place was a miracle.

"What do you need to do for the spell?" Zac asked.

"It's part potion and incantation," she replied, reading through the pages again.

"Okay, so it's an outdoorsy thing," he said simply.

"If you want. The spell will leave a calling card of sorts, attached to the place it was cast. It would lead the Witch Hunter here, if here was the place we chose to do it," Gabby explained, leaving the choice up to the brothers.

"The old cemetery," Zac said. "I don't want any witchy residue in the house."

"I have to go get a few things. I will meet you there in an hour." Gabby slipped the grimoire into her bag and made for the front door, not waiting for an answer. She hardly believed they had roped her into helping them in the first place. When Liz found out, she'd be furious.

The cemetery was located on the edge of the main manor grounds, off to the side of the original plantation. Over one hundred and fifty years, the land had been reclaimed by nature, the swampland encroaching back to its original form.

Most of the cemetery was overgrown, falling out of repair as the locals forgot it ever existed. It was full of people who had died over a hundred and fifty years ago, many Degaud plots among the headstones, their family having been one of the first to have settled in the region. The cemetery was technically located on private property, which was mostly the reason for the lack of upkeep. A space was cleared in the centre, which Gabby had worked on herself months before the brothers had returned to Ashburton. It was the place she came to learn her powers.

The vampire brothers lounged in the afternoon sunlight. Winter was leaving and the humid summer months were creeping closer. Zac had hated the humidity of the swamps since he was a young boy. Traveling north with the Confederates had seen a summer devoid of air and uncomfortably heavy with moisture—something he had never experienced before. The Civil War had opened his eyes in more ways than learning how to kill a man. War had given his human life purpose when his meagre accomplishments were a disappointment to his family. It'd also given his new life the release he'd needed.

"You know I have misgivings about this," Sam said. "We have no idea what meddling with this ancient spell might do. Who it might be calling."

Zac sat on a cracked headstone, his feet dangling over the edge, tapping on the side. "Well, too bad. What other option do we have?"

"We could find another witch. One who has more experience."

"Don't let Glinda hear you say that."

"I'm serious, Zac. We're dragging her into something she doesn't understand. Not that we do, either."

"I understand well enough."

"Oh, c'mon," Sam said. "Even you're not convinced by this harebrained scheme. It's written all over your face."

Zac folded his arms, detecting the hesitation in his brother's plan. "A million bucks says you wouldn't leave in the first place."

Sam sighed and cocked his head to the side, letting him know Gabby was approaching. They'd continue this later, no doubt.

The witch strode into the cemetery, the grimoire in her arms and a bag slung over her shoulder. "Let's get this over with." she said, getting right down to business.

They watched as she picked up a long stick and drew a rough pentagram in the dirt. Once it was complete, she placed the bowl in the centre and poured a plastic bottle filled with a dark brown liquid into it.

Sitting on the ground at the base of the pentagram, she drew her bag close and pulled out a hunting knife. "I need some of your blood. Who wants to do the honours?"

"Why?" Sam asked.

"Vampire blood must call vampire blood. It won't

work another way." She gestured for one of them to come forward.

"Fine. Use mine." Zac held his hand out. The sooner this was over, the sooner they could deal with the bigger issue. It wasn't the greatest feeling to be stalked by a rogue witch from beyond the grave. He'd done some horrible things in his time, but self-preservation was more tantalising than repenting.

Gabby cut his hand with the knife and wasn't gentle about it, either. Clenching his fist, he remained silent as blood dripped into the potion, the brown liquid sizzling as each drop collided with the surface, even though it was ice-cold.

"Now, read this while I do the incantation." Gabby held out the translation of the spell she had written on a scrap of notepaper.

Snatching it from her, he read the incantation and scoffed, "You witches just love your poetry."

Gabby rolled her eyes. "It's what was written in the grimoire. Just read it and shut the hell up."

Reluctantly, he read as she chanted in some old language they'd never heard before. Witch speak, most likely. "*Blood of my blood, I summon thee. Blood of my blood, I beseech thee. Blood of my blood, in Heaven and Hell, come save me.*"

The potion burst into flames and they leaned away from the sudden heat and smoke.

"I guess that means it worked," Gabby said.

Zac glanced around the cemetery. "If it worked, then where is the vampire?"

"It doesn't work that way," she told him. "We put out the call, now we wait for an answer." She stood and gathered her things.

"So...we just go home and wait?"

"Yes, you wait. I didn't want to do this, just remember that. And it's all I can do, so you'll just have to be satisfied."

"C'mon, Zac." Sam walked away. "If the Witch Hunter wants to come, then they'll come on their own time."

He watched Gabby's receding form until she disappeared through the trees. Listening to the cemetery closely, he heard nothing but the normal sounds of the forest and Sam's heavy footsteps.

How could he wait when he was the one being stalked by God knows what? He knew there was nothing else he could do but follow his brother home and keep one eye open at all times.

CHAPTER 4

Three days had passed since Gabby had cast the summoning spell, and for three days, nothing had happened.

Zac was a very impatient vampire. Ironic, since he had all the time in the world. Strangely, he'd been more patient as a human. In those days, it took a lot longer to get anywhere other than where you were. Knowing how fast things had become in the modern world, he didn't know how he managed it.

"You know, I'm sick of all this waiting. There's got to be something we can do." He sighed, looking out the window of the parlour to the garden beyond.

Sam glanced up from his book. "It's only been three days."

The front door slammed closed, but neither of them looked to see who it was. They knew Liz was walking down the hallway.

"Are you going to tell her?" Zac raised an eyebrow at him.

"Are you?" Sam retorted.

"Where have you two been hiding the past few days?" Liz asked as she walked into the parlour. "Wait. Maybe I don't want to know the answer to that."

"Then why did you ask?" Zac grinned wickedly at her when she rolled her eyes.

"Where were you when I came looking on Sunday? I thought we were going to do something?" Liz asked Sam, who glanced at his brother, not knowing what he should say.

"We were out with Gabby performing blood sacrifices." Zac winked at her, a mocking tone in his voice. "Why are you asking anyway? I know Gabby told you."

"How did you know?" she asked, confused.

"I didn't, you just told me." He ducked as a cushion flew at his head.

Of course, Gabby would tell her. They shared just about everything with each other and it stood to reason that she'd share this bombshell as well.

"When were you going to tell me?" Liz objected.

"I knew you'd disapprove," Zac said, leaning against the windowsill.

"Yeah, of course I do," she cried. "Did you think any of it through?"

"Of course, I did."

"All of five seconds!"

"Look, if we had told you, we would've spent ten years arguing about whether we should do it or not. And if you hadn't noticed, I think ten years is a bit of an optimistic time frame for planning our defences." Zac smiled sarcastically. "That's why I'm me and you're you."

Liz sighed dramatically, sinking onto the sofa, arms folded across her chest. "Fine. It's too late now."

Zac shook his head. "Anyway, you guys are getting hungry. Have you thought about the chihuahuas?"

"We've had to go farther afield to hunt," Sam replied. "It's getting harder to dodge them."

As far as they knew, the werewolf pack lived in a smaller town nearby. They weren't an issue to the brothers when they'd first returned home, but that may have had something to do with the vampires trying to lead human lives. Once the wolves caught on that vampires were living in the area, they did all they could to inch them out—especially once they knew that Sam and Liz only fed on animals. They'd started claiming even more territory and now it was becoming a dangerous threat.

"They're pushing us out so they can claim the town," Liz said.

"That's because they know they can't win a fight against all of us together," Zac scoffed. "They're using dirty underhanded techniques to get their way."

"I know what you're trying to insinuate, Zac," Sam warned. "Look what happened with Alistair."

"That was different. Besides, this is our home and I'm sure as hell not going to let some dog screw with you," he argued.

"The moon is almost full."

The werewolves would be stronger the closer it came to a full moon, when their compulsory transformation neared. It would be stupid to go out into the forest at night, even they would be overpowered. Werewolves could change whenever they wanted but were at the mercy of the phases of the moon, their strength waxing and waning with it.

"Fine, I won't start anything with them," Zac huffed. "But if they come at you or Liz, I'll do what I need to."

Sam nodded. "Understood."

"You know I'm coming with you tomorrow, right?"

"You finally want to try a squirrel?"

Zac snorted. "Hilarious, Samuel. I'm more into wolves."

"Their bite can change a human... God knows what it can do to a vampire," he said in a last-ditch effort to dissuade Zac.

"What do you take me for? I ain't some green recruit, Sam. I'm an expert."

"That's what I'm afraid of... You can come with us, but don't start anything. We can't afford it right now."

"Aye, aye, Captain. Oh wait, that's me." Zac laughed at his own joke, earning a slap in the head with another cushion from Liz.

Zac grinned to himself. Tomorrow at sunset, it would be vampires versus werewolves, one way or the other. His bet was that the dogs would start it.

The late afternoon sun burned orange through the treetops, casting long shadows over the open yard in front of the manor.

Zac was perched on top of the brick fence, waiting impatiently for Sam and Liz to arrive home. When he finally caught sight of them coming up the driveway, he jumped down and went to meet them.

"About time," he said.

"Chomping at the bit as per usual, I see," Sam said, thumping his brother on the shoulder.

"Sooner we go, the sooner it's done."

"Just stay back, okay?" Sam asked, holding his hand up. "If it looks like trouble, then do what you have to."

"Fine. I'll be your little escort service. I won't touch the stinking dogs unless they try something."

Sam assessed his answer for a moment before he nodded and turned toward the forest. Just as he said he would, Zac kept his distance, perched up in a tree some distance back, watching and listening.

It didn't take long for their presence to be noted, as if the pack waited for the vampires to hunt tonight. As the werewolves sauntered through the forest in their human forms, Sam and Liz stood deathly still in the middle of a clearing, waiting for the inevitable while Zac lingered in the shadows.

"I thought we told you vamps not to come here anymore," the hulking man they understood was the alpha declared as they came close.

"Do you really want us to feed on innocent humans?" Sam asked. "That's all we're doing here."

The man snarled, "We want you dead or gone, whichever comes first."

"We only feed on animals," Sam tried to reason. "We don't want to hurt anyone. Surely we can make a deal."

The wolves laughed, the menacing sound carrying around the dark forest.

"Do you hear that?" the wolf asked. "He wants to make a *deal*."

"There ain't no deals, boy," another man drawled. "Never will be."

"Change it up, boys," the alpha said to the others, his eyes beginning to glow a deep amber. "Let's get us some vampers."

Liz stared in horror as the alpha began to shift, his teeth elongating into the sharp incisors of an enormous wolf while silver hair sprouted all over his skin. He tore his shirt and jeans off with no regard for modesty. Roaring as much in pain as to intimidate them, every bone in his body began to snap and twist as he slowly transformed.

As the rest of the werewolves followed suit, Zac

jumped from tree to tree, only slightly rocking each one as he landed. Before the alpha could complete his transformation, he dove from the tree above, savagely striking him in the head. The half man, half wolf fell heavily to the ground, his pack mates howling and snapping as they completed their change.

"*Run*." Zac turned to Sam and Liz, pointing to the dark forest behind them.

"What about you?" Sam asked as he took a few steps backward.

"Are you stupid? Run!" he yelled. He turned back toward the pack, growling deep in his throat.

As Sam and Liz ran in the opposite direction, Zac jumped over the snapping jaws of the werewolves, intent on luring as many of them as he could away from the others. Bolting in the opposite direction, he bit open his wrist, dripping a trail of blood for them to follow.

He knew this land better than the back of his hand. The vegetation had changed somewhat since he was human, but all the dips and rises were the same. Making a mental note of his location, he veered right, flanking the swamp. It'd receded some but was still there.

One wolf was right on his heels, snapping at every opportunity, looking for its mark. The river was directly ahead, along with a sharp drop that plummeted into the muddy bank below. If he was lucky, he would give the wolf a surprise he wouldn't forget.

Breaking through the trees, Zac almost missed the edge, jumping at the last minute. Barely clearing the breadth of the river, he threw his weight forward, grasping a low branch. There was a sharp yelp behind him as the wolf desperately tried to slow itself, but the drop had appeared too suddenly. It fell in a shower of decaying leaves and earth, landing heavily into the thick mud below. Zac hauled himself up onto the high bank on the opposite side and glanced down. The werewolf was well and truly stuck in the bank below, struggling to free itself from the sucking mud with no avail. If it changed back into human form, his hulking body would weigh him down even more.

Zac sneered at the pathetic sight and turned toward the manor where he knew Sam and Liz would circle back to. Running as fast as he could through the trees, he caught the scent of another wolf. As it lunged for him out of the shadows, he jumped, grasping a limb above him, causing the wolf to sail past. His feet had barely touched the ground before he'd turned, grasping a fallen branch like a baseball bat.

The wolf scrambled back around and faced him, its eyes reflecting in the moonlight. Snarling, it advanced slowly. Incisors that had to be at least four inches long dripped with saliva, ready to tear through his flesh.

They stared each other down for a moment, then the wolf lunged. Its jaws widened, aiming for his jugular. The branch swung and connected with the furry flesh of the wolf with a sickening thud, the blow sending it crashing back through the trees, howling in rage as much as pain. The forest fell into silence as its limp body came to rest somewhere in the darkness.

Pausing for only a second, Zac dumped the branch and continued on toward the rendezvous point.

Coming up on the clearing, he caught sight of Sam and Liz, who were surrounded by four wolves. As the lead wolf tensed to attack, Zac was on it. He wrapped his arms around its middle and crushed its ribs with a sickening crack. Tossing the wounded wolf aside, he put himself between the vampires and their immediate danger.

Crouching down so he could look the four wolves directly in the eye, he called, "*Here puppy, puppy, puppy…*"

Then there were five wolves, the one Zac had embedded in the mud nowhere to be seen. Amber eyes flashed in the darkness as they fixated on their prey. Suddenly, one wolf feigned a lunge from Zac's left, distracting him long enough so a large, rust-coloured wolf could launch an attack from the right.

Knocked flat on his back, Zac roared in anger, grasping the neck of the werewolf and used all his strength to keep its snapping jaws at a distance. He quite liked his face. It'd be counterproductive if it was ripped off.

Abruptly, the wolf was torn from him, and it let out

an ear-piercing yelp as its bones crunched. Scrambling to his feet, Zac hissed as he laid eyes on an unfamiliar vampire standing over the twisted remains of the werewolf who, only moments before, had been an inch from his face.

The clearing fell silent, the wolves falling back to a safe distance. The unknown vampire silently assessed them before glancing back to the vampires behind him.

"This one has been marked," the vampire snarled at the assembled wolves, pointing to Zac. "He does not die until it is appointed." He kicked the remains of the wolf toward the pack.

The wolves backed away, snarling, one of their number grasping the body of their fallen comrade by the scruff of the neck, dragging him with them.

Then the three vampires were alone with the intruder, the one obviously sent by Katrin. He turned and sneered at them with contempt, like they were an annoyance he'd rather deal with the same way. Blatantly assessing Zac, he gave him a look that dismissed him as harmless. Turning without a word, he disappeared into the darkness of the forest.

"Well, it's safe to say that we're being watched," Zac announced to no one in particular, annoyed that the fight had ended prematurely.

"Do you think they know about...you know?" Liz asked quietly.

"No," Zac replied, still staring in the direction the

vampire had disappeared. "If they knew, then this would have ended differently."

They stood in silence for a few minutes as if waiting for the shadows themselves to come and fight them. A mournful howl in the direction of the river broke the heavy silence, making Zac smirk in satisfaction.

"Let's go home," Sam said, taking Liz's hand and leading her away.

Zac stared after the unknown vampire, his blood boiling.

They'd solved nothing with the wolves, but maybe now they would be spooked enough not to try anything. Only time would tell if they could venture out into the forest without incident.

But he was more worried about Katrin. Until now, her threat had seemed empty. Life had continued as normal, the ramifications of staking Alistair non-existent.

Zac sighed. Perhaps he didn't know as much as he thought he did.

CHAPTER 5

Drawing her first breath burnt her disused lungs and she coughed uncontrollably. Sitting bolt upright in a panic, she looked around wildly, disoriented. *Where the hell am I?* Her thoughts scrambled to make sense of her situation, her heart hammering against her chest.

The air was dark and damp around her, thick with the scent of earth. Slowly, her murky vision cleared and she realised she was in the cave where she escaped the unbearable draw of killing. The reek of blood had stained the fields above and she couldn't take it anymore. The aura of death had driven her to the precipice and the thought of killing a human for pleasure disgusted her. Now, she remembered.

"My name is Aya," she whispered, the reminder sorely needed.

I escaped to this cave for the long sleep, she thought. *To clear myself of the urge to kill. To let an age pass before I could walk the Earth again. I am below the fields of southern America. Ashburton, Louisiana.*

The haze in her mind cleared and she carefully stood, stretching her disused muscles. Casting her mind above, she felt nothing but silence.

Aya was a vampire, but she had been granted other skills. She could sense emotions, which was a blessing and a curse. Recalling the battlefields above, she shuddered. Too much concentrated emotion always threatened to overwhelm her and she had to be careful. War was enough to drive her mad if she didn't protect herself. The American Civil War... She was glad she'd slept through that.

She brushed the dust and cobwebs from herself and ran her fingers through her long black hair. She really had to remember to bring a blanket next time. Who knew what'd lived in here with her over the years?

She was starving. How long had she been sleeping?

She had to find her way outside, find something to eat, and wash before exploring the world above.

Aya made her way from the cave, down a passageway she barely remembered. She'd entered this place so abruptly and never fully took in her surroundings. It was hidden from the outside, of that she was sure.

Still at the mouth of the cave was the heavy rock she'd placed to block the small hole that served as the cave entrance. With no effort, she pulled the boulder aside and light poured through the opening along with the fresh, crisp air of the world.

The sun was still climbing in the sky as she emerged into the day. Blinking furiously, she held up her hand, shielding herself from the glare as her eyes became accustomed to the brightness.

The land outside the cave had changed somewhat. The vegetation was thicker and a little wilder than she remembered. A short way off, she caught the glimpse of light reflecting off water and recalled a lake being there. Cautiously, she made her way toward it, ready to catch the scent of any nearby animal. She was bound to have more luck closer to the water's edge.

Chance happened that she came across a lone deer grazing, separated from its mates. Once Aya had taken the edge off her hunger, she went to the water's edge.

The lake was dark, the surface rippled by the light breeze that flowed from the east. Aya, content that no one was around for at least a mile, peeled off her dress and tiptoed into the lake. She washed herself with the gravel that littered the bottom, rinsed her waist-length hair as best she could, and scrubbed her dress. She wondered how the times had changed and if her clothing would pass until she found more. She was still very eighteen-hundreds, but at least she had some decent boots under her cream shift dress.

Naked, she sat on the shore amongst some weeping willows that were still devoid of their leaves and ran her fingers through the drops of light that spilled between the curled branches. Her clothes lay on some rocks nearby, drying in the early morning sun. By the surrounding air, she guessed it was late winter or early spring, though the temperature didn't bother her much. A vampire in the sun was an abnormality, but she wasn't a typical vampire.

Musing about her awakening as her mind became clearer, she remembered a dream...and she rarely saw anything while she was asleep. She remembered walking through a forest that was thick with ancient trees, their trunks covered in moss and vines. They were the purest green she'd ever seen in all her long years. Reaching out, she laid her hands against the trunk of the closest tree, listening to the surrounding sounds. A humming grew around her that became louder and louder until she realised it was a voice. *Blood of my blood...* It was the faintest whisper and she almost didn't catch the words. Looking around, her blue eyes sparkled in the dappled sunlight, and she gasped.

Aya jerked her head up, suddenly awake. She'd dozed again at the memory of the dream. Someone had called her—that, she was certain—and they had used an ancient spell to do so. There was some unknown power at play here. She could walk into a trap if she wasn't prepared—others hunted her as she hunted them.

Who had called her and what did they need her for? These were the questions she needed answered, and for that, she needed to find the spot where the spell was cast. Only then could she track for other answers.

Pulling on her dress, she wandered the shore of the lake, sending out her senses to feel the land ahead. From the abruptness of her awakening, she gathered the spell was cast nearby, perhaps within a few miles. Someone from the village, perhaps? She wondered what had become of the people she'd befriended in her brief time here during the Civil War. Lived and died, presumably.

It wasn't long before she felt the faint emanations of power from the forest. Wandering lithely through the trees, she came across a graveyard. It was so overgrown, it seemed to seldom hold visitors. The headstones were spotted with yellow lichens and green moss, some dating back to the former part of the seventeen-hundreds. The few family crypts were in a sorry state with broken windows and doors that had become unhinged and rusted. Aya didn't have much respect for the dead, so the neglect did not bother her that much. She much preferred how nature had claimed this place back.

An area in the centre of the site had been cleared, the earth newly churned. Dead leaves and twigs were swept to one side, and fallen branches and weeds were removed and put into a pile by the fence. The ground underneath was bare, with the faint traces of footprints and indentations where objects had lain. Aya noted the markings bore the resemblance to a circle of power, the corners of a pentagram. *Witch work.*

At the very centre, she felt the residue of magic she'd noticed from the lake. Kneeling, she felt the disturbed earth with long, pale fingers. Yes, this was where it had happened. Aya heard the subdued humming she recognised from her dream. A potion was made here, and it'd had blood in it.

Strange...potions never sung like this. Perhaps it was the calling card the spell had left or the blood itself. It was like a song was being performed only for her to hear, something she had never experienced before.

Standing, she brushed her hands together to remove the dirt and smirked. Find the source of the song and there her caller would be. One and the same.

On her way to the town, Aya came across a farmhouse.

Inside, she heard the movements of the humans who dwelt there and at the rear, she found a clothesline where a youthful woman was pulling in dry laundry. While she watched, a man's voice called the woman from inside and she disappeared into the house, leaving the wicker washing basket on the ground.

Aya noted what the woman was wearing—a white shirt with no collar or sleeves and dark-coloured trousers—and darted across the lawn. She pulled similar clothing from the line and disappeared, the humans none the wiser.

Aya dared not move any faster than need be, so it took her some time to reach the outskirts of the village —now the town, of Ashburton. Even in the muted darkness she remembered how this place was, a small, sleepy village that grew more prosperous as time went by. Now it was a bizarre place. It was much larger and full of strange technology, but more alive and colourful than she'd expected.

The streets were hard, no longer packed dirt, and there were no horses to be seen. Shiny metal vehicles lined the street instead, and artificial orange light washed over her surroundings. She stared as one of the vehicles flashed past, with bright lights shining on the front.

A little overwhelmed by the changed world, Aya pulled the lapels her stolen jacket closed. Compared to other women who were around the streets, she passed as ordinary enough, but she was a little surprised at how promiscuous the fashions were. Skirts that finished above the knee, low-cropped blouses, and loose hair. It seemed acceptable, normal even.

Across the street, she spied a restaurant and bar that seemed to be where most people were gathered. The clock on the town hall a few doors down stated it was seven-thirty p.m. The bar was her first and best option to gather information. People talked more freely with a bit of alcohol.

She crossed the garden square and moved through the people gathered on the sidewalks. A few men glanced at her as she passed and their female partners cast her withering glares, which she disregarded without so much as a glance in their direction.

Aya opened the door to the bar and stopped just inside the doorway. In a split-second, she'd surveyed the room and found three vampires, a witch, and a werewolf. What a small-town supernatural hub. Ashburton had really come up in the underworld.

Perhaps her rude awakening wouldn't be such an unpleasant thing after all, but she had to be mindful of who these creatures were. The town would be claimed by one of the groups and by the intensity in the bar, she guessed it was up for contention.

She strode toward the bar at the far side of the large, open room, aware that eyes were following her progress. The place was not that busy as it was still early evening, but busy enough that she brushed past her fair share of alcohol-fuelled boyish men. Young, *human* men.

She shook her head, pushing away the impulse. This was reconnaissance only. Fresh, warm, human blood straight from the source was an indulgence that too often turned her into something darker than she ever wanted to be.

At the bar she ordered a triple scotch, straight up.

The bartender eyed her with a little awe—she didn't have to read his emotions to know that he was a little turned on by the thought of a woman like her drinking hard liquor. "On the house," he said with a little compulsion. Strange enough, the alcohol helped with her control, but it took a lot of the stuff to make her drunk.

As the scotch slowly disappeared from the glass, her inner compass noted the lay of the bar behind her. She sat on a stool, studying the bottom of her glass, taking a moment to acclimatise to the odd new world. The lights, music, and people were so alien to her that her head spun.

She listened to conversations, trying to hear anything that would be of use—from assimilating into this slightly insane new era, to locating the source of the singing blood.

It didn't take long for her to realise that the world might be different, but people never changed. Humans were still obsessed with the same things—money, sex, and power.

Two vampires were seated with a witch at the rear of the bar. She couldn't help but notice that they were staring at her and not making any effort to hide it, even if her back was turned. The third vampire seemed to be with them but was flitting around, talking to many young humans. She felt young herself...almost newly made. The werewolf, a young testosterone-fuelled male, stood to Aya's left, ordering a couple of beers. He was unconsciously fidgeting and leaning toward her as if he could sense she was something else...and he reeked of sweat and blood.

The wolf left, taking his stink with him, but to her annoyance, he was replaced with one of the vampires.

He leaned against the bar with the pretence of ordering drinks, but she could feel the curiosity dripping from him. Tall, dark, and handsome was such a cliché, but an apt description.

He feigned a casual glance in her direction and caught her gaze. Green eyes assessed her from under his messy black hair and she wondered how old he was, though she knew he was nowhere near her actual age. No vampire in this country was, at least before she went to sleep. It was a new age and a lot more things seemed accessible, even for the undead.

"Hi." He smiled at her.

She looked away, not wanting to encourage him.

He held his hand out, flashing a warm smile, ignoring her brush off. "I'm Zachary Degaud, and you are?"

She turned her head slightly and looked him up and down. "And what am I going to do with a Zachary Degaud?"

The faint trace of a smile touched his lips. "Just rolling out the welcome wagon."

"Zachary is such an old-fashioned name."

"What can I say? Old-fashioned parents." He

leaned closer, flashing a wicked smile. "But you can just call me Zac. And your name is?"

She could tell he was one for playing games. Asking casual questions to gain morsels of information. In other circumstances she would have had a lot of fun with this one.

She looked him up and down again and decided to play the game. "You can call me Aya."

"Aya." He tried her name out, pleased she'd taken the time to assess him. "Aya, what?"

She smirked. "Just Aya."

"I haven't seen you here before, *Just Aya*. Are you new to town?" He winked. "And your accent... Do I detect a hint of British there?"

She narrowed her eyes. "Just passing through."

Not new to town, I can remember being here long ago, she thought. What a unique place it was. She wondered if he knew how dark Ashburton's past really was.

"I was born in Britain," she added before she could stop herself. Well, her accent was unmistakable.

"Only passing? Sounds like you'll be gone soon. Do you mind if I join you for a drink? I'd hate to miss the opportunity to get to know such a beautiful woman."

Aya unsuccessfully stifled a laugh. He obviously suspected she was more than human, but trying to glean information from her under duress of flattery? It was a manipulation she was well-acquainted with and at least a little fond of. She was also aware that his vampire and witch friend had not stopped watching them. They were listening in on every cringeworthy word that he dribbled.

"I don't think so, Zachary. I'm not one for falling for cheap flattery from strange men in bars." The lack of emotion in her voice was chilling as she shot him down. "You need to improve your game."

His eyes widened ever so slightly. He obviously wasn't used to being turned down. He was rather handsome in the dangerous kind of way...seduction was a weapon for him.

Before he could retort, the door opened with a crash and a group of rowdy men burst in, laughing and wrestling. Aya cursed under her breath. She couldn't help but breathe in their scent as the wind blew around them. They stunk of human blood and sweat and violence. *Werewolves.* Werewolves who had obviously been on the hunt in their human form. Zac visibly stiffened.

Aya raised her eyebrow at him. "Friends of yours?"

"Not in the slightest." He glanced back to his friends, who were looking a little unsettled, but both groups kept their distance at opposite ends of the bar.

These were the groups fighting over the town. Now she was sure of it.

Repulsed by the emotions emanating from the wolves, she scowled. Hunting was one thing but killing innocent humans for sport went against all that she'd worked for.

She seethed, their stink fuelling her primal anger. *It would be so easy to tear them apart, to strew their body parts through the forest. It wouldn't take long...*

Aya felt her eyes clouding at the thought. Blinking, she cleared her mind and turned back to Zac. She had to be careful. There was still the issue of finding the one who had called her, and she wanted to do it without revealing herself, at least not at first.

"Well," she declared, "this town is flavoursome."

"Never a truer word spoken." Zac snorted. "Are you sure I can't join you?" His wicked grin had returned.

Aya glanced over her shoulder. Perhaps Zac was the one who'd called her. It would explain why he was sniffing around; vampires didn't usually bother one another unless there was something in it for them. He did have a witch friend hovering in the wings who could've cast the spell, but perhaps he was just trying to figure out if she was a vampire, someone whom he could enlist in the war over territory.

She glanced toward the witch and for the first time, met her gaze. She was a young woman with pale olive-toned skin, long dark hair, and a warm radiance of muted power. A power that was very familiar—one to watch.

"No," she said, answering his question. "I was just leaving."

"Will I see you again, Miss Aya?"

She looked at him with a note of amusement. "Maybe."

It was time to withdraw from this supernatural hotbed—all the underlying vendettas that were emerging in this place were overwhelming her still groggy senses. She'd only been awake for a few hours and had slept a lot longer than she'd planned. Another mystery.

Her cool blue gaze met his. "Good night, Mr. Zachary." Then she promptly stalked across the room and slunk through the door while the three supernaturals watched her smooth exit.

CHAPTER 6

Zac watched Aya as she left, his head spinning.

Her clear blue eyes were haunting, almost otherworldly, but as the wolves had come in, he was sure they'd clouded over. Not like his own black vampire eyes; hers were chillingly white.

He was now positive she wasn't entirely human… but what was she exactly? He had absolutely no idea.

Was Aya the Witch Hunter? He wasn't so sure—she didn't seem the type on first meeting.

Returning to their table, Zac sank down into his seat, frowning.

"You could've brought some drinks back, brother." Sam feigned exasperation then added, "She didn't give much away, did she?"

Zac nodded. "I have to find out more about her. I don't think she's a vampire, but she's certainly not one hundred percent human, either."

Gabby raised her eyebrows. "I think I should be the one doing the digging. I might get a read on her."

Sam shook his head. "Your powers aren't developed. What if she is the Hunter and doesn't like the fact that we summoned her? She could rip you apart."

Zac tilted his head to the side as if he were listening to something. "I can still feel her outside. I'm going to follow her."

Sam grabbed Zac's arm as he made to stand up. "I know you're keen for some action, but I don't think you should push it. The wolves are still here. I know you can smell the blood on them. They've been hunting."

Zac's face became dark with anger. "Let me be, brother. You and I both know that I was made for this. I spent the last one hundred years stalking death and tormenting the living, and that's not a skill easily forgotten. And if you are thinking about stopping me, remember that I am stronger than you. *You still feed on squirrels.*"

Sam let him go. "I thought you were trying to change. Let this one go."

"You can't change a vampire's basic nature, Sam. The sooner you realise that, the happier you'll be." He was halfway across the bar before Sam could formulate a response.

Aya knew he would follow.

She stood on the sidewalk some distance away from the bar, the heavy night air clinging around her tightly. Pulling back into the shadows, she watched as he stepped onto the street and looked around, listening. As he turned her way, she sidled into the ally beside her.

It housed a few dumpsters and fire escapes...and darkness. The perfect place to linger. She jumped to the top of the fire escape two stories up, crouching back into the shadows, and waited.

Zac stopped at the mouth of the alleyway, silhouetted by the light of the streetlamps. He was using all his strength to look for her, that she could tell. *Look all you want, vampire. You won't find me.*

He took a few cautious steps into the darkness, listening. She was confident he couldn't sense her, but he continued into the alley regardless. He looked around a moment and turned to leave but halted when he saw what awaited him. The five werewolves from the bar stalked into the opening, blocking the way, their bulky forms silhouetted by the orange glow of the streetlamps.

Sniggering, they circled Zac, their breath vaporising in the chilled night air.

Aya heard the faint growl of warning that came from deep inside Zac's throat as he looked at each of the wolves in turn. "Best you go back to your kennels, boys, before you do something you regret."

They all laughed, elbowing each other.

"Five against one, blood sucker, and the moon's almost full," the largest of the men said.

"When we kill you, it will be a message to yer brother and his whore," spat another. "You kill one of ours and we kill one of youse."

"Oh, but that wasn't us who ripped his head off," Zac drawled. "Honestly, I'm disappointed it wasn't me who got to do the honours."

"We don't give one shit about vamper business. We want you out of this town fer good," the alpha drawled as he approached Zac.

Before the vampire could react, the two wolves behind him lunged forward, wooden stakes dropping out of their sleeves, and stabbed him through both shins.

He fell to the ground, howling in pain. "Oh, you'll be sorry you did that, *dog*."

The wolves howled with laughter, circling him. "Man, you're the dumbest vamper we've ever had the pleasure of beatin' ta death. We'll love takin' our time stakin' you."

Zac rolled over, pulling the stakes from his legs, grimacing as each came free. "Like to see you try, Fido."

His eyes misted black and he bared his fangs, lunging for the alpha, but the others were on him. He was flung across the alley and hit the brick wall of the adjoining building hard. Before he could rise, a wolf staked him in the shoulder. Collapsing with a cry of rage, Zac kicked out and tripped his attacker. In one swift movement, he tore the stake from his shoulder and stabbed it through the wolf's knee, hobbling him.

Enraged, the pack was on top of him, trying to hold him down while the alpha kicked and punched. There were audible snapping sounds as he broke Zac's arms and jaw.

Aya winced. Could she hold herself back from this? He was a vampire and they were werewolves—neither were innocent. It wasn't what she fought against and it was not her right to interfere.

Zac was on his knees, blood pouring from dozens of wounds and dripping from his mouth. The smell of it was overwhelming, intoxicating. The alpha punched him savagely in the ribs, the crack audible as several snapped under the impact.

Zac doubled over crying out in pain as the wolves yelled, "Die, vampire!"

Aya hissed as the scent of blood tore at her resolve. The filthy dogs would kill him. She wasn't thrilled to reveal herself so soon—it was too much too soon. The blood, the pain, the resigned fear emanating from the vampire...even the pure joy the wolves felt at the promise of murder.

Before she realised, Aya had silently appeared behind the alpha. The wolf had Zac's head in his hands, his muscles tensing as he made to snap his neck.

Before the others realised she was there, Aya sunk her fingers into the alpha's back and tore him in two. Shoulder to groin, he fell apart in a shower of hot, sticky blood and insides.

Aya tasted the blood in her mouth and her eyes clouded over, her own blood quickening. Zac's eyes were wide with disbelief as he collapsed onto the pavement, his strength gone.

Aya turned her face toward the next closest wolf, who backed away. She was on him in a flash, tearing his head from his body.

The three remaining wolves ran, but they never made it more than a few steps before they too were torn apart.

Aya crouched over the last and sunk her teeth into his neck and drank her fill while he still twitched. The wolf's blood was sour with the stench of torture and malice as it ran down her throat.

It was Zac's moaning that finally brought her back from the frenzy.

Shaking her head to clear her eyes, she rose, her gaze moving to the broken vampire. She stood over him, assessing her next move.

He rolled onto his back with a twisted grimace and startled as he saw her standing over him. He tried to scramble backward, the sight of her sparking unexpected fear in him.

Aya, still hazy from the wolf's blood, grabbed Zac by the neck and threw him against the wall. She pressed herself against his broken body and dug her fingers into his neck, partially crushing his airway. He grabbed at her hands, trying to free himself as he gasped for air.

"Listen to me, vampire," she hissed into his ear. "I'm not here to make your life difficult. I am not here to hurt you. I could squeeze your pathetic head from your shoulders with no effort at all. I saved you tonight and delivered you control over this pitiful town. You'll do well to remember that and stay out of my way." She let him go and he fell to his knees, gasping for breath.

"What are you?" he rasped, clutching his broken ribs with one hand and rubbing his crushed neck with the other. "Your eyes..."

Aya stared down at him, wondering how far she should go. She'd already crossed the line in revealing herself to him in such a violent way, but that couldn't be helped now. He stared up at her with his deep green eyes, half in fear and half in awe, and suddenly she was uneasy.

She crouched down so she was at his eye level. Tensely, she raised her hand to touch the marks she had left on his neck. Before her fingers could brush his skin, she pulled back. His blood was familiar somehow. *Was he the one?*

Then she realised she could hear the humming sound again at the edges of her awareness. She tasted the blood on her fingers, a combination of werewolf and vampire. Her eyes widened slightly when, for a split-second, she could feel the starlight on her shoulders—something she hadn't felt for a very long time.

In that moment, she knew it was Zac's blood that had been used to call her. The song she had heard at the cemetery was all around him.

Zac reached out to her and she jumped backward, standing to her full height. "Was it you?"

"What?" Zac grimaced as he dragged himself to his feet.

Aya didn't answer. There was something terrible about him, something different. Now that it was in front of her, she became even more uncertain. His blood sang to her in a way she had never felt in all her long years. It wasn't lust or love…it was something else.

And it frightened her.

"You're the Witch Hunter," he stated suddenly, stumbling backward into the wall in surprise. "I knew something was different about you, but—"

Aya darted forward and pinned Zac against the wall again. He didn't struggle this time, but his eyes gave away his fear. "When I've gone from this alley, you will wake up and forget that I was ever here. You will forget that it was I who killed the wolves. You'll wake up and *forget*." She prayed that she'd had enough blood for the compulsion to work.

As she dropped Zac, he fell to his knees again.

Then, she disappeared.

Sam, Liz, and Gabby came to an abrupt halt as they entered the alley. Gabby turned and promptly heaved into the gutter.

The scent of blood was thick in the air, and Sam gasped at the carnage that littered the alley about him. Severed limbs, guts, and gore littered the dark alley. He had no idea what'd happened. Did Zac do this?

What. The. *Hell.*

They were the werewolves...or what was left of them.

Sam cursed, hastily avoiding the gore, and approached his brother. Zac was healing from numerous injuries, his clothing torn and mostly covered in his own blood. He looked as mystified as Sam did.

They'd left the bar a few minutes after the werewolves, but a few minutes was all it took. Turning back toward Liz, he noticed she was hovering at the mouth of the alley, agitated.

"I can't, Sam," she said, hugging her arms about her. "It's too much."

He knew straight away that the blood was messing with her control and he beckoned to Gabby. "Can you take her home? I'll deal with this..." He gestured around him.

Gabby took Liz's hand and led her away. Once he

was certain they were gone, he turned back to Zac and grimaced. "What the hell did you do?"

Zac shrugged and looked up.

"Zac, now is not the time to—"

"I don't know what the hell happened, Sam!" he yelled, throwing his hands in the air. "The dogs beat the crap out of me and were happy to keep on going until I was dead. The alpha was about to rip my head off...then I woke up on the ground and they were all in bits. That's *all I remember*."

Sam grabbed Zac's face, moving it side to side, looking into his eyes.

"What the hell, Sam!" He jerked away.

"I don't think you were compelled. I can't sense anything." He frowned, not sure what to believe. They had to clean up this mess before anyone discovered it or there would be trouble.

"We can't be compelled," Zac said angrily, his face betraying his doubt.

"We've not come across many vampires older than we are. Perhaps it is possible," Sam wondered, though a little alarmed. "Do you think the spell worked?"

"You think the Witch Hunter did this?" Zac balked. "Why would they help me against *werewolves*?"

Sam tried to keep his voice calm. "I don't know, but we need to be prepared for anything."

Snorting, Zac rose, his gaze turning to the body parts. "The only logical explanation is that I blacked out and..."

Sam's brow furrowed in concern. "A frenzy?"

Zac sighed and pinched the bridge of his nose with his bloodstained fingers. "It wouldn't be unheard of. I was never a dog person."

"Maybe you're right. They got you pretty good." Sam turned to help his brother, already tired of thinking about the unexplainable.

Grimacing, Zac popped his ribs back into place with a sharp jab with his fingers. "Yeah, my jaw is still broken."

"The sooner we get this swept under the rug, the sooner we can get you something to eat." Blood would help him heal and regain his strength. *Clean* blood, that was.

It took them all night to dispose of the bodies and wash away the blood, alternating trash detail with keeping watch. They didn't speak, resigned to listening to their own thoughts. Sam didn't know what had happened to the woman Aya, where she had disappeared to, or if Zac had even found her, but it seemed like the least of their problems right now. Five wolves didn't exactly make a pack and he could only pray that no one would care enough to come looking.

Once the night began to lighten into a murky pre-dawn grey, the scene was erased and the brothers headed home after yet another night of fighting, with more questions raised than answered. One problem solved and another gained.

CHAPTER 7

With dawn came the sun. Monsters of the dark couldn't walk here, but for Aya, it was never an issue. She could walk wherever she chose.

She was strolling through the gardened square in the centre of Ashburton, marvelling at the flowers and manicured hedges lining the paths. It reminded her of an age long past, of another life where she was at peace.

The winter's day was crisp and clear, blue sky overhead, the humidity of the swamp non-existent. It was now the twenty-first century—she'd read it on a discarded newspaper along with the headlines. She had slept for one-hundred and fifty years, which was a lot longer than she'd intended. If it wasn't for the summoning spell, she wasn't sure when she would've woken.

Aya already liked this time. Apart from the technological advances—smartphones, cars, and electricity—it was the social ones she liked the most. Women were so much more free and powerful, and the fashions they were allowed to wear were seductive. She'd already found a liking for rock 'n' roll music and the clothing the sale's woman had picked out for her. What did she call it? Motorcycle jacket, dark jeans, singlet, and combat boots...*rock chic*. Aya liked the sound of that. When it came time for payment, Aya stared into the woman's eyes and made her ring it all up for free.

After her shopping trip, she ventured into some other stores along the main street. Her favourite was the large bookstore where any question she had about this time was answered. They even let her sit and read as long as she liked without bothering her.

Outside, it was the town square and adjoining gardens that captured her attention. It seemed most of Ashburton was out and about, enjoying the unseasonable cloudless day. It had never taken her so long to adjust to a new era after waking, but the world had become so different in such a short time.

Exploring was exciting, but she couldn't get the vision of what she'd done the previous night out of her head. Losing control like that was unforgivable. She'd wanted to rip those wolves apart so badly, but not until they had cornered that annoying vampire, Zac. Then she'd ripped them apart, into a million tiny pieces.

But if she hadn't, she would never have found the

blood that'd called her. She'd had to taste it before the song began. Before the stars called to her...

She was so distracted, she tensed when she realised someone was watching her. Without looking up from her newspaper, she sent her mind out and felt the now familiar hum of blood.

Zac was in the square.

And in the daylight.

She sensed another vampire with him, the younger sociable female from the bar, as well as the baby witch. She was not sure about Zac, but the other vampire... she was new, how could she tolerate the sun? The witch didn't seem powerful enough to spell a trinket for her to wear, let alone place one on her body.

Casting her hearing out, she could tell they were arguing about something. Approaching her, most likely.

We don't know who she is, Zac. Trust me, Liz. Be careful, she heard amongst the buzzing of his blood.

Rolling her eyes, she turned around and glared at them. Getting up, she wandered down the closest path through the gardens in order to escape their gaze. She needed time to think over her options. She needed a plan of attack after the previous evening and to think about her loss of control, among other things.

The taste of Zac's blood had awoken senses she hadn't felt since before she was turned, and that could be dangerous. Not to mention their motives might be malicious. Others hunted her as she hunted them. Deals had been done for less.

Strolling down the path, her gaze wandered to the surrounding gardens. The plants were well-looked after and landscaped into intricate patterns. She marvelled at a display of small grey ground cover grasses that'd been grown and trimmed into a simple mandala.

"What do you think, miss?" She heard at her shoulder.

Turning, she found a young human man with short, messy, red-tinted brown hair and chestnut eyes smiling at her. From his dirt-encrusted overalls and wheelbarrow full of cuttings, she gathered he must be the gardener.

"It's beautiful," she replied. "Did you do this?"

"Yeah." He blushed. "At first the boss didn't like me spending so much time on them, but I used to do it on my days off. When we won first in the annual county comps, he didn't mind so much."

"Well," Aya said, turning back to the garden and ignoring the gardener's blush, "the entire garden is wonderful."

"Thanks." He laughed nervously. "Oh, I'm Alex."

"Aya." She shook his outstretched hand, hoping he wasn't trying to come onto her.

"Very pleased to meet you." He smiled shyly. "So, do you work around here or are you a visitor?"

"Oh, um..." She raised her eyebrows, not sure what to say.

"Sorry, I don't mean to pry. Just a little small-town hospitality."

"No, it's fine." She shook her head. "I'm just...not used to people noticing."

Alex raised his eyebrows. "Then they're fools."

If her blood could actually flow the same way a human's did, then she might have blushed.

"I've got some work in the area," she said. "Temporary work."

"Oh, right. What doing? If you don't mind me asking, that is."

Aya winked. "If I told you, I'd have to kill you."

Alex hesitated for a moment and laughed. "You almost got me with that one."

"How long have you worked here?" she asked, quickly changing the subject.

"About three years. I was an apprentice builder, but gardening seemed more my thing."

"Sure is."

"And you? You seem into nature. Do you garden at all?"

She laughed. "No, I'm more of an appreciator. My family was..." She clamped her mouth shut. This Alex guy had an uncanny way of making her feel at ease.

"Hey, I'm sorry. I didn't mean..."

She turned and smiled at him. "It's fine."

He sensed that she was uncomfortable and to

change the subject, he said, "If you keep going down that way, there is a forested section with some nice ferns and Spanish moss in the trees." He pointed ahead, then gestured to the right. "That way is a cottage garden, English style, though it's out of season for most of the flowers."

"Thanks," Aya said and began to move off. "It was really nice meeting you."

Grabbing the handles of his wheelbarrow, he smiled and nodded, continuing back the way she'd come.

Zac watched Aya from across the square. Gabby and Liz flanked him, following his gaze, both equally deep in thought.

Aya had, without a doubt, caught his interest, especially after last night. She sat with her back to them on a park bench, reading a newspaper, seemingly oblivious to the world around her. Though he seriously doubted that.

When he'd left the bar last night, he'd sensed her presence on the street as clear as day...until he'd reached the alleyway. It was as if she'd disappeared into thin air. He was positive that she wasn't human, but what exactly was she? That was still a mystery.

"Maybe you should give it a day or two. Especially after what had happened last night," Liz urged.

"*Pfft.* I'm one hundred and seventy years old and I'm already dead," he scoffed. It'd be stupid not to admit to himself that he was rattled by the gruesome end to their dog problem but admitting that to someone else... *Never.* A frenzy like that wasn't unheard of and the circumstances were right, but he didn't remember a shred of it. That was the only thing that unsettled him about the entire fiasco.

Gabby wasn't entirely convinced. "C'mon, Zac, if she's the one, then she's at least six hundred years old, right? That would make her stronger than you by far."

"Yeah, but I'm charming."

Liz sighed. "If you have to, then just be careful, okay?"

"Yeah," Gabby said, looking toward the gardens. "There's something strange about her I can't quite put my finger on."

"You got that right, Glinda." He used one of his favourite nicknames for her. "Have you ever heard of a vampire with white eyes?"

Gabby frowned. "No. What makes you say that?"

He shrugged. "Last night, when the wolves came in, I swore her eyes changed."

Gabby looked at Liz, who mirrored her confused expression. "I've never heard of it. But it's a clue, at least."

"Hmm," Zac murmured, lost in thought. "Stay here, I'm going to see what I can get out of her."

"Whatever, Zac. I've got to go back to work." Gabby walked away, clearly over it.

Liz followed Zac, determined to keep him in line. "We don't know who she is."

He turned and placed a hand on her shoulder to stop her. "Trust me, Liz."

"*Be careful*," she said.

"I always am."

"Liar."

Zac smiled. He'd do whatever he wanted. He always did.

Catching sight of Aya speaking with the human gardener Alex, Zac moved closer so he could listen to what they were saying, determined to expose her.

***

Aya continued around the path in the direction of the forest. This area of the gardens reminded her of her home. No, the place she was born. It stopped being her home once they'd defiled it.

Lingering underneath an ancient, gnarled cypress, she could almost imagine her brother climbing amongst the branches, teasing her from above. Allowing the daydream to creep into her mind, she closed her eyes while the yellow light filtered through the canopy and warmed her cheeks.

Lost in her memory, she hadn't noticed Zac approach from the opposite direction. Her eyes snapped open and she stared at him, making her expression as unreadable as she could.

He sauntered down the path, his blood buzzing like an annoying bee circling a flower.

Grinning, he said, "Hello, Miss Aya."

"Zac." She nodded curtly, hoping he would go away.

"Beautiful day for a walk in the gardens," he said with a wink.

"Do you enjoy following young women to dark corners, Mr. Degaud?" she drawled, all tact flying out the window. She wondered how many women he'd stalked down dark alleyways in his desire for blood. All vampires did, it was folly to deny it.

Zac narrowed his eyes and she knew she'd struck a nerve. "My brother works here." He shrugged, disregarding her cold question.

A vampire gardener. Aya snorted at the ironic notion.

In the distance, she could see the young woman he was talking with earlier, the one he'd called Liz. She was trying her hardest to look elsewhere, to remain casual, but her body was tense and angled toward them.

"Your girlfriend is staring at us." She nodded in Liz's direction. "What's her deal?"

"She's not my girlfriend," he replied, looking away. "That's my brother's girl."

"Looks like it bothers you." She stared, making him visibly uncomfortable.

"We're not talking about me," he said curtly.

"And what are we talking about?"

"I'm much more interested in you."

"What's new soon becomes old, you know. Give up while you're ahead," she told him.

"I'd much rather chase pretty girls around for the rest of my days than give up. With all the women in the world, there's a new one for every day," he said with a laugh. "I'll start with you."

"Very smooth, Mr. Degaud." A player in every sense of the word.

"Just keeping the old-world charm alive."

"What do you want?" She raised her eyebrows, cutting to the chase. "Do you want me to join your super-secret cult or was there something specific you wanted?"

He laughed again, running his hand through his messy hair. "It's hardly a secret that I want something."

She looked at him, waiting for him to say something else, feeling the uncertainty radiating from him...along with that annoying hum. Glancing across the park, she saw Alex look up from his work. As their gazes meet, he mouthed, "Hi." She smiled at the casual gesture.

"You're blowing me off for Alex?" Zac feigned disgusted surprise. "I'm much more handsome than he is."

Aya glanced at Liz this time, who was still pretending not to notice them. She looked bothered, worrying the hem of her T-shirt with long pale fingers. "Are you always this shallow?"

"*Ouch*," Zac said mockingly. "Are you always this brutal?"

"Only to the those who deserve it." Aya raised her eyebrows when Zac didn't move. "That's your cue to move along, Casanova."

"Fine, fine." He raised his hands in mock surrender. "I know when I'm defeated. I'll see you around."

He backed away a few steps, then turned and walked toward Liz. He then looked back at Aya with a lopsided grin.

Catching movement out of the corner of her eye, she turned as Alex jumped over a low box hedge at the side of the path. "Was he bothering you?"

"Yes, he is bothersome." Aya sighed.

Zac was someone who was used to getting his way and doing whatever it took to get it. She knew his type all too well. He reeked of recklessness and that could mean trouble for her if she wasn't careful.

"He's the brother of a guy who works here." Alex cocked his head toward the direction Zac had disappeared, confirming what the vampire had said earlier. "Don't worry too much about him. It's mostly bravado. If you want me to have a word with him..."

Aya smiled. "It's okay. I can handle his kind...but thank you."

He blushed and picked up the hedge clippers from the turf. "Well, I better get back to it." As an afterthought, he added, "Hey, if you're staying a while, you should come to *Max's* tonight. It's the bar across the way there. I usually meet Sam and some other friends there after work for a few drinks and a bit of pool. I dunno, could be something to do…"

Aya smiled. It had been a long time since anyone had invited her anywhere without an ulterior motive. She sensed she had to be careful that she didn't lead Alex on. He seemed like one of the few genuine humans out there. Clueless, but genuine.

"Okay," she conceded, after a moment's thought to the contrary. "Perhaps."

CHAPTER 8

Aya was worried about going to the bar that evening. Having spent the afternoon at the bookshop and the library, she was more than ready for a few drinks but less inspired about the questions Alex would ask. Innocent questions, but ones she couldn't answer with truths.

They'd want to know about her, where she was from, what she was doing here, about her family, her likes and dislikes. *Normal things.*

There was no hiding her accent, she was undoubtedly British. She spoke many languages, but the accent was something she kept hold of. It was a part of her that she couldn't seem to shake, no matter how many centuries had passed.

The bar was busy, full of people winding down on a Friday afternoon desperate to forget their working week. She pushed through the doorway and immediately felt the presence of two vampires over by the far-right wall. Glancing in their direction, her eyes found Alex sitting with them, laughing at some joke someone had just told.

It was the other male and the girl, Liz. Walking toward them, she smiled as Alex raised his hand to wave her over.

"Hey," he said, getting up. "Glad you could make it. This is Sam and his girlfriend, Liz. This is Aya." He gestured to the two vampires and she realised he didn't have a clue that his friends weren't human.

"Oh," she said, extending her hand. "Pleased to meet you. Sam, you work with Alex, right?"

Sam smiled warmly and shook her hand. "I see he's been telling you a few things. Hopefully all nice things."

"Not much." Keeping her expression even, Aya smiled, turned to Liz, and shook her hand. She found the blonde was still as annoying as she had been earlier that morning...and she hadn't even opened her mouth yet.

"I was just telling them that Zac was harassing you in the gardens today," Alex said.

Aya shrugged. "You call that harassing? Really, it was nothing I couldn't deal with."

Sam let out a laugh. "From what he said, it sounded like you mortally wounded him. Whatever you've done, keep doing it. He needs to be taken down a peg or two." He winked at her.

"Ah," Aya said. "So, you're the brother."

"Unfortunately, yes." Sam grimaced and winked again. "Luckily, I'm the nice one. Zac likes to play the bad boy, but underneath it all, he's a decent guy. He just doesn't like showing it."

Aya heard Zac approach from behind, betrayed but the sound of his blood.

"Oh, I see. Like a defence mechanism, right?" she asked a little sarcastically. "To cover up his pure, wounded heart?"

"You got it," Zac said darkly. "I gotta protect myself from the big bad world."

"I could use a defence mechanism right about now." Aya rolled her eyes and turned to face him.

Zac frowned and ran his hand through his hair. "Look, Aya. We've got off on the wrong foot. I'd like to start again."

Sam snorted behind her, making Zac glare even harder.

Aya grinned up at him. "I'll think about it, but you'll have your work cut out for you."

The others laughed again. She could tell he was having a hard time admitting that he'd been an idiot. This was probably the best she would ever get in the way of an apology.

"Well, let me start by getting you a drink," he added. "Scotch?"

"Very observant of you, Mr. Degaud." She smiled as he walked away.

"So," Liz began, "how long are you staying for, Aya?

Alex mentioned you were only here temporarily."

"I'm not sure yet. It depends on my work." Which, technically, wasn't a lie.

"What do you do?" Sam asked casually.

"If she told you, she'd have to kill you," Alex said with a smile, obviously remembering their conversation that morning.

Aya noticed the fleeting looks of panic on Sam and Liz's faces before they laughed.

"Really, it's boring," she told them. "I consult with local governments over their building ordinances. Heritage...*stuff*."

"You're right," Alex said. "Sounds like a hoot."

"What do you do for fun, Aya?" Liz asked.

What did she do in her spare time? She thought back to the 1860s. She'd come to Ashburton to find and punish a naughty witch. What she did for fun was play with people's emotions and drink their blood, though she could hardly tell them that. "I travel a lot, so I like to learn about the places I visit. It helps with work."

"A history buff, huh? You'd get along with Alex's sister. Too bad she's in England studying," Liz said and turned to Alex. "Where is she again?"

"Oxford," Alex said with a sad note in his voice. "Where's your family from, Aya?"

"A tiny village in the Lake District," she replied, which was mostly the truth. "Grasmere. It's quite a way from Oxford, in the Northwest."

There was an annoying buzzing sound that grew

louder and halted in a crescendo as Zac placed a glass of scotch in front of her. She gave him a half smile in thanks and took a large mouthful. Sam raised his eyebrow slightly at her thirst for alcohol, but she ignored him.

"Why did you come to the States, then?" Alex asked.

"A job offer." Aya shrugged. "It was too good to refuse, if you know what I mean."

"What about your family?"

Her eyes narrowed slightly. "I don't speak to them." That was true and the table became silent. Aya took advantage of the break in the questioning to down the rest of her drink to help curb her annoyance.

"So, you two are gardeners," she said, changing the subject when it became apparent no one knew what to say next. "What do you two do?" She looked at Liz and Zac.

"Well," Liz began, "I work over at the coffeehouse for the moment. I'm thinking about college in the spring or next fall. And what do you do, Zac?" The last part came out with a note of sarcasm.

"I do a lot of stuff," he said.

"He does nothing but be a nuisance all day," Sam explained.

"I don't need to work, so I don't see the point."

"Isn't it boring?" Aya asked.

"Nope. Not when there's so many people who rise to the occasion," he said, prodding for a reaction.

"I've never risen once."

His eyes narrowed. "Not yet."

Aya turned to Sam, ignoring Zac's last statement. "So, where do you live, exactly?"

"We own the old manor and plantation grounds on the east side of town," he replied.

"Ah, the Degaud Manor. Obviously."

"Do you know it?" Alex asked.

"Of course, she knows it," Liz told him with a huff. "She works with heritage building laws."

Aya remembered the manor when it was newly built, but she contemplated what she'd read in the library's archives earlier that morning. Rumours swirled about the house and the grounds, circling for decades until an urban legend had gained traction. Now, the human population of the town seemed to only know the diluted story.

The Degaud massacre was a dark piece of town history that wasn't dwelt upon...and for good reason.

The urban legend said that back in the weeks after the Civil War had ended, a servant had become insane. They'd slaughtered everyone who lived in the house and plantation, mutilating their bodies beyond recognition. The few slaves that'd escaped claimed it was the work of voodoo spirits and wouldn't set foot near the land again. Soon after, they disappeared, too. The manor had been abandoned ever since, only caretakers going to check the property every so often.

Most people kept away, spooked by the ghost stories that'd been made up about the place.

"Yes. I've read the stories," she said. The massacre was, undoubtedly, the work of vampires—it had all the calling cards.

"And I can safely say there are no ghosts or voodoo spirits lurking anywhere near the place," Sam told her. "They're all just scary stories."

"Well, that's reassuring." She smiled, knowing that ghosts—or rather, spirits—did exist. She'd assisted with a few exorcisms in her time.

After that, the subject changed to lighter topics. It was all gossip and stories about people and places she had no knowledge or interest in, so she let her mind wander. Keeping one ear on the conversation, she watched each vampire's mannerisms as they spoke.

She picked Sam to be the kinder of the brothers. He was rational and used his head more often than his heart.

Liz was young, and the way she spoke and held herself said she was inexperienced at life.

Alex was undoubtedly human in that he followed his heart in almost everything, but he was naïve in trusting that everyone around him had some good in them. That would be his downfall one day.

And Zac, who said very little the whole evening, showed himself to be arrogant and impulsive by the way he held himself. He was more concerned with what he could get out of someone to use to his advantage. *Typical vampire.*

But all of them were holding onto the human parts of themselves, some more than others. Liz and Sam were holding the tightest, almost desperately wanting to be the immortal humans capable of doing good. And Zac...? His hold was reluctant at best. It wouldn't take much to push him over the edge.

"I need to freshen up," Liz proclaimed, snapping her out of her daze. "Aya, come with."

"I'm fine thanks," she replied, raising her eyebrow.

"Oh, Aya. C'mon. I want to talk to you without the boys listening in." She winked at them, then took Aya's arm and led her toward the ladies' room.

Liz closed the bathroom door behind them and put her bag on the basin. The stalls were empty, and the dull roar of the busy bar was the only sound that filled the room. She took out a compact from her purse and dabbed powder on her face.

Aya leaned against the basin and eyed the young vampire in the mirror, feigning smoothing her hair down.

"What does your name mean?" Liz asked after a moment.

She shrugged. "It's just one of those strange names. My parents were free spirits."

"Right, I get it. Like the English equivalent of hippies? We had a girl at our school once who was named Rainbow Apple." She laughed at the insane notion.

"Well, that seems unfortunate," Aya said, reacting to the tone in Liz's voice. "How long have you and Sam been together?"

"Oh, about a year. He helped me through a rough patch and it kind of just happened. It's easy between us."

"That's a pretty ring." Aya reached out and took Liz's hand so she could see the jewel. It was a small onyx stone set in an ornate silver band. It tingled with the charm she knew it was infused with, and that magic was old. Surely, it was the trinket that allowed her to walk in the sun. Their witch couldn't have spelled it for her.

"Thanks. Sam gave it to me," she said, taking her hand back nervously, pretending to look at it herself. "You don't wear any enamoured. How come?"

"I never really saw the point. Maybe if someone gave me something, I would."

"Like a handsome man." Liz giggled, winking at her.

Aya pursed her lips. Girl-talk grated on her insides, but it was a means to an end. Playing along, she replied, "Maybe."

"Do you have anyone back where you're from?"

"No. No handsome man is waiting for me. My life is in America, at least, for now." She hadn't had to lie yet, but then again, she was good at manipulating her truths.

"Well, the guys around here are all falling over themselves over you."

"Really?" Aya frowned.

"Yes! Of course, they are. Aya, you're hot. You could have any of them you wanted." Liz offered her some lipstick.

She shook her head. "I never noticed."

"I can tell Alex thinks you're beautiful. Zac, too."

Aya scoffed at the notion, "I don't have time for romance."

Liz took the opportunity to push her toward the other brother. "Zac's really not that bad. Overprotective of his brother and he can say a lot of inappropriate things, but he's a decent guy under it all. He just likes to put on a show."

"I know the type." She rolled her eyes. "And it gets *very* old, *very* fast."

Liz frowned, but covered it up with a grin. "C'mon. I think we need more drinks. Make a late one of it." She linked her arm through Aya's and pulled her back out into the bar, trying to appear like her new best friend.

As they emerged from the bathroom, Zac stepped in front of Aya, blocking her way. He'd obviously decided to try another tactic. Liz's arm slid from hers and she stopped and turned back. Seeing Zac there, she winked at Aya before continuing back to their table.

"Yes?" Aya prodded when he said nothing.

"What are you really doing here, Aya?" he asked, stepping closer than she would like.

"Well, I thought that would be obvious. I'm having a drink with some nice people I met. Then *you* came along."

"Oh, don't play coy with me." He ran a finger down her cheek and along her jawline.

She noticed that his pupils were dilated slightly. She couldn't believe the gall of this man—he was trying to compel her! It would never work, not in a million years, though it angered her more than it should have.

Her expression darkened and she drew back and slapped him. For her it was the lightest of touches, but his head snapped to the side with the force of the blow. His hand went to his face in surprise.

Stalking back to the table, Aya let her expression darken with anger.

"Oh, Aya, I'm sorry," Liz cried when she sat down heavily. Of course, they'd been watching. "After what I said..."

Aya shrugged. She had expected no less from him. In all her years, it was rare to find a man who didn't only think about one thing where women were concerned—especially when they were trying to coerce information from her.

She caught sight of Zac as he pushed through the exit. He wasn't used to being shot down, that much she could tell. She sighed and took a long draught from her glass, already tired of his game.

Why had he cast the summoning spell at all? To get laid? If so, these people were beyond her help.

***

Alex and Sam were in deep conversation by the bar as they waited to be served. The place had really filled up and it was taking a long time for the staff to work their way through the queue.

Sam was asking his friend about Aya. Alex told him she'd been wandering the gardens that morning and he'd run into her, got to talking, and invited her to join them. He seemed enamoured with her after that one simple meeting.

There was nothing about her that gave away that she may be a vampire, but if she was as old as they had suspected, then she would be an expert in hiding her true self from the world. At least she'd seemed to have picked up on Alex's feelings and had kept herself at a distance. That one Sam would give her.

"Yeah," Alex said. "She seems real nice, but she doesn't seem to like to talk about herself much."

"No," Sam agreed, "she doesn't at all." So far, all her answers had been vague at best.

When they reached the table, they noticed Gabby

had joined them and Zac had disappeared. Aya seemed to be wound up about something, and his brother's absence seemed to be part of it. He wondered what he'd said this time.

"Liz and I have been friends since the seventh grade," Gabby said.

"And I've known Alex since grade school." Liz smiled at him as they approached.

"She's the one who taught me to put sand down other kid's pants." Alex looked at her with mock disapproval. "And I got into a lot of trouble for it, too."

"What happened to Zac?" Sam asked, sitting back in his seat.

Liz rolled her eyes. "What do you think happened?"

Sam looked from Liz to Aya and said, "Sorry."

"It seems like you apologise for him a lot," Aya told him. "I'd stop while you're ahead."

Sam ran his hand through his hair and laughed. "You're probably right. I guess it's just habit."

"I'm sorry, but I have to go." She stood abruptly. "It was nice to meet you all."

Sam went to protest, but she'd already turned and was several paces away. Looking to Alex, he shrugged. He would get the report from Zac later, no doubt. Clinking glasses with everyone, he promptly put them out of his mind.

When Sam got home, he found Zac in the parlour, lying on the sofa with an empty bottle of whiskey. If he were human, he'd be considered an alcoholic, or at least, in the hospital with alcohol poisoning.

"Let it rip, brother," Sam said as he sat in his usual chair. The way they sat was very doctor-patient.

Zac sat up and scowled. "I tried a different tactic since talking wasn't getting anywhere. If she was human, then she could be compelled."

Sam stifled a laugh. "You tried to *compel* her? And?"

"And it didn't work," he snapped.

"So, you automatically think she's not human?"

"She makes Gabby uneasy. Hell, even I can tell something is off. Don't tell me you can't; I wouldn't believe it if you did."

"Fine, yes. Something is off," he conceded. "I'm assuming that you've had enough time to think of another plan while you've been here licking your wounds?"

Zac rolled his eyes. "Of course, I have. I am an evil mastermind." *Well, he'd gotten the evil part right.*

"Spit it out, then."

"What are the three things that we can use on her to verify she's a vampire?"

Sam sighed, but played along. "Silver, sunlight, and..." He groaned. "A human barrier."

"Sunlight won't work, we already know that," Zac went on. "So, we need a house that a human lives in."

"Alex. You want her to go to Alex's and see if she needs to be invited in."

"Not only that," he declared. "Invite her over to dinner and spike her food."

Sam snorted. "That's a little childish, isn't it?"

"Maybe, but it's simple enough and foolproof."

"Maybe we should just ask her, Zac. All this tiptoeing around—"

"If she's not supernatural, or the Hunter, then she could be one of Katrin's," Zac told him. "We have to play this carefully, Samuel."

Reluctantly, Sam agreed. They didn't have the time to sit back and wait. They had to take the offensive. He knew Zac would need him to suggest the plan to Alex without him catching on, making it seem like it was his friend's idea to invite Aya over for dinner.

"Right," he said, running his hands down his face. "Leave it with me. I'll get Alex to invite her and make sure she turns up."

Zac grinned. "That's my boy."

CHAPTER 9

By Monday it was hot and muggy, the lingering moisture in the air annoyingly heavy.

It made work in the gardens difficult for Alex. Sam, not so much, though he complained to keep his friend happy. They were working on repainting the bandstand for the upcoming Spring Festival organised by the local Historical Society. An entire weekend of pre-Civil War era activities was an awkward blast from the past for Sam, who'd been there the first time around.

"Hey, we haven't had dinner in ages," Sam said suddenly. "We should do it this weekend."

Alex jumped down off the ladder, wiping the sweat from his brow with the back of his hand. "Oh, yeah. Sounds cool. I think it was my turn, right?"

"I don't really remember. But if you want to do it, I'll convince everyone to bring something."

Sam felt bad about manipulating his friend like this, but too much was at stake. The Witch Hunter hadn't shown up yet, and they were their only lead. Who knew when Katrin would rear her ugly head? Testing Aya seemed like the proactive thing to do.

"Okay, deal." Alex threw his paint-stained gloves into the barrow at his feet. "Speaking of food, it's lunchtime and I'm starving. Wanna go over to the café?"

Sam heartily agreed and they walked together towards Mrs. Greene's café.

Alex nudged him as they crossed the street, motioning toward the window of the bookstore. Inside, sitting on a sofa, reading a book about the Hubble space telescope, was Aya. She seemed rather enthralled in the workings of modern space exploration, so much so, that when Alex tapped on the glass, she jumped.

Sam chose to hang back as Alex ducked into the store. He cast his hearing out after his friend, hoping he'd catch a few words through the open door.

"Hey, Aya," Alex said as he approached her.

"What's up?" She smiled at him.

"I just wanted to know if you wanted to come to dinner on Friday," he asked, but quickly continued when she hesitated, "Oh, it's a dinner party type thing. There will be some other people. Gabby, Liz, Sam…"

She still seemed hesitant. "Oh, that sounds nice."

"Okay, well, it's at my place at seven. Friday night," he said, then gave her the address.

Aya's gaze flickered to Sam's through the window. "Sure. *I'd love to.*"

Alex grinned, backing out of the store. "Great. I'll catch you later, then."

Sam sighed and turned away from the window. Alex had invited her, just as they knew he would. He couldn't help feeling guilty as he came out of the bookstore, a grin plastered on his face. Sam elbowed him and they went to collect their lunch.

Thankfully, Friday came with no outside issues.

Sam told Liz and Gabby about their plan, and they arrived at Alex's early. They'd decided it would be best if they were there before Aya arrived so they could prepare.

Alex suspected nothing, glad for the help in the kitchen where Zac and Liz were currently holed up under the pretence of opening the wine.

"She doesn't wear any jewellery," Liz murmured. "How can she be out in the daytime?"

"That's irrelevant. It could be because she's old enough or a witch spelled her body," Zac explained as he popped the cork from one of the bottles and handed it to her.

"I thought that didn't work on you?" she asked, confused.

"Just because it didn't work on me the first time, doesn't mean it didn't on her," he replied sarcastically, taking a jar from his jacket pocket.

"And what's that?"

Zac shook the small jar so the powder moved inside. "This is silver." He took off the lid and sprinkled it over the mashed potatoes Liz had dished up on Aya's plate, careful not to let it touch his skin. Picking up a fork, he mixed it through. Taking out another jar from his opposite pocket, he sprinkled a clear liquid into the bottle of wine with the least left and shook it.

"And what was that?"

"This is a little something I got off a person of dubious nature," he said with a wink. "It's something like garlic."

"But garlic won't do anything."

"True, but if concentrated enough it will bring blood to the surface. Ingested, it will make her vomit it up by the bucket full."

"Zac, I'm not sure about this..." Liz shook her head. "It's over the top. We should just stick with the silver."

"Now, now, Liz. We have to be sure what she is. The last thing we need is another threat on top of an insane dead witch. I think she's a vampire and this is a foolproof way of finding out. If Alex gets to the door before one of us, he'll invite her in, so we need a backup plan." He turned and placed the plate back into the oven to keep it warm. "Just make sure you give her the right plate and all will be okay. I don't want to be the one vomiting over the dinner table."

"What about Alex? He doesn't know about any of this?" Liz wrung her hands together with worry.

"I will deal with Alex if need be. A little compulsion never hurt anyone."

"It doesn't feel right to me, Zac."

He waved her off. "Just blame it all on me. I'm used to it."

They returned to the dining room where Gabby, Sam, and Alex were seated, drinking the wine that Liz had brought with her. Zac placed the bottle he'd spiked next to Liz and winked.

"You told her seven, right?" Sam joked when he saw Alex fidgeting.

"Yeah." He jumped when there was a sudden knock on the front door.

Alex rose awkwardly, almost knocking over his glass. Zac followed him from the dining room, waiting to see what would happen.

Alex strode to the front door and opened it to find Aya standing on the other side. The human gasped a little as he took in her appearance.

She wore a tight-fitting black blouse and dark grey skinny jeans that clung in all the right places, and in all the right ways, and she'd had a haircut. Her black hair still hung halfway down her back, but it was all different lengths.

Alex blushed a little and said, "Hi."

Smiling brightly, Aya stepped inside and hugged him. "Lovely to see you again," she chirped.

Zac hid his look of confusion. She hadn't been invited in *at all*. She just stepped through the door like it was the most ordinary thing in the world. It *was* ordinary, but she had so many vampire tendencies he was sure she couldn't come in...and she couldn't be compelled, either.

Was he wrong?

He snapped back to reality as he realised Aya was speaking to him.

"Earth to Zac." She snapped her fingers in front of his face.

"What, don't I get a hug?" he asked, a wicked tone in his voice.

"No."

"Aya, you wound me." He clutched his heart as she glided past him into the dining room.

***

Aya could hardly hold back her laughter when she caught Zac's expression. Human thresholds weren't an issue for her, much like the sun. He'd obviously been counting on Alex giving her an invitation before she stepped inside.

Liz, Sam, and Gabby were seated at the dining table as she walked in, drinking wine and laughing at some joke Sam had just told. Upon seeing her, Liz got up and poured her a glass from the near-empty bottle and handed it to her. "Aya! It's great that you could make it. Here, have a glass."

Aya took the wineglass and sat at an empty spot at the table, Zac sitting across from her. She took a sip, aware that Zac was watching her closely, pretending to be distracted by something else. "Thank you to Alex for inviting me." She inclined her head toward him as he came back in from the kitchen.

"Oh, it was no problem." He blushed. "Everything's ready if you're hungry now?"

"If you like."

Liz stood abruptly and said, "I'll help you, Alex."

"It's a good wine," Aya said, swirling the red liquid around the glass as they disappeared into the kitchen.

Zac slumped back in the chair, almost disappointed.

"I picked it out," Gabby said. "I'm the only one who knows what's good. Otherwise, we would have gotten the cheapest one."

Sam laughed and agreed as Liz put a plate in front of Aya. When they were all seated, they began to eat.

"Meatloaf." Alex shrugged almost apologetically when Aya raised her eyebrow at him.

"How American." She smiled politely and ate a few mouthfuls, selecting a little of everything on the plate.

She made a conscious effort to taste every bite and make every chew count.

Everyone but Alex seemed to be watching her.

"This," she said, gesturing to the plate with her fork, "is delicious."

"*Great.*" Alex beamed. "It's about the only thing I can cook."

"Well, you can cook it well, that's for sure," Liz said.

Aya couldn't help herself. She coughed loudly, feigning choking on a mouthful of potato. Zac sat forward in his chair, his expression hopeful. She thumped her chest and took a mouthful of wine.

"Went down the wrong way," she declared brightly.

After that, the conversation naturally turned to things that were more familiar to the host. Things were quickly turning into one of those boring dinner parties where people told annoying personal jokes. Unfortunately, she was the odd one out, having only been around a week. It reminded her of the formal dinners and cocktail parties she had attended back in the day.

'The day' being somewhere around 1860. Empty pleasantries, childish gossip, and blatant social climbing. She longed for something interesting to talk about. Murder, mayhem, and general chaos...those were things she was used to.

After dessert, she excused herself to the bathroom to get some distance. Zac's constant hovering was driving her insane and it was all she could do to tune out the annoying hum of his blood.

Closing the bathroom door behind her, she sighed loudly. Staring at her reflection in the mirror, she weighed up the information she'd learned. After observing them for the last few days, she still didn't have any clue as to their motivation for calling her.

Walking into the house like she did had certainly thrown them off her scent. They'd spiked the wine and the food with something that Zac had obviously thought would influence her. *Silver and garlic? Really?*

She grinned at her reflection when she recalled the look of mingled confusion and anger on his face. She'd developed quite a liking for infuriating him. He always rose to the occasion, not the other way around, and would be furious when he finally caught on that he was the one being played.

She couldn't wait to see the look on his face.

Alex was being attentive, but she knew it was because he was developing a crush on her. He had no idea that his friends were vampires. Especially Liz, who seemed to be a friend of his since early childhood. She felt a little sorry for him, knowing he would find out eventually, when he grew old and she did not. Liz would have to leave town before people asked questions about the eternal twenty-one-year-old.

Splashing cool water on her face, Aya wondered what their problem was. She'd sensed nothing malicious in the town at all, other than the werewolves. She'd dealt with them easily enough, but the vampires were still sniffing around, trying to expose what she was. Were they working with someone else who was out to get her? No, even that didn't sit right.

Looking up into the mirror, she froze as she caught sight of a figure standing directly behind her.

Without turning, she knew no one was there. Not *really*. She glared at the reflection and finally understood.

The woman behind her looked the same as the day she'd delivered Aya's death sentence. Tall and slim, with fiery auburn hair that fell in waves over her shoulders and that same cold, calculated expression that never shifted.

"Katrin." Aya rolled her eyes. "You don't look a day over a billion, you old hag."

"My dear," Katrin purred. "I've been looking for you for a long, *long* time. You've been a naughty little vampire."

Aya couldn't help laughing. "It was a shame you weren't home when I killed your demon spawn, you murderous bitch."

"Oh, but dear, I'm already dead." Her expression didn't waver. "Never in my wildest dreams did I imagine that boy in all his stupidity would deliver you to me."

Aya hesitated. *Of course. Katrin had marked him.*

"Oh, he hasn't told you about his little predicament yet?" Katrin asked in mock surprise.

She didn't reply.

"It's past due that I should send my children to pay you a visit," Katrin continued. "All four of you together again, *how wonderful*. Now we know your whereabouts, I'm sure they won't be long. Perhaps I will just send your favourite? I know he's longing to see your pretty face again. After all, he did fall in love with you."

"Send them all. I'm collecting the entire set," Aya snarled. "And I will enjoy killing him most of all."

"So be it. You will regret using your power again, little girl. This time it will destroy you."

"It's a little late for that don't you think?"

"Oh, it's only just begun."

The witch's form shimmered and evaporated, then Aya was alone again.

Taking a deep breath, she hit the bench top with her fist. It would do no good getting angry. She knew Katrin wouldn't focus on Zac anymore, but would use all of them to get to her. She had unwittingly implicated her new 'friends' in an age-old blood feud. She was a much greater prize than an annoying brat of a vampire.

For the rest of the evening she fought to keep herself in check, exchanging pleasantries with the vampires, the witch, and their human host. Her heart wasn't in it, the need for her previous charade slipping. When it was time to say goodnight, she asked Gabby for a ride to town. She needed some alone time with the elusive witch.

As they filed out of the house and down the driveway, Aya heard the annoying buzz that announced Zac was following them from the house.

"Aya," he called. "Can I speak to you a moment?"

Gabby glanced at her, a note of sympathy on her face, and kept walking to the car. Aya turned and raised her eyebrows at Zac, who stood with his hands jammed into the pockets of his jeans.

"I just want to apologise for the other night," he said with a grimace.

She looked him up and down. "You say that like you don't mean it."

"I do." He wasn't even convincing himself.

"You don't apologise often, do you?"

He sighed through his teeth, the breath drawn out.

"What's your deal, Zac?" Aya prodded when he said nothing.

He frowned. "What do you mean?"

"I might not know you very well, but I'm switched on enough to tell that you're acting strange." She crossed her arms. "What do you want?"

She knew very well that he wouldn't come straight out and ask her the million-dollar question. It would mean that he had to reveal himself, but she was curious to see what lie he would come up with.

"I—" He couldn't bring himself to say anything and it annoyed her more than she thought it would.

"Why can't you just act like a normal person?" She shook her head in annoyance, speaking more to herself than Zac.

"Like Alex?" he said like it was an insult.

"Not that it's any of your business, but Alex speaks to me because he *likes* to, not because he *wants* something. Perhaps you should take a page out of his book." Aya spun on her heel and strode to Gabby's car, sliding into the passenger seat.

Gabby glanced at her and started the car. Pulling away from the curb, she said, "He's the biggest ass in the entire town. I wouldn't take anything he says to heart. There's no filter from his head to his mouth."

"So people keep telling me..."

She wasn't worried that much about Zac and his mood swings. Katrin had unsettled her entirely and it was time to out herself. She knew Gabby would be the most understanding. They were so alike.

"Gabby, there is something that I need to tell you, but I think it would be best if you pull over."

Gabby glanced over at her, concern etched in her face. The car came to a stop and she turned off the engine.

"Aya, what is it?" she asked warily, a note of fear in her voice.

Aya took a deep breath. *Here goes nothing.*

"I am the one known as the Witch Hunter, and I know it was you and Zac who called me. Not half an hour ago, while I was in Alex's bathroom, the witch

Katrin threatened me. I believe you know who I'm talking about."

Gabby's face drained of colour.

"You have nothing to fear from me, Gabby. I wish to help you."

It took a few minutes for Gabby to work up the courage to speak. "Then we have a lot to talk about."

CHAPTER 10

Gabby opened the front door of the manor. It bothered her that the brothers never locked it, but they were vampires. Surely, it didn't matter either way.

Walking into the parlour, she found everyone assembled. She wasn't sure how she should break the news to them. Aya's confession the previous night had come as a shock, but deep down, Gabby wasn't really surprised.

Aya was more than a vampire, Gabby knew this, but *what* she was, was a mystery. That much Aya had proved at dinner.

They'd talked for a long time once she'd admitted who she was. Gabby remembered how much she'd said, but how little she'd revealed. It'd taken some time to convince Aya to come to the manor to speak with everyone, especially after Zac's behaviour. She still had a lot of questions and was sure everyone else would have just as many.

"So, what's the big scandal, Gabby?" Zac lounged back on the sofa, annoyed.

Gabby crossed the room and dumped her bag on the coffee table, placing her grimoire carefully beside it. It was best she just came out with it. Rip it off like a band aid. "Last night after leaving Alex's, Aya confessed to me that she's the Witch Hunter."

"What?" Sam exclaimed, standing up to face her. "And you believed her?"

Gabby shrunk back slightly. "She gave me no reason not to. She told me that Katrin had threatened her while she was at Alex's. While we were all in the house."

Zac sat up, worry etched on his face. "Katrin was in the house?"

"She said she appeared to her in the bathroom mirror." Gabby took a few steps back before she continued, "I told her to meet us here."

Zac was on his feet. "Gabby, be careful what you say next."

"She can answer a lot of our questions, Zac." Sam placed a reassuring hand on his arm. "If she's the Witch Hunter as she says, then we would have no chance against her."

Zac glared at Gabby. "Well, she sure has a talent for manipulation. She could be anyone or *anything*."

Gabby crossed her arms over her chest. "Well, she's coming here any moment, so you can ask her yourself."

"We don't even know who she is," Liz, who'd been listening in horrified silence, exclaimed.

"I, for one, don't believe that the spell would be in the grimoire unless we could trust it," Gabby told them. "It hasn't led me astray yet, and now more than ever, I truly believe it was our only option."

"Oh, now you agree with the spell," Zac huffed. "Good going, Tabitha."

"Now that I've spoken with Aya, yes," she said, her eyes narrowed. "Now who's the one with regrets?" Zac snorted. "You begged me to cast the damn spell, Zac. Besides, I don't think she's just a vampire. She can do things you can't."

"And what else could she be? You think she's some kind of super freaky hybrid?"

"I'm not entirely sure…"

"Nice work, Gabby. You're a wealth of knowledge." Zac rolled his eyes and clapped his hands.

"Oh, shut up, Zac. It's your fault we're in this mess in the first place. Next time be careful who you piss off and you wouldn't need my help."

"What can I say? I do a lot of things I don't need to do, but I do them anyway."

"That's enough, you two." Sam's calm voice cut through the tension. "We should hear what Aya has to say first before jumping to any conclusions."

Aya had arrived some minutes ago.

She remembered the house that'd once stood here near the edge of the swamp. It'd been rebuilt after it burned down, but its current incarnation could only be described as dilapidated.

She wondered what really had happened, but she knew vampires had been responsible for this and much of the destruction in the South, so it could've been anything. Even the walls seemed to echo with some kind of supernatural interference.

Aya could hear raised voices coming from down the hall. *Of course, they would be arguing.* The brothers especially—they seemed as different as night and day.

She strolled toward the action, taking in the old paintings along the walls—landscapes and portraits of long dead southern plantation owners. Very French.

She stood in the doorway of the large sitting room and surveyed the scene. Zac and Gabby were bickering like children in front of the massive fireplace, which was popping away merrily. Sam was being the level-headed mediator, and Liz was rolling her eyes in frustration. Liz had so much to learn about life, her stupidity made her gag. Although no one had noticed her, she feigned throwing up on the carpet. Silently, she made herself comfortable on the ancient brocade sofa and watched the show.

"We at least need to ask her what she knows,"

Gabby said. "She told me she knew the witch Katrin. If she knows her, she might at least know where we might look next."

"I don't trust her," Zac growled. "She played us for fools."

"She's the female version of you," Sam said, earning himself a menacing glare.

"And you are a fool," Liz snapped.

"Oh, yeah, Liz. Your entire life was my fault," Zac snarled.

Liz went to slap him, but Sam put his hand on her shoulder to calm her. "Shut it, Zac. I don't care whose fault this is, but you're my brother and that makes it my problem."

Zac took a step back and raised his hands. "Fine. The sooner we talk to this ancient bitch, the sooner we can kill Katrin."

"I wouldn't call her that to her face…" Gabby raised her eyebrows. "I bet she could snap you in half."

Aya lounged back on the sofa and watched them argue about her. They still hadn't noticed she was a mere two meters away. She really was too sneaky for her own good. "You know," she quipped, "it's impolite to talk about someone behind their back." She grinned in satisfaction as they all jumped.

"How long have you been there?" Zac exclaimed.

She smiled wickedly. "*A while.*"

"Hell, Aya. Do you want us to trust you or not?"

She paused a second and pretended to think it

over. Shaking her head, she said, "Doesn't bother me. We want the same thing, to a certain extent. Trust is optional."

"To you, maybe." Liz stepped forward. "But it's important to us."

"To twenty-first century do-gooders, maybe. Trust is not a huge priority when dealing with vampires." Aya moved forward fluidly until she was directly in front of Liz. "Is it exhausting holding onto so much of your humanity? Denying what you have become?"

"Back off," Sam warned as Liz visibly cringed under her imposing presence.

Aya glared at him from under her eyelashes, the light from the fire making her expression almost demonic. "You decided to cast a spell in a moment of desperation not knowing what would happen. Now I am here and here I will stay."

"But we know nothing about you," Liz said protectively.

Aya narrowed her eyes at the young vampire. "And what would you know? You've been a vampire for less than a year. To me, that's a blink of an eye. *A drop in the ocean.*"

"Then, how old are you really?" Zac asked from behind her.

Looking back over her shoulder, she stated, "I think it was about the year forty-six. Anno Domini, but I could be mistaken... Your mind deteriorates when you're an *ancient bitch.*"

Zac narrowed his eyes and said nothing.

"But, that would mean you're...you're nearly two thousand years old," Sam said in a small voice.

"Is it really so hard to believe?" It felt good not having to hide herself anymore, letting her anger guide her words. They all looked alarmed at the notion of her being so old. They mustn't know much about their own kind at all. "And how old are you?"

"Why do they call you the Witch Hunter?" Gabby asked, changing the subject before it came to blows.

"That's self-explanatory," she replied sarcastically. "If a witch uses their power for evil, then it's the end for them." Aya dragged her finger across her throat.

"Why witches?" Liz asked.

She raised her eyebrows. "Why not?" The tone in her voice suggested that this was her final answer on the subject.

"Why is Katrin after you?" Sam asked gently.

"Probably the same reason she's after him." She pointed to Zac, avoiding his question. "Because we all pissed her off."

"And now she knows you're working with us," Zac huffed.

"Am I now?"

"Two birds, one stone," Gabby whispered, shaking her head.

"We don't really have an option. That's why they used the spell," Sam said.

Aya curled her lip in a snarl at the memory of

being forced awake by it. It'd felt like she'd been doused with a bucket of cold water.

"Do you know who wrote the spell in my grimoire?" Gabby asked, picking it up and turning to a place marked by a slip of paper.

Aya looked at the page Gabby pointed out and sighed. "Once upon a time I helped your ancestor. I can't believe that idiot wrote a spell. At least it's not specific, but troublesome."

"What do you mean, troublesome?"

"I've done a lot of things to annoy many people. None more so than Katrin. I get followed by her thugs more often than not, so you can understand why this spell is inconvenient. Change a few words around, add a bit of you... You get the picture."

"Is that why you hid yourself from us? For fear that we were working with Katrin?" Sam asked.

"One reason," Aya confirmed. "Though, fear had no part in it."

Zac snorted. "Of course not."

"Why could you come into Alex's house without being invited?" Liz asked.

Aya thought for a moment, then said, "I can walk wherever I want."

"But why?"

"Because I can." The statement was final.

"Zac, remember the vampire you killed? He was one of Katrin's, wasn't he looking for someone?" Sam prodded. "And he's who started the mess with the werewolves."

"And what happened to them?" Aya asked, knowing full well she was what had happened to the wolves.

"Gone. They won't bother us again." Zac glowered as if remembering something horrible. "He was looking for you."

"What makes you say that?" she asked.

"I remember because I made fun of him. He said he was looking for a woman that was 'black of hair, blue of eye'. And you're the only one fitting that description around here."

"What was his name?"

"Alistair something. Payne? I don't really remember."

Aya cocked her head. "And you killed him?"

"Yes."

"Good. He was annoying."

"You knew him?" Sam asked.

Aya snorted in frustration. "It doesn't really matter now. Unfortunately, I've lost the element of surprise, but we can work with that. Katrin was watching you somehow." How the hell had they tracked her here? *Again?*

"How could she be watching us?" Liz looked horrified.

"Katrin is an ancient witch, Liz. She stopped her spirit from passing on, thus remaining in an in-between place to continue influencing the living. She has many vampires and witches in her following and can see many places through the eyes of others."

"So you think there's someone physically watching us?" Zac asked, knowing full well that at least one vampire had them under surveillance.

"Perhaps. It's hard to tell. Usually, I can sense who's around, but a witch can help shield them. Especially now that Katrin knows I'm here, that's even more likely."

"Then it would all be in our best interests if you stay here with us at the manor," Sam stated. "As you said, they're after you as well. There's plenty of room, and I'm sure Zac won't mind."

Zac glared at his brother. "Actually, I do mind. What's to stop her from killing us in our sleep? All we have is her word and after all the lies she's told us—"

Aya rolled her eyes. "If I wanted to kill you all, Zac, I could have done it a million times by now. Besides, I've only ever told you the truth...with a few omissions." Zac huffed in annoyance. "Katrin has caused me much trouble in the past, so I would like to get rid her. I have no issue with you other than the fact that you're an arsehole." Gabby let out a laugh at Aya's statement. "I won't murder you in your sleep. *Cross my heart.*"

"If you cross the line, Aya, be warned—"

"What are you going to do, Zac? Punch me like a

twenty-pound weakling?" She walked around him, sizing him up. "I'd like to take you down a few pegs."

"Cut it out, you two," Sam said firmly, ever the level-headed mediator.

Gabby cleared her throat, changing the subject yet again. "So, what do you suggest we do? Go on the offensive or defensive?"

"There's not much we can do until either Katrin shows herself or one of her followers appears. Which won't be long." Aya shrugged. "Once the witch has come out of hiding, we need a way to break her hold on the living and send her to the other side. There's some witchy homework for you, Gabby." Aya doubted that she could find a way, she seemed unaware of her potential. It radiated all around the young witch but telling her as much would defeat the purpose. Gabby had to find it for herself.

"I'm only new at this, Aya. I don't know what good I can do." Gabby tried to hide the panic in her voice, but it wavered, giving her away.

"I'm sure you'll find something." Aya smiled for the first time. "We'll have a lot to keep us entertained in the meantime."

Zac was still annoyed. "Like what?"

"Staking vampires, thwarting assassination attempts... You know, all the fun stuff." Aya sighed at the awkward silence that followed. What a boring bunch of vampires. Even she had a taste for a little persuasive violence now and then, but perhaps not quite as persuasive as ripping apart werewolves had been.

"Well," Liz proclaimed to cover up the awkward silence, "it's rather late, so we better be going home. Could you give me a ride, Gabby?"

"Sure." Gabby looked relieved as she gathered her things, her mind preoccupied with the task Aya had entrusted her with.

"Speak to you tomorrow." Liz gave Sam a quick kiss on the lips as they left the parlour, the front door closing a moment later.

Zac glared at Aya and disappeared from the room without a word. Sam shrugged apologetically. "Do you need to go get anything?"

Aya shook her head. "No."

"Nothing? No clothes or anything?"

"No."

He seemed a little taken aback. She supposed most people had some things. A change of clothes would be normal, even for a vampire. She wasn't really what constituted as 'normal'.

"I'm not attached to possessions," she told him.

"Well, let me show you upstairs. We have a spare room you can use." He cocked his head toward the door.

Sam led her up the stairs and opened the first door next to the landing. "You can use this room. The bathroom is through there. It joins to my room on the other side. If you need anything, let one of us know. If you want to buy anything, I can give you some cash. We don't make a habit of compelling people if we don't have to." He turned and walked back to the bedroom door. "Oh, and we don't eat them, either."

Aya nodded her understanding and he closed the door behind him.

How the hell had she wormed her way into the Degaud Manor? She didn't intend to harm any of them, but it was way too easy. This took their desperation to a whole other level. She made a mental note to have a word with Sam about security.

Looking around the room, Aya sighed.

Here we go again.

CHAPTER 11

When Aya opened her eyes, it was light outside.

She sat up, taking in her surroundings in the stark light of day. The room they'd given her was modest, but the bed was comfortable. Better than the slab of rock she'd slept on the last one hundred and fifty years, but even a bed of nails would be better than that.

Aya cast out her hearing, but there was no sound coming from the bathroom or the room beyond. It seemed Sam had already left for work.

She showered and dressed in the same clothes she wore yesterday, making a note to get some more later.

Venturing out into the hallway, she caught the faint hum of Zac's blood somewhere on the manor grounds. Keeping a note of his general location, she explored the house. They'd invited her in, so to speak, so she took the liberty to snoop.

The brothers had done a lot of work to the house

since moving in. They'd wired the entire place with electricity and soft, tasteful lighting drenched every room. She wondered how many workmen they'd compelled to have this done. Then again, their parents had been rich plantation owners and a hundred years of interest in their bank accounts would have made them even more well off. They were a boon for the local economy.

She passed the door to the master bedroom she knew was Zac's and kept walking. She shuddered to think what was in there. It could remain a mystery.

Tiptoeing down the stairs, Aya wandered to the back of the house where the kitchen was located. It was attached to a formal dining room which held a long mahogany table with twelve chairs. What looked like the original chandelier hung from the centre of the room and landscape paintings were displayed on each wall, but otherwise it was bare.

She wandered back down the hallway, coming to another closed doorway. Running her hand along the frame to the door handle, she listened for a moment and turned it quietly, the door creaking inward.

She found herself in the study. An enormous mahogany desk stood to one side, covered in old papers and books. The entire wall behind it was lined with bookshelves filled with more books and trinkets than she could count. Opposite were floor-to-ceiling French doors that opened up onto the veranda. Outside, she saw the wisteria that'd once grown in manicured fashion had overtaken most of the railings, ventured up to the second floor, and probably onto the roof as well.

It'd been a long time, but she remembered this room as if it were yesterday. Actually, considering her current predicament, it was only last week.

Approaching the bookshelves, she ran her fingers across the spines, reading the titles as she went. There was a layer of dust, which gave away that no one had moved anything from the shelves in a very long time.

They all seemed to be ledgers from the old plantation. Expenditure, profit...until she placed her finger on a copy of Shakespeare's *Julius Caesar*. Her heart stopped for a beat or two. She'd known a few dangerous Romans once upon a time.

Pulling it from the shelf, she flicked through the pages, finally looking at the inside cover. In a perfect script was written, *For Louis, Many happy returns on the day of your birth, Arthur Risom.*

Arthur Risom. The name sounded familiar.

"What are you doing?"

Aya turned to find Zac at the door. He was glaring at her, his arms crossed over his chest.

She hadn't heard him appear and she should have by the sound of his blood alone. Placing the book back, she said nothing, silently scolding herself.

He scowled at her. "Do you always sneak around?"

"*Pfft*," she hissed. "I don't sneak."

"Then what were you doing?"

"*Sneaking.*" She grinned wickedly, biting her lower lip.

"I don't know what you're looking for, but I don't appreciate you poking about in my father's study."

"Whatever." She threw her hands up in mock defence. "Touchy this morning, aren't we?"

"Only because you're here," he sneered, looking her up and down.

"Then perhaps I should go watch the show from the sidelines." She sauntered over to him and looked into his strange green eyes. "When they come for you, you'll beg me to *poke around*." She glared and pushed past his bulky frame into the hallway. Walking down the hall and into the parlour, she heard him following her for round two.

"Aya," he said, not trying to hide his exasperation, "just leave that stuff alone. It belonged to my father. I don't want anyone to touch it, okay?"

She turned, raising an eyebrow at him. "Whatever. If it means that much to you, then I won't go in there again. Satisfied?"

He didn't look convinced, but he nodded and sat on the sofa in a huff.

"You know, this place could really use a duster. It's not as nice as I remember it," she jabbed. "I pity those with allergies. This place is a death trap."

"You've been here before?" He sounded surprised.

Nodding, she said, "I never left."

"What do you mean?" he asked, confused.

"I was asleep since 1860-ish. I don't usually keep track of the date."

Zac didn't mask his surprise. "You've been asleep in Ashburton for the last one hundred and fifty years?"

Aya shrugged, running a finger across the dusty mantelpiece. "If you hadn't summoned me, I probably would still be down there." Truthfully, the fact that she had slept so long worried her. Who knew when she would've woken if not for Zac and his reckless stupidity? It could only mean she was becoming weaker...and she hoped that wasn't true.

"Down where?" he asked, not fathoming the mechanics of it.

"The cave by the lake," she said matter-of-factly.

"Then you would've been here when Sam and I..."

"Louis Degaud was quite the gentleman," she said absently.

"My father?"

"Yes. I believe so."

"Did I? Did Sam..."

"I think you would have remembered if you'd met me," she told him. "I had quite a dramatic presence back then. I believe Louis' eldest son was away fighting in the war, which was quite the scandal. His youngest... well, I don't really remember. Mrs. Degaud, what was her name again? Marie. She was as polite as they came in those days, which meant she'd stab you in the back if you were to come between her husband and her money."

"When did you leave?" he whispered, his expression somewhat shocked.

Aya frowned at his tone. "About the time your parents received word of their son's heroic death fighting to uphold the rights of the *slavery* of the South."

Zac's eyes narrowed. "If I had a choice about it now, I wouldn't have gone."

"Whatever helps you sleep at night."

"*Aya.*"

She shrugged. What did she care?

"So, you were here when…"

Aya sensed there was something he thought she knew but was uncertain of asking. "The last I knew of this town and the world was in the 1860s. Whatever came to pass after that is unknown to me, along with the so-called massacre. It has the stench of vampires all over it but fighting over territory was nasty in those days, especially with the witches."

Zac was silent for a moment, as if he were trying to decide what to tell her. "I died in the Civil War," he said finally. "I was shot and left for dead. But before I died, a vampire came. I supposed it was because of all the blood. I was the only one still alive in that pile of corpses. She saw I was a captain and took me for her own gain. When I finally understood that she was using me, I left…only to find she'd reached my family before I could."

He stood and walked to the window opposite with

his back to her. She could feel it troubled him. Who was his maker? Obviously, a callous bitch by the sounds of it. This was the vampire who had massacred every last human at the plantation after all. No wonder Zac was such an asshole.

Aya felt sorry for him but stopped herself from saying it out loud. She felt sorry now, but back then, would she really have done anything to stop it? Instead, she asked, "Did you kill her?"

"Yes," he declared, still looking out the window, carefully hiding the emotion in his voice.

"Good." She clapped her hands together and stood. "Then that problem is solved. The wicked vampire is dead. What was her name?"

Zac turned and frowned at her. "Victoria."

"Oh! Victoria. Long, curly, auburn hair? In America, by the way of France? Up-herself English bitch? Are we thinking about the same cold-hearted vampire?"

"How did you..." he whispered, his eyes wide with surprise.

"Bitch got what she deserved. I hope you made it slow and *painful*."

Zac's expression was horrified. He'd met his match in her, that was glaringly obvious.

"Well, thanks for the little chit chat." Aya smiled brightly. "Paces to go, people to eat. You know how it goes." And she was gone before he could open his mouth.

Liz was relieved when Gabby came into the coffeehouse. The previous night was weighing heavily on her and it was all she could do to remain focused on work. Making herself a coffee, she went and sat with her friend in a booth by the window.

Gabby, seeing Liz was wound up, produced a flask from her bag and handed it to her under the table. Mrs. Greene wouldn't take too kindly to her staff drinking on the clock and at midday, too. She hadn't tested how much it took to make her drunk these days, but she assumed it was a lot.

"To the Irish." Gabby grinned as Liz dumped the contents of the flask into her coffee.

"Thanks, Gab. I really need this today," she said with a sigh, relaxing back into the booth, conscious of the surrounding customers.

"What kind of friend would I be if I didn't pick up on these things?" She winked. "Besides, with the weird stuff we have to deal with, a little whiskey never goes astray."

"Mental is what it is," Liz groaned. "But we're in it now, I guess."

"Up to the eyeballs." Gabby leaned closer. "Tomorrow—"

"I don't want to think about tomorrow," she interrupted. "What do you make of her?"

"Who, Aya?"

"Yeah."

Gabby thought for a moment. "Well, she's over two thousand years old. That's gotta screw with your head after a while."

Liz groaned, letting her head loll backward. "I don't want to think about age."

"Sorry."

"It's okay. I guess thinking about where I'll be in two thousand years is a bit of overkill." Liz laughed at the idea.

"Well, as for Aya, I believe her, but there's a lot she's not saying. I'm not sure if we should be worried or not."

"She also implied that Katrin was hunting her as well," Liz pointed out. "I wonder what she did?"

"And I wonder how long she's been hunted," Gabby added. "Alistair was looking for her, and he was linked to Katrin."

"You're right." Liz took a gulp of her coffee. "It makes my head hurt."

Gabby frowned, her mind having drifted to something else. "What I don't understand is why she would help my ancestor. Vampires and witches don't usually get along. I can understand her hunting them, but forging alliances?"

"You get along with Zac and Sam," Liz said, "and me."

"Yeah, but you guys fight your vampire side. You

want to be as human as possible. Aya seems like a force all her own."

"She's not like vampires are meant to be."

"No, that's my point. She's not like you, she doesn't hold on to anything that's human...or doesn't seem to. She's holding onto something else," Gabby said, frustrated. "I just wish I could figure out what."

"Maybe she was a witch. Before, I mean," she offered.

"No. Witches become ordinary vampires when they're turned. All connection with any power and earth sense is lost."

"How do you know?"

Gabby smiled. "The grimoire is more than a book of spells and potions. It also acts as a kind of journal. A connection to those who came before."

"Like a family record?"

"Kind of. More like passing along advice," she replied. "Which I really need since I'm on my own."

"I think we should be on our guard where Aya's concerned. She's obviously got her own agenda." Liz sighed, catching sight of Alex over Gabby's shoulder. He was frowning at them, clasping his lunch so hard his thumb had dented the sandwich.

She waved at him. "Alex!"

Approaching, he smiled weakly. "Hey Liz, Gabby."

"Hey." Gabby turned around, catching the uncertainty in his voice. "Everything okay?"

"Yeah," he said, looking toward the exit. "I'm just running late. I'll see you later."

Before they could say goodbye, he hurried away and was pushing through the door. Liz glanced at Gabby. "Do you think he heard us?"

"I don't know," she said, shrugging. "He could have."

"I feel bad, you know. Keeping all of this from him."

Gabby sighed. "I know. It's for the best, though. The more people that are involved—"

"The more people get hurt," Liz finished her sentence.

"Right." She smiled. "On that note, I have to go back to the office."

"Thanks for the Irish." Liz winked, heading for her space behind the counter.

Her thoughts had calmed, but she was no less worried about Aya...and now, Alex. They were just trying to protect him from all of this, but she wondered how good it was for him to keep pushing him away. Making up stories, excuses. She knew she would have to leave him behind one day, but until then, she wanted to hold on to some sense of normalcy and Alex was a link to her old life.

She knew she was being selfish and deep down, Liz hoped it wouldn't blow up in her face.

But those were some famous last words.

Alex flopped onto the ground heavily beside the garden bed he'd been mulching before lunch, his sandwich well and truly mangled. He'd overheard the end of the girls' conversation and it worried the hell out of him. He swore that they had been talking about witches, but that didn't seem right. Then Liz had voiced her distrust over Aya's agenda.

What the hell?

He jumped when Aya sank down gracefully beside him, her eyebrows raised at the sight of his mangled lunch.

"Nice sandwich," she said. "What did it do to you?"

He tossed the sandwich aside, suddenly not hungry. "I guess I don't know my own strength."

Aya frowned at the gesture. "What's up?"

He shrugged. "Nothing. I just heard Gabby and Liz talking about something I shouldn't have overheard."

"Like what?"

Alex hesitated. "They were talking about you."

She laughed. "I bet they were."

"What do you mean?"

"Well, as of last night, I'm staying with Zac and Sam at their fancy manor house in the swamp," she said with a flick of her hair. "It was unexpected, but it beats paying for a hotel. Liz isn't that thrilled for whatever reason. It's only been one night and of course, Zac and I aren't getting along."

"I'm not surprised."

Aya chuckled. "I'm sure they all have some colourful things to say about that."

"Wait, you're living at the manor?" He seemed surprised.

"Yeah." She grimaced. "It was Sam's idea, obviously."

"Oh." Alex fidgeted with the hem of his shirt.

Aya, as if sensing his discomfort, stood and said, "I'll leave you to it, Alex. I've got stuff to do."

Alex watched her disappear across the street. She seemed happier than when he'd first met her.

The more he thought about it, the more he couldn't help but wonder if she did have an agenda like the girls were talking about. She'd never really told him what she was doing in town and her job description seemed vague at best.

The obvious FBI and CIA scenarios ran through his mind, but he snorted at the ridiculousness of it. Like she'd be a spook. That stuff only happened in the movies.

But he couldn't shake what he overheard. If Aya really had an agenda, then what the hell would it be?

When Zac walked into *Max's* that night, he was surprised to see Liz sitting at a table on her own with a glass and bottle of Jack. Something was bothering her big time. Sauntering up behind her, he grabbed the bottle and took a mouthful.

"What's up, beautiful," he said, sitting across from her.

Groaning, she snatched the bottle back from him.

"What?" He raised his hands, grinning, waiting for a response.

"Ass," she hissed.

"Yeah, so what?" Zac laughed, tapping the tabletop.

She shook her head. "You act like you're not even worried about anything."

"And you are?"

"Of course, I am, Zac!" She kept her voice low, growling at him. "Aren't you afraid of being killed?"

"We've all done it before."

"But the next time you won't come back."

"Afraid you'll miss me?"

Liz sighed heavily, pouring herself another glass of Jack, pushing the bottle toward Zac. "Is everything a joke to you?"

He frowned, the smug smile fading as he took a long draught straight from the bottle. He played with the idea of telling her what he could hardly admit to himself—that he had some semblance of feelings for her. He thought about his brother and that welded his big mouth shut.

"No," he said, staring into her eyes.

Uncomfortable, she sighed heavily, looking away. "I

think Alex overheard me and Gabby talking about Aya today."

"You think, or you know?" he asked, the most truthful moment he'd had in the past month dissolving into nothing.

"I think," she said, glaring. "I don't trust her yet. This whole thing scares the hell out of me."

Zac looked at her for a moment, realising he hadn't thought of her safety once in the past two weeks. He had been selfish and impulsive—his best two traits. "You'll always be safe if I have anything to do with it." He grabbed her hand under the table.

"I know," she whispered, pulling back awkwardly.

"Liz, I..." he began, but fell short when he caught the unmistakable reek of a werewolf that'd just entered the bar.

She looked at him, her expression confused, but turned when she caught the scent.

The man walking toward them was heavyset, the rough stubble of a new beard covering his chin, and he looked as angry as a bee in a jar. His rough appearance and plaid shirt made him look like a lumberjack. Except it wasn't the frontier; they were in the middle of a humid, smelly swamp.

"I want to know what happened to my brothers, vamper," the werewolf spat, pushing Zac roughly as he stood.

He hardly remembered it, even though it was only about two weeks ago. A lot had happened since then.

Psycho witches and ancient witch hunting vampires trumped five mutilated werewolves. *Only in a vampire's world.*

"What are you implying, dog?" Zac snarled.

"You know exactly what I'm talking about, you blood sucking piece of shit."

<hr>

Aya couldn't help but laugh as she walked into *Max's*.

Zac was standing face to face with a werewolf, Liz cowering behind him like a little girl. Her gaze met the young vampire's and it was all she could do not to fall on the floor with laughter. Her silent plea for her help was hilarious.

She'd certainly guessed correctly about Zac; he was always getting himself into trouble. Perhaps this town wouldn't be so boring after all.

Aya decided it was time to send everyone a little message. She'd won this town from the wolves and they needed to keep their hands off it *for good*. Before, she was content to let Zac keep it, but now it was going to be more fun if it was hers.

She stopped beside the two men and placed her hand on the werewolf's shoulder. She turned him about and flashed him a smile.

"Now, now," she crooned, "a handsome man like you shouldn't be so angry. I bet you'd rather have a drink with me." She looked him up and down and smiled wickedly, biting her lip. "That idiot isn't even worth it."

Without looking back, she could tell Zac and Liz were stunned as she led the wolf by the hand to the bar. Suddenly he didn't seem to care that he'd come here for revenge. He didn't even sense she was also a vampire.

The dog was more engrossed in her looks and whatever was in his pants to bother. She didn't even have to use compulsion. She ordered him the strongest drink she could to curb his bloodlust and sighed. *Stupid dog.*

"What's a handsome man like you doing in a hole like this?" she asked breathlessly. "What's your name?"

The werewolf could hardly contain his elation. "Ralph."

Ralph? Hell, it just got worse.

"Well, *Ralph*, it sure is a pleasure to meet you." She ran a finger down the buttons of his plaid shirt. "We're going to have some fun. I hope you're up for it."

Ralph leaned over her shoulder, picking up his drink and inhaling her scent. By the look on his face, she could tell he was in her thrall. He downed the drink in two gulps and slammed the glass down on the bar.

"That's an alluring cologne you're wearing," she flirted, leaning closer to breathe in his ugly wolf stink. She caught Zac's eye and winked as she led her catch into the bathrooms at the back of the bar.

Checking to see if all the stalls were empty, she locked the bathroom door and turned, looking Ralph up and down. He stepped forward, clutching her around the waist and went to kiss her, but she grabbed the side of his head and smashed it into the basin, the force cracking the porcelain. The wolf fell to the floor, blood pouring from a gash on his forehead.

"What the hell!" he howled. "You bitch!"

"Listen to me," Aya soothed, crouching on the floor and shoving him over so he could see her face. "The next time you come into this town and threaten any one of those vampires, I will tear you to shreds and send back the pieces to your pathetic little pack. This town is *mine,* and I do not appreciate the peace being broken by a *dog.*" She grasped the front of his shirt, pulling him closer. She let her eyes cloud over into two ethereal white pools and licked her fangs. Ralph cried out in horror and put his hands in front of his face. Dropping him back onto the tiles, she stood over him and ground the heel of her boot on his chest.

"I got it! I got it!" he whimpered. "What the hell are you?"

"I'm your worst nightmare." Aya looked up into the mirror, fluffed her hair up and smiled down at him. "You have a nice night now, you hear?"

The bathroom door shut heavily behind her.

Zac raised his eyebrows as she approached. "What the hell did you do to him?"

Aya looked at him nonchalantly and took a sip of his drink. "He won't bother you anymore."

Suddenly, the bathroom door crashed open and the werewolf stumbled into the walkway. Catching Aya's eye, he visibly stiffened. The gash she had given him had healed and he'd washed most of the blood off, the hair at his temple wet and stringy. She raised her glass and he looked away, totally panic-stricken, and made a dash for the exit.

Aya laughed and Liz glanced at her warily. "What exactly did you do to him, Aya?"

She stood and grabbed their bottle of Jack. Winking at Liz, she left the bar, not bothered whether she explained herself or not.

CHAPTER 12

Zac glared at the corpse hanging on a pole like a twisted scarecrow and cursed.

The last thing he expected to find first thing in the morning was a corpse in the front yard—much less a vampire corpse. And he knew that there was only one person who would've put it there. Scowling, he took out his cell and called Sam. Before he could say hello, he barked, "Have you seen Aya?"

Sam sighed. "No. Did she take the cell I gave her?"

"It's still in her room." He couldn't keep the annoyance out of his voice, even if he tried.

"Zac, she hasn't been awake for long. Perhaps she doesn't see the usefulness of it yet."

"Do you know where she is?"

"No, I haven't seen her today."

"Well, if you see her, tell her I'm looking for her. I want to talk to her about the corpse in the front yard."

"*What?*" came the reply from the other end.

"A desiccated vampire is sitting in the yard like a scarecrow. And only one person we know could've done that." He hung up abruptly.

Getting in his car, he cursed Aya all the way into town. When he caught up with her, he'd give her a piece of his mind. How stupid could she be? Leaving a corpse in the front yard for anyone to come along and see. He knew it was too good to be true, their shaky alliance was a joke. *Two thousand year-old idiot.*

Parking the car at an awkward angle by the main square, he stalked down the street, catching sight of Alex in the distance pruning some box hedges.

"Have you seen Aya?" he asked, coming up behind him. He didn't bother saying hello.

Alex turned, scowling when he saw it was Zac. "Depends why you're asking."

Zac rolled his eyes. "C'mon. Have you seen her or not?"

"She went to the bookstore." Alex pointed across the street.

He leaned forward, thumping him on the shoulder. "Thanks, buddy. That wasn't so hard, was it?"

"Just don't be...*you*, Zac."

"Me? *Never.*"

He stalked across the street through a break in traffic and glanced through the front windows into the store. There were lines of shelving and displays along one side and CDs and magazines in the centre. There was a gift section by the registers and a café tucked away at the rear, so there were lots of little corners she could hide in. Quickly surveying, he couldn't see her, so he walked inside and looked down each aisle before spotting her amongst the magazines.

She was reading a copy of *National Geographic*.

He came up behind her, ready to give her a piece of his mind, but she said, "This is such a wonderful magazine." She'd made no gesture that suggested she knew he was there, and it irritated him further.

"We need to talk," he said through his teeth.

"I'd never heard much of this solar system business. I knew it was all there, but the names humans give things is intriguing. And this Amazon rainforest... I'd like to go there. It sounds wild and dangerous. Have you been?"

"No," he replied impatiently, shuffling from foot to foot.

"Well, I'd like to go before it disappears. Some things aren't as immortal as others. Before I was asleep, the civilised world told us that it was a land of savages, but that's not true."

"As much as I'm enjoying the history lesson, I want to talk to you about something else," he hissed into her ear.

Aya placed the magazine back on the shelf. "And what do you want to discuss?"

"I want to discuss the *corpse* you left in the front yard," he hissed again, looking around to see if anyone was listening.

"Oh, that," she said.

"Yes, *that*." He took her arm and forcefully guided her from the shop, smiling at the attendant at the counter, who was eyeing them suspiciously. He took her across the street to the square where he was sure no one was close enough to hear them.

Turning her to face him, he scowled as she laughed. "What the hell is so funny?"

"You. Getting all worked up."

"It's not funny, Aya. You left a desiccated corpse in the front yard for everyone to see."

"Not true. No one knows the house is lived in. No one comes to visit and the gates are meant to be locked because it is a site of 'historical significance'. No one is going to see the corpse. I left Dean there to serve as a warning to his buddy who has camped out somewhere in town."

"Oh," Zac said, throwing his hands up in exasperation, "so, the corpse has a name?"

"Yes," she replied as if it were the most normal thing to be talking about. "When his friend stops by tonight, he'll try something else and I will be waiting for him to expose himself."

"You can't just do things and not tell us! I nearly died when I went outside!"

She laughed again. "Well, I really wish I'd been there to see that."

"Then why is it there and not someplace else?" He crossed his arms, glowering at her.

"Well, you wanted my help. This is me helping. Dean was already in the house while you were sleeping, princess. If I hadn't been there, it would have been curtains for the Degaud brothers."

"And how do you know his name was Dean?"

"I asked him."

"You asked him?"

"Yes, right before he told me about his friend. Then I killed him. You should've been there. I was brilliant."

"Jesus." He ran his hand through his hair in frustration.

"I met a Jesus once," she said. "He was all right."

Zac stared at her dumbfounded. The things that came out of her mouth. Enduring her mood swings was like having a bucket of icy water dumped on his head. "Just get rid of it before anyone sees it."

"Aye aye, Captain," she said, mock saluting him. "I will deny Dean his proper burial so his soul will wander for eternity."

"Just as long as it doesn't wander anywhere near the house."

***

Aya began the walk back to the manor in a huff. She couldn't wait until she came to the forest so she could run. Those boys had no sense of humour at all. Typical men, always thinking they're right.

Glaring, she brightened slightly when she saw Alex

by the path ahead. He was pruning the hedge that bordered the sidewalk. Hacking would be a better description. He was annoyed, too.

"Hello," she said as she came level with him.

He looked up at her and went back to his work, giving a grunt in acknowledgement.

"Are you okay?" she asked, concerned.

Alex shrugged. "Yeah." He didn't really convince her, but she didn't press the subject, either.

"Do you want to get a drink later?" she asked. "Tonight, I mean." There was no reason she couldn't go out and have a bit of fun. The more she was out, the more she could learn about the town and notice who was lurking about, especially that other vampire. He'd probably hang about the town once the sun went down. She knew she would.

Alex seemed unsure as he said, "I dunno."

"I have to go to the manor and take care of something, but I'll come and meet you after, okay?" She raised her eyebrows to force a response from him.

"Yeah," he said with a shrug.

Something was still bothering him, but for now she had to go deal with Dean, the corpse in the front yard. She smiled and began walking, leaving Alex to finish hacking the hedge.

There was a prickling feeling at the back of her neck as she walked. It felt like someone was watching her, but glancing around, she saw no one was paying her the least bit of attention. It was better to assume one of Katrin's cronies were around by default. There was no doubt in her mind that all of them were being watched and she guessed it was Dean's mate. They wouldn't try anything in such a public place, but she better be on her guard.

She continued through the park, her mind, eyes, and ears all out watching for something amiss.

That night, Alex strode down the gloomy street, his mind wandering. It'd been a long afternoon alone with his thoughts. Ugh, why had he agreed to meet Aya tonight?

Ever since he overheard Liz and Gabby, he couldn't stop thinking about what they'd implied about Aya. The more he thought about it, the weirder it sounded. He was ignorant and they were shutting him out. They'd never kept him out of anything before and it hurt.

He couldn't shake the feeling at all.

He really liked Aya, but there was something about her... She'd never really told him what she was doing in town—she'd never seemed to have worked her 'job' once. As a matter of fact, she hadn't really told him anything about herself at all. Nothing specific, anyway.

Perhaps he should confront her. That might be the only way he would get any answers. Liz had acted like nothing was amiss, but maybe Aya wouldn't. She seemed the type of person who told things straight.

He was so engrossed in his thoughts that he jumped as someone bashed into his shoulder. "Hey, watch it, buddy," he exclaimed.

The young man who'd bumped into him, turned and put his hand on his shoulder. "Hey, I know you."

He was built like a football player, with wide shoulders and thick arms; his blond hair cut into a severe crew. The kind of guy that used to beat him up in high school.

"No, I don't think so." Alex shrugged the guy's hand away and turned to keep walking.

"I'm positive." He followed Alex down the path into the square. "I know you."

"Look, buddy. I don't know you, okay?" If he didn't try to look the guy in the eyes, hopefully he'd leave him alone.

The square had become quiet and empty, the people who'd dotted it before had all disappeared. Alex's heartbeat began to pick up. If this guy wanted to beat him up or mug him, he had the perfect opportunity.

Alex wasn't the best fighter. High school bullies had only taught him to run. If he had to take a swing—

Before he could do anything else, the man grabbed him from behind and turned him around. All Alex saw was the guy's fist hurtling toward his face. There was a smack as he was punched square in the eye.

Alex cried out, falling to the ground and clutching his face. "Just take whatever you want. Take my wallet, I don't want a fight."

"I don't want your wallet," the guy snarled. "I want you as bait."

"What the hell?" Alex tried to scramble backward, but the man grabbed his leg and pulled him across the garden into the woodland area of the park.

He was pushed roughly against a tree, his head cracking against the trunk. Dazed, he blinked hard, his hand clutching the egg-shaped lump that was already starting to rise. He yelled for help but was punched again, this time his lip splitting against his teeth. The cut was bleeding, the coppery taste of his blood filling his mouth.

"Shut up," the blond guy hissed. He pulled a branch from the tree with a superhuman strength that made Alex gasp in fear. Who the hell was this guy?

"Stupid human," he muttered. "Just *bleed*." Alex tried to shield himself with his arms as he was hit again and again with the branch, his skin breaking open and bleeding from hundreds of tiny cuts. The blond guy laughed. "That's it. They'll come now with the blood. They'll want to *save you*."

Alex couldn't understand what the guy was talking about, he seemed completely insane. If he didn't do something, he'd be beaten to death with a *branch* by a crazy person.

He tried to kick out, but couldn't connect with

anything, but at least the assault from the branch stopped. Scrambling to his feet, he was too late to see the branch come at him from the left. It tore a gash in his forehead, ripping through skin as the force threw his head to the side.

He was jerked to his feet, a hand clutching his throat. Alex cried out in surprise as he was wrenched in close to the crazy guy's face. His eyes were black and his teeth… His teeth could only be described as fangs.

Alex shook as terror overtook him. *What the hell was he?*

He cried out as the guy leaned in and bit his neck. He tried to struggle, but he was held tightly. *Jesus*, he was being eaten alive by a vampire-wannabe weirdo.

He panicked and tried to struggle harder, but he was losing blood. His limbs felt like they were filled with lead.

Then the guy wasn't there anymore, and he fell to the ground, landing heavily on his knees. It barely registered that his attacker had been thrown fifty feet away into a tree.

Sam was pulling him up, propping him against another tree. Sam, his best buddy to the rescue. But when Alex looked again, he had the same eyes as the crazy cannibal who'd attacked him.

"*Jesus*," he yelled, but couldn't make his limbs work.

"It's okay, Alex," Sam said. "Sit tight, I'll explain everything. I've just got to deal with this guy."

Slack-jawed in shock, Alex could only nod.

When Sam caught the scent of Alex's blood on the breeze, he knew it wasn't good. He ran as fast as he dared toward its source, trying not to draw any attention from the surrounding people on the street.

In the distance, he caught sight of two figures between the trees. He roared in fury as he realised a vampire had Alex and was feeding on him.

He had to protect his friend, no matter what. Even if he found out, he had to save him.

Grabbing the vampire from behind, he threw him clear across the path into a tree. A sickening thud echoed as his body collided with the trunk before it fell to the ground.

There was so much blood, he couldn't help it when his eyes misted over into black. He grabbed Alex, heaving him up against the tree behind him.

"*Jesus*," Alex yelled in shock as his eyes focused on his face. He would have to explain to his friend later.

"It's okay, Alex," Sam said. "Sit tight, I'll explain everything. I've just got to deal with this guy."

The vampire had picked himself up and was advancing on them. As he came within striking distance, Sam punched the side of his head and a sickening crack echoed through the park. The vampire was either newly made or older than Sam was because the punch didn't seem to bother him at all. His fist connected with Sam's jaw, the force sending him backward. He landed heavily on his back, the air pushed from his lungs.

As he lay gasping for breath, his eyes widened in surprise as he caught sight of Aya perched on a branch above him. She pressed her index finger to her lips to silence him and gestured toward the vampire and then back down to him.

Without giving away her position, he got up as quickly as he could…and not a moment too soon. The vampire was on him again, viciously punching him in the ribs. As he doubled over, instinctively clutching his side, he was kneed in the face and blood gushed from his nose and split lip.

Sam didn't even have a second to regain his composure before he stumbled back under the tree. The vampire had him around the neck in the blink of an eye, laughing in triumph. "Looks like I won," he crowed.

But Sam had already lured him into position. Aya dropped lithely from the tree onto the vampire's back and wrapped her arms around his neck.

"Hello," Aya crooned in his ear. Before he could compose himself, she sunk her fangs into his jugular, making him lose his grip on Sam's neck.

Sam, now free, tore a branch from the tree and plunged it through the vampire's heart, barely missing Aya as she let him go.

"Hey," she cried, shoving the now dead vampire aside. "*Watch it*. We're on the same side, remember?"

Sam smiled, his chest heaving. "You knew what you were doing."

Aya smiled wickedly. "I see you're the one who got all the book smarts."

"Thanks," he puffed, wiping his bloody nose on his sleeve.

They turned back to Alex, who was fixed to his spot against the tree in absolute terror. Sam glanced at Aya and she nodded.

She knelt next to their hurt friend and put her hand on his. "I'm sorry, Alex. We came as fast as we could. Where are you hurt?" Her voice was soft, concerned.

He was obviously afraid of them but didn't scream or try to run. "I'm cut all over my arms. My face…"

Aya nodded and turned to Sam. "You have to heal him."

"Why?" he asked, confused. "Can't you?"

"My blood will make it worse. If he has enough, it will kill him…and you. Make sure you remember that," she said firmly, gesturing for him to kneel.

At the mention of blood, Alex's eyes rolled back into his head and he fainted. Frowning, Sam leaned over his unconscious body and wiped Alex's brow with his sleeve. The blood didn't bother him—he'd worked hard to keep that side him under control—but head wounds bled profusely. It was in all their best interests if he healed that first.

It was a secret they kept close—that vampire blood

could heal a human's wounds and much more...with one caveat. If blood was given too late, then it was vampirism for the human.

Sam wondered why Aya's blood would do the opposite and act like poison. She wasn't an ordinary vampire, perhaps that had something to do with it. He made a mental note to warn the others.

"That was one of Katrin's, right?" he asked.

"That was Dean's friend," Aya replied. "I was waiting for him."

"Who's Dean?"

"The corpse-crow."

Sam rolled his eyes and dripped his blood on each of Alex's wounds.

As soon as he was done, Aya herded him toward his car as he carried Alex's limp body, eager to get their friend home and safe.

Zac found Liz at the same table as the day before, but this time with a bottle of Johnny. Really, he didn't know why he came to the bar on today of all days. His brother was supposed to be here, but he was nowhere to be seen.

He sat across from her, cocked his head to the side, and waited for her to speak first.

Instead, she pushed the bottle across the table, staring at her hands.

She was upset and obviously didn't want to talk about it. All dressed up and no do-gooder boyfriend in the vicinity. He wondered what Sam was doing, standing Liz up when he knew today was important.

They finished the bottle in silence and when it became obvious that Sam wasn't coming, Zac took her arm and they left the bar. Hovering outside on the sidewalk, he wasn't sure if he should take her home or not.

Finally, she spoke. "It was today, you know," she said, shivering.

He glanced sidelong at her, gauging her expression. It had been a year since she'd died, since she had become a vampire. The anniversary had become lost, forgotten in the chaos of his stupid mistake and Aya's chaotic presence.

"Yeah, I know," he told her.

They stood awkwardly on the sidewalk for a moment. Liz was upset and he wanted to be there for her. Selfish as it was, his heart ached.

Turning, Zac gazed at her as she looked out into the darkness of the gardens across the street. He'd wanted to kiss her at least once before he had to give her up. *Just once.*

Liz turned, returning his stare.

Reaching down, he ran his thumb across her cheek and drew a sharp breath as she sighed. Drawing close, he kissed her softly on the lips, lingering, testing her response, but he didn't need to.

She kissed him back with a fire he didn't think she possessed.

"Liz," he whispered, completely in her trance. He was ripping a hole in his brother's heart behind his back, but he couldn't stop himself even if he tried. Regardless, he pulled back.

"I..." he began, but this time, she kissed him and whatever he'd been thinking about was lost.

***

Only twenty minutes had passed when Alex sat bolt upright, gasping for breath. Sam and Aya had bundled him into Sam's car and brought him home. The beauty of a small town was that it never took long to get anywhere.

They were still out the front of his house when he came to, having just put him on the bench on the porch.

Sam looked at him warily, unsure what his reaction would be. If he totally flipped out, he was prepared to compel him if it protected his sanity. Alex was his friend and while he disliked the idea, he knew he had to protect Liz and Zac first. He was sure Aya could protect herself.

Alex put his face in his hands and groaned. "What the hell are you, Sam?"

There was no use hedging around the topic.

"I'm a vampire. And Aya..." he glanced at her, "Aya is a vampire, too."

Alex stood and leaned against the front door. "I heard Liz and Gabby talking about Aya. This is what they meant, wasn't it?"

"Probably," she replied.

Alex glanced at Aya. "How old are you really? I mean, you're not twenty-five, are you?"

"No. I'm a lot older than that. I've been around quite a few more lifetimes that I had originally planned, but I'm flattered that you think I'm twenty-five."

"How old?" he whispered.

"I think you should tell him your age first," she said to Sam. "Ease him into it."

Sam grimaced. "I'm one-hundred and sixty-seven."

"You say that like its normal!" Alex threw his hands up in annoyance. "And you?" He jabbed a finger at Aya.

She balked. "I'm two thousand, give or take."

"And Zac?" His eyes widened. "Liz? Please don't tell me Liz is one, too?"

"Yes, we all are. But not Gabby," he added. "Gabby is a witch."

"Holy shit!" Alex's hand slapped his forehead in disbelief. "I'm in the *X-files*!"

Aya frowned. "What's an X-file?"

Sam glared at her. "It's a TV show."

"TV?" She cocked her head, confused, then exclaimed, "Oh! The picture thing... I get it."

Alex stared at them dumbfounded.

"Alex, we're still your friends," Sam said seriously.

Aya smiled at him. "And you're the first human who's liked me for *who* I was and not *what* I was."

"You're all crazy," he said backing through the front door. "You need to leave me the hell alone."

"Alex, please," Sam said.

"Just go away, Sam. I was attacked by a vampire, something that isn't meant to exist. Then I find out all my friends are vampires, too!"

"And Gabby. Don't forget about Gabby. She's a witch," Aya quipped.

Sam glared at her. "*Not helping.*"

"Will you just go away?" Alex snarled. "I don't want you coming near me and I don't want you in my house."

"Then take back your invitation," Sam pleaded. "Then I won't be able to come in."

Alex glanced warily from him to Aya, suspecting a trick.

Aya nodded. "He's right. Rescind both our invitations. If you choose not to speak to us again, we cannot come inside."

Sam knew it wouldn't work on Aya. She wasn't entirely vampire, but he was a little taken aback. He didn't think she had it in her to be kind.

"Well," Alex spat, "I take back both your invitations. I rescind Zac's and I rescind Liz's."

Then he slammed the door in their faces.

"Full. Stop," Aya declared as they stood on the porch.

Sam's eyebrows rose. "You can't help but have the last word, can you?"

"*Nope*. It's a total power move."

"I should've compelled him," Sam said as they walked back to the car.

Aya disagreed. "Alex won't say anything. You need to trust him, not the other way around."

"How do you know?" He didn't sound so sure.

"The one thing I know about Alex is that he's loyal. He won't talk, at least not until he's had a chance to talk it through with Gabby and Liz."

He sighed and asked, "Why did you tell him that? To take back your invitation? You never needed one."

She shrugged, leaning against the car. "If it makes him feel safer, then I will let him believe."

"I must admit, I'm surprised."

"Surprised?" She raised her eyebrows. "That I'm not one hundred percent monster? Thanks for the vote of confidence."

"That's not what I meant, and you know it." He

waited for a response, but soon realised he wasn't going to get one.

Aya, only now noticing that he was dressed up, said, "Hot date, Romeo?"

"I was meant to meet Liz," he replied. "It's one year today since she was turned."

"Oh, so you celebrate them?" she asked sarcastically. "Did you get her a cake?"

"No! It's just a hard day for her and all. She hasn't had the best time with it."

Aya laughed. "Does anyone?"

He frowned and didn't reply..

She snorted at his grimace. "Well, at least you wore a black shirt. The blood doesn't show up unless you look hard enough."

"Thanks for the encouragement." He rolled his eyes. "If you don't mind, I have to go find Liz and apologise. If you're going to the manor, can you tell Zac?"

Aya groaned, tapping the car boot. "Only if you get rid of the body."

"Just do it with a little tact, Aya. I don't want him doing anything reckless."

"Yes, sir," she said sarcastically and opened the passenger side door, then slammed it shut, electing to go on foot, rather than get in the car with Sam. "But don't blame me when he does anyway."

The manor was dark when Aya made her way up the driveway.

She wasn't used to answering to others, let alone to the most annoying vampire in the history of the world—Zac Degaud. She worked her best one on one. *Alone.*

Thankful for the alone time, she lit the fire in the parlour, preferring the warm natural light to the artificial electric ones. It was more homely in the big old house.

Stoking the coals, she watched the sparks whirlwind onto the hearth, her thoughts spiralling with them, the embers bringing back memories she'd rather forget. The castle she knew so intimately emerged from the coals; the details vivid even after two thousand years. The place where she was turned. Closing her eyes, she tried to will away the image. The stone and wood structure built by the Britons, sacked by the Romans, and the same she was destroyed in flame.

The adjoining door to the hallway burst open and she spun, hissing deep in her throat as Zac and Liz stumbled in, their hands all over each other, kissing like it was their last day on Earth. Zac's shirt was open, and he was pulling at the hem of Liz's. They hadn't even noticed she was in the room and if she moved, they certainly would.

She scowled, her heart wrenching in her chest. *Poor, Sam.* Sam, who loved this girl.

Zac pulled Liz's top off and trailed kisses down her jaw and the length of her neck.

Aya felt her heart lurch. She could stand it no more and coughed loudly.

"Oh my God!" Liz exclaimed, covering herself with her arms.

Zac took a step back, drawing in a sharp hiss of breath when he saw Aya. Her expression was darkness as she scowled at them.

He swallowed hard. "Aya, I didn't know you were here."

Aya snorted her disgust. "Maybe you should check who's in the room before you screw your brother's girlfriend in it."

They stared at her, not sure what to say, as if they were trying to gauge what she would do next.

Aya made to leave the room, but Liz grabbed her arm. "Please don't say anything."

Aya snatched her arm back, looking Liz up and down with contempt. Saying nothing, she stalked from the room. *How dare she.*

She flew down the hall into the study, coming to a stop in front of the French doors that led onto the veranda. Opening them, she walked out into the night air. She felt more at ease here amongst the overgrown wisteria and the light breeze and willed her anger to melt away. Once upon a time, the forest was her home, a safe place from the evils of the world.

She ran her fingers across the vines that twined

around the banister. Her earth sense had vanished when she turned, a loss that cut to her very soul. She missed the music of the plants, the shifting land beneath her feet. Casting her mind out into the night, all she heard was the soft hum of Zac, who had followed her outside. He leaned against the doorframe, his open shirt flapping in the breeze.

Aya scowled as she felt her anger simmer up again. Without turning she said, "You could have at least dressed yourself properly."

He hastily buttoned up his shirt and came to stand beside her. Why was she so mad? Did she have feelings for him? Was that what that annoying thing was in the pit of her stomach? She wasn't even sure what that meant. All she knew was the biting taste of revenge and destruction. She didn't know what love was, and he obviously didn't, either.

"Aya, I'm sorry—" he began.

"Why are you apologising to me? It's not my back you're going behind," she interrupted, not tearing her eyes away from the dark, cloudy sky that eerily reflected her mood.

After a moment he said, "You like the garden."

He was too observant, having noticed the way she stroked the wisteria. She didn't dare reply. God, he was so annoying.

They stood in silence for a while, neither looking at each other. Aya silently willed him to go away, but he didn't budge.

None of them were blind, they could all see that Zac was drawn to Liz—Alex, Sam, Gabby. They all knew in some small way but trusted that Zac wouldn't cross the line. Sam, least of all, didn't expect Liz to reciprocate. It was Sam Aya felt sorry for.

Surprised at her train of thought, she felt the memory rise of the first night she'd met Zac. The wolves had attacked him in the alley by the bar and she'd saved him. She'd compelled the memory from him, but still couldn't fathom why she'd intervened in the first place.

The greater mystery was how she'd stopped the frenzy and not ended him along with the pack. Perhaps she would never understand.

Zac shuffled nervously beside her, bringing her back to the present. She glanced at him out of the corner of her eye.

The fact that his blood made that sound was a mystery. It was something that drew her, but she still didn't think it had to do with love or lust. Perhaps he was something else as well, but she didn't think so, either.

"Alex knows what we are," she said finally.

She felt him tense beside her.

Sighing, she walked back inside, leaving Zac to stew in the storm of his own making.

It was late when Liz finally climbed the stairs leading to her apartment above the small hardware store on the end of Main Street.

She'd made a terrible mistake. She was hurt, alone, and Zac was there. It wasn't an excuse, but it had happened that way, regardless.

She was glad that Aya was there to stop them, but she feared she'd hurt her, too. Was there any end to her stupidity? What the hell would she tell Sam? Where had he been all night? There was no doubt that she was attracted to Zac, otherwise she wouldn't have let it go so far, but he wasn't blameless, either.

Maybe what she'd done was worst of all. She knew Zac had feelings for her. Feelings he'd kept buried, but not forgotten, because she'd chosen Sam.

As she came up the last flight of stairs, she saw Sam sitting by her door, waiting for her. His expression was closed, and her heart skipped a beat. She knew he heard that.

"Sam," she said when he didn't look up.

"I'm sorry," he whispered, smiling sadly at her.

Instantly, she knew something had happened.

"What's wrong?" she asked, trying to hide the guilt in her voice.

"Alex was attacked by a vampire," he replied. "Luckily Aya was there or I wouldn't have been able to save him."

"Oh my God." Her hand flew to her mouth in shock. "Is he okay?"

Sam nodded. "He knows about us, Liz. All of us."

She sat next to him on the landing and murmured, "I take it he didn't react very well."

"He's scared and confused, with good reason. He's just found out his friends are vampires and it took being attacked by one to find out."

They sat in silence for a few minutes as she processed what'd happened. How had everything gone so bad so fast? Alex, Zac...

"Where were you?" he asked. "I went to the bar and you were already gone. I came here, I looked in the gardens. I even went to the forest before coming back here."

Liz felt the guilt wrench in her gut. If Aya hadn't been at the manor, she would've slept with Zac. And now she knew Sam was off saving Alex from certain death. She felt awful.

She was afraid if she told him, she would've ruined the best thing that'd ever happened to her...all because she was weak.

But if she kept it to herself, her guilt would tear her apart.

"I was with Zac," she said, struggling to keep her voice from cracking.

"And?" he whispered as if he already suspected.

"I... We kissed," she sobbed, unable to keep it to herself. "I was hurt. I needed you, but now I know you were with Alex. Saving him... I'm horrible..."

He snorted and his head dropped into his hands. "Liz, please tell me it was all him. Not you."

She didn't know what to say. She'd kissed him as well. Sam took her silence as an admission of guilt and stood.

"Please, Sam," she pleaded. "Stay."

He sat back down heavily, and Liz took his hand. They would work it out. She loved him and he loved her. They would be okay.

They had to be.

***

The harsh light of day didn't make Zac feel any better about himself. If Liz kept it to herself, there was no need to tell Sam. No reason to hurt him whatsoever.

He took in his reflection in the bathroom mirror and snorted. She would crack and tell him eventually. Hopefully by then, he would have his feelings sorted out. He'd taken advantage of her vulnerability. Then again...

He pushed the thoughts away, splashing his face with cold water.

Thumping down the stairs, he hovered in the doorway to the parlour. Aya was lying on the couch, facing away from the door, reading a book. She looked a lot calmer than she had last night.

"What are you reading?" he asked, standing over her.

"Something about kids fighting to the death in a woodland arena. It's terrible." She tossed it aside. "There's not nearly enough blood in it for a death match."

"That's a bit much, isn't it?" he huffed.

She grinned up at him. "What do you want me to say? I'm insatiable."

"Does this mean I'm back in your good books?" he asked warily, remembering the bite in her words the previous night.

Sitting up, she asked, "Were you ever in my 'good book'?"

Running his hand through his hair, he replied, "Probably not."

"What's that thing you said that time? 'I do a lot of things I don't need to do, but I do them anyway'," she mocked his tone of voice.

"You heard that?"

"I hear a lot of things." Her eyes narrowed, but he caught the note of amusement in her voice.

Zac couldn't help but grin. If they could ever stop bickering, he was sure they would have a good relationship.

He thought back to the previous night—the relief he'd felt when he kissed Liz and the burning need that coursed through him, feelings he hadn't felt for a very long time. But that memory would always conclude with the look of mingled anger and something akin to jealousy that had been etched on Aya's face.

His smile faded and his head turned toward the front door as it slammed, signalling Sam's arrival home.

"Aya, I'm sorry. I..." He didn't know how to put it into words.

Her gaze flickered to the doorway behind him and she shook her head. By the look on her face, it seemed that Sam wasn't happy and that could only mean...

He turned around to face his brother.

Sam was glaring at him and Zac instantly knew that Liz had caved.

Aya looked at them back and forth then said, "I'll be in the study." She couldn't help prodding him one last time.

Liz had followed Sam into the room, her eyes red and puffy, her expression hollow.

"You just couldn't help yourself, could you, brother?" Sam sneered.

"It goes both ways."

"You don't get to mess with this, Zac. You hear me?"

"Sam, please. Calm down," Liz cried, trying to push them apart, but they were both stronger than she was.

Ignoring her pleas, Zac spat, "Who died and made you king of the world, brother?"

"You don't love her, Zac. How could you when you don't respect anything or anyone?"

Zac's expression darkened and the room seemed to disappear around him. "Who are you to tell me who I can and cannot love?"

"Oh, so that's what this is about? You doing what you want, whenever you want." Sam was in his face, refusing to back down.

"Perhaps you should stop following me around like a pathetic lap dog."

"Really? You want to get into that as well?"

"Get it all out, Sam. Tell me what you really think. Tell me what you want to do to me."

"Stop it! I'm not going to fight you. Is that what you want?"

"I know you want to take a couple of swings, little brother."

"Yeah, I want to hit you, so what?"

"Then do it. Hit me, Samuel." When Sam didn't move, Zac grabbed the front of his shirt, pulling him close and snarled, "*Hit me.*"

"You're insane. You don't want any help, do you? Has the last forty years been a joke to you?" His expression fell into one of disappointment. "You want to be a monster."

Sam's words cut into him right where it hurt. That, right there, was the worst thing he could've said, and in that moment, he knew this was about more than Liz. She was the catalyst for something that'd been brewing between them for a long time.

Zac's jaw set as he ground his teeth together. He couldn't contain his rage anymore. As it simmered over, his eyes darkened and in one fluid motion, he snapped Sam's neck. His brother fell limply to the floor with a dull thud.

"No!" Liz cried and fell to her knees, pulling him into her lap. She sobbed, stroking his hair and glared up at Zac. "How could you? *He's your brother!*" She knew he would wake in a few hours, but this was too far.

Zac's expression slowly changed into one of horror. They'd fought before, come to blows, but neither of them had gone this far. He'd killed his brother over *a woman*. His brother, who he loved more than anything. It was the most human emotion of all that had driven him to be the monster he truly was. The monster who he thought he'd made peace with.

He saw the way Liz was holding Sam. She truly loved his brother, not him. She never would, he finally realised. He would never have what Sam had—Victoria had taken it all away.

Zac had to get out of there. He couldn't deal with this.

He was out the front door and gone before he could think twice about it.

Aya flew out of the study when she heard Liz scream at Zac. She was just in time to see the front door slam shut.

So, he'd run instead of facing his problems. *Typical.*

Standing in the doorway of the parlour, she took in Sam's temporarily dead body on the floor in front of the fireplace. Liz leaned against the mantle and sighed in frustration. She jumped when Aya materialised out of the shadows.

"You scared me," she said, clutching her heart.

Aya scowled. "Do you think I can't see what you do to him."

"What are you talking about?"

"God knows why, but he loves you. And you love Sam. The selfish thing is that deep down, you want Zac as well. You're leading him on and it's horrible. You are with Sam. Do the right thing and let Zac go." Aya's face didn't betray her feelings, whatever those were.

"And why do you care so much? You're the ice queen, Aya. *Butt out*." Tears streamed down her cheeks.

She snorted and shook her head. "After two thousand years, it's all still the same."

"What?" Liz glared, her fists shaking.

"Stupid little girls playing with fire."

"I love Sam, Aya. It will always be him," she cried. "He was the one who found me and helped me through the change. He was there to help me get the cravings under control. Zac helped me as well, but I never thought... I knew he cared for me, but..."

"Which one changed you?" Aya asked, her voice low.

Liz looked up at her with a tear-stained face. "No! They didn't do this to me! Aya, no, don't think that!"

Aya visibly relaxed. "I was already dead when Sam found me. I must have had vampire blood in my system because I woke up. He was there holding me, thinking I was gone. We'd become friends before... before it happened. Aya, I don't know who changed me. We never found them."

Aya wasn't convinced. Sighing, she knelt and heaved Sam's bulky form onto the couch with little effort. She was so slight, it was easy to forget that she trumped them all in the strength department.

She sat on the chair opposite as Liz sat on the couch with Sam's head in her lap.

When it was obvious Aya was going to wait, Liz asked, "Was all that stuff you told us about yourself... Was it all true?"

"Yes," she stated. It was hard to get more than a brisk answer to any question that was asked of her.

"Two thousand years is a long time. What have you done with it all?" Aya looked at her like she had said something offensive. "I mean, you must have seen a lot of things..." Even Liz knew she sounded lame.

"Yes," Aya stated again. "But it's not story time and they don't all have good endings. I wouldn't want to frighten your sensitive heart."

Aya knew she intimidated Liz. What the young vampire thought about her didn't bother her, but she had to sit here for who knew how long until Sam woke up. Her staring was making Liz uncomfortable, like she was ready to run if she made a move. But Aya could never help herself.

"What will you do when it comes time to leave?" she asked.

Liz stared at her for a moment as if she was trying to comprehend her question.

"It's a straightforward question, Liz."

"I-I don't know," she stammered, wringing her hands.

"The eternal twenty-one-year-old. Never ageing, frozen in time. How will you explain that?" She was crossing a line, pushing her like this, but the brothers had coddled her. Protected Liz from the inevitable choices she would have to make, and Aya just had to press on the nerve. Perhaps her need came out of jealousy more than anything.

"The time will come," Liz murmured. "And I will be ready then, but for now, I can be who I was meant to be while I can. Why are you so heartless, Aya?"

"I prefer the term realist," she sneered.

"Is this what I have to look forward to? Losing every inch of humanity? Becoming selfish and mean like you?" Liz shook her head in denial.

Aya snorted. "I try to help people, Liz. I'm not always a scary vampire. I don't kill for sport. Perhaps in a few hundred years you'll get it and get the hell over it. Look, I'm here to help with the whole Katrin thing, and if that means sitting here waiting for your boyfriend to wake up, then so be it. I will not answer your questions and put up with your insecurities, and probably never will, so save your breath."

Aya leaned over and grabbed the book she'd been reading from the coffee table and kicked her legs over the arm of the chair. She'd rather read a terrible book than suffer through Liz's uncomfortable silence.

***

The sun had long set by the time Sam gasped for air, sitting upright.

"Thank God." Aya sighed dramatically, tossing her book into the fire.

Sam rubbed his neck, grimacing. "I can't believe he snapped my neck."

"We have to go after him," Liz whispered. She glanced at Aya, who just looked annoyed.

"Love triangles are so last century." Aya rolled her eyes as Liz turned to pour Sam a glass of scotch.

"We've been together for a hundred and fifty years. I'm not going to abandon him." Sam couldn't keep the tears from his eyes. Disappointment or heartbreak? Who knew?

"Tell me what you want me to do and it's done." Liz handed him the glass.

"I fear what he might do, Liz. It doesn't take much to set him off and he's snapped. I know him better than I know myself. He'll leave a trail of bodies behind him before he comes to his senses. The last time it took him years and *we don't have years.*" Sam threw his glass into the fireplace, shattering it into pieces. "Katrin could have already killed him."

Liz wrapped her arms around Sam's waist and lay her head against his back. "Then we will do whatever we can to find him."

Aya shifted uncomfortably. She felt like an interloper, an imposter to this private moment. Liz's gaze flicked to her and she smiled kindly. Aya glared in return, not wanting her sympathy.

"The problem is, I have no idea where he could've gone." Sam held his head in his hands and sighed.

Aya frowned, knowing she had to tell them about his blood. If she tried, she could track him. She was alarmed at how much she cared for this unlikely group of vampires and their one human ally. No one had ever come close.

Her gaze stayed on the floor as she whispered, "I can find him."

Sam looked up at her in surprise. "How?"

Closing her eyes, she took a deep breath. "I can track his blood."

"What do you mean, you can track his blood?" Liz asked. "No vampire can do that."

"I can hear it."

"I don't understand..." Sam said.

Aya scowled. "It buzzes in my head like an annoying mosquito you just can't manage to squash. It doesn't matter how. *I can.* That's all that matters." She stood abruptly. "Don't worry about anything. I will find him and bring him back, whether he wants to come or not."

"Aya, thank you." Sam gave her a look filled with relief.

She sharply nodded and crossed the room without a backward glance. In a second, she was outside, slamming the front door behind her. Breathing deeply, she cast her mind out, listening for the familiar music. She caught a faint trace at the very edge of her limit.

Northeast.

She had a long way to go.

CHAPTER 14

The night was pitch-black as he stood deep in the shadows, waiting.

No moon hung in the sky. The only light was from the streetlamps that were spaced too far apart to be of any use.

The alley that extended behind the shops and restaurants was lined with dumpsters, empty cartons, and pallets, all stinking of rotting food. The deserted lot on the other side was overgrown with weeds almost as high as the chain-link fence. It was a dumping ground for things that didn't want to be found.

The sound of a door slamming and the jangle of keys reached him as he lurked in the darkness. A young woman emerged from behind a row of dumpsters by a restaurant and began walking toward the street at the opposite end of the alley.

He inhaled deeply as she passed his dark hiding

place. The smell of her blood was tantalising and made him even thirstier. He could feel the burn in his throat. She walked the length of the alley, oblivious that she was being watched.

He silently followed her as she finally turned down the adjoining street, her heels tapping against the pavement. The light from the main thoroughfare ahead shone like a beacon of safety as she made her way toward it. She didn't know it yet, but she would never make it.

He stood in the mouth of the alley, wreathed in shadow, listening to her powerful heartbeat. The woman turned back, finally sensing his presence. He heard her gasp as she saw his silhouette and her pace quickened.

The sound of her heart was intoxicating, even more now that it had accelerated in fear. In the blink of an eye, he was in front of her.

She came to an abrupt halt, her eyes widening in fear. She fumbled for something in her bag, her hands shaking, and pulled out a can of pepper spray. Pointing it at his face, she took a few fearful steps back.

"Come closer and I'll scream," she shouted at him, a wild look of panic written on her pretty face.

He laughed at the futility of it all. Before she could react, he had her pressed against the wall, hand over her mouth to stifle the screams that would undoubtedly follow. As the pepper spray clattered to the ground, he considered compelling her before disregarding the notion. He liked it more when they tried to fight.

"*Shh…*" he soothed, running a finger down the woman's exposed neck. "It won't hurt much, *I promise.*"

The woman whimpered as he leaned into her and inhaled deeply, his fangs scraping the delicate flesh around the pulsing jugular.

Before he could sink his fangs into her neck, he was pulled upward into space. Disoriented, he landed heavily on concrete, the air pushing from his lungs. On his feet in a flash, he found himself on the roof of the adjacent building. Eyes black and teeth bared, he lunged for his attacker and found himself pinned facedown, a knee in his back. Struggling was useless. He was firmly in place, but he did anyway, blind with rage.

"Bloody hell, calm down," a female voice hissed in his ear, a voice that was vaguely familiar.

He struggled harder against the knee in his back, trying to flip his assailant to one side, but hands clamped down over his wrists, driving him mad. He was denied his kill and would get it back any way he could.

"Zac," the voice whispered in his ear, "don't struggle. It'll only make it harder. Zac, please come back. We need to talk."

He stilled. The voice was familiar somehow. Where

had he heard it? Probably in a dream somewhere. But he remembered he didn't dream anymore.

Suddenly, he was on his back and the most beautiful raven-haired woman was astride him, pinning his hands above his head. Her eyes were icy blue but melted his black eyes back to their usual green.

"Zac, it's Aya. *Please*."

Aya? Yes, now he remembered.

"What are you looking at?" he hissed at her. Why did it have to be *her*?

"I'm looking at you," she hissed back. "Now get up and come with me."

"Why did you bother."

"Why did I bother coming for you?" Her eyebrows rose in surprise. "Because you're worth bothering about, Zac. That's why."

The tension slacked in his body and she loosened her grip. Even if he tried anything, it wouldn't work. She was countless times stronger than he was and more cunning to boot. The last thing he wanted to do was go back to the manor and talk about it, but he doubted he had a choice.

Aya stood and held out her hand. "Come on, Zac. I have a room not far from here. We can talk."

Zac stood on his own. "I don't want to talk, Aya. I want—"

"To kill and terrorise innocent women?" she interrupted, anger contorting her face.

"I didn't kill any of them."

She seemed to ignore him. "You're better than empty violence. If you don't want to talk, then please, at least come with me. In your frame of mind, you're getting sloppy. If I have to compel another one..." Aya shook her head and held out her hand, motioning for him to take it.

Begrudgingly, he took it, absently running his thumb across her knuckles. Infuriating as she was, he liked the feel of her hand in his.

Still scowling at her, she led him to a tiny motel at the edge of town. He noticed his car in the lot and his eyes grew dark. How long had she been following him?

She let them into the motel room and made sure the door locked behind them. The place was dark and cold and had a slight smell of mould. The neon sign outside flashed *vacancy* through the window, the red colour mirroring his mood.

"How long have you been following me?" he hissed, struggling not to raise his voice as Aya swept the curtains closed.

She glanced at him as she flicked the lamp on, her expression unreadable. "Long enough." She gestured for him to sit on the bed beside her. Reluctantly, he sat stiffly on the cheap floral duvet.

The silence was palpable between them.

Finally, she said, "You need to come back. Katrin is still out there and she will use us all to get to you, no matter where you are. We are all in this together, there's no going back."

Zac snorted. There were a lot of things he was refusing to think about, but then again, they were just new items on an already long list, but he'd never gotten to the point of killing this brother before. They'd come to blows the way only vampire brothers could, but nothing they couldn't come back from.

He'd crossed the line utterly and totally with Sam this time. He remembered the sickening snap Sam's neck had made and flinched. *What had I done?*

"He's okay, you know," Aya murmured. "A little angry, but he doesn't blame you. You can both come back from this."

He turned to look at her, his green eyes full of anger. "I don't know how to come back from this, so how could he? I do nothing but think about it..." He paused and sighed painfully, closing his eyes. "How could one woman drive us apart? We've been brothers for a hundred and seventy years."

Aya smiled almost sadly. "The heart can do strange things, even to us."

He couldn't help but let the faint glimmer of his own smile answer her. He knew deep down that unrequited love would eventually destroy him. Liz would go on with Sam, but he would be left alone to love an empty dream for all eternity if he chose to.

Deep down, he knew it wasn't just this that'd made him run. Sam wanted him to be more than he was, more than what he knew, and that was being good. That was what he was really rebelling against. He was lost and always had been.

"Why did you come after me? Why didn't Sam?" he asked.

"Because..." She sighed, pausing as if she was trying to decide what she should say. "I was the only one who could track you."

"What do you mean?"

Aya frowned. "Your blood sings to me."

Zac's eyebrows rose. "My blood sings to you?"

She laughed, almost nervously. "It's hard to explain. I cast my mind out and I can hear it. I just followed, and I found you."

"Simple as that?"

"Simple as that." She clutched his hand like he needed reassuring that she wasn't crazy. "You don't have to do this, you know. The more alone you are, the farther you'll slip away from your humanity until it's gone forever."

"Do other people... Does their blood...sing to you?" he whispered, not quite sure what it meant.

"No." She shook her head but didn't continue.

"What does it mean..." he mused to himself, gazing at Aya. She looked confused, her hand still clutching his. He gave it a slight squeeze. "Afraid I'll run away?"

"Something like that," she whispered, shifting closer.

"But you'll be able to find me again." His voice was almost inaudible.

"Yes."

He stared down into her eyes and wondered why he never noticed how clear they were before. She was unusually beautiful, her features seemed almost alien and he couldn't tear his gaze away. Reaching up with his free hand, he tucked a strand of long black hair behind her ear, stroking her cheek with his thumb. He felt her breathing quicken as she leaned into his hand, closing her eyes.

Why did his blood sing to her?

He couldn't fathom it, but he suddenly wanted her. She was irresistible. Tilting her chin up, he kissed her lightly on the lips, the contact pulling at his heart. Drawing back, he looked into her eyes as if he was asking approval to taste her lips again. Her hand clutched the front of his shirt, pulling him closer, and this time, she kissed him with a need that took his breath away.

Where had this come from? Didn't she hate him?

Unable to stop himself, he pushed her back onto the bed and was on top of her, his hand running down her side, caressing the curve of her waist. His palm slid over her hip, down her thigh, and pulled her leg up around him, all the while his lips never leaving hers.

Aya rolled him over, her lithe form melding into his. In that moment he knew he'd do anything to please her, *anything.*

Abruptly, she pulled away, gasping for breath. He followed, clutching her hips, not letting her break contact. They were face to face, his gaze searching hers.

"I'm sorry."

"What for?" he whispered huskily. "I'm not."

"I can't do this with you. No matter how much I want to." She looked pained, the confusion clear on her face.

He cocked his head and went to speak, but her hand was on his mouth, stopping him. He was utterly in her trance. The feel of her hand on his lips was heady and he kissed her palm. She scowled, gazing into his eyes. "Sorry about this..." she murmured.

"Sorry about wha—"

When Zac woke, the morning light filtered through the cheap curtains, bathing the room in a disgusting budget motel shade of mustard. He could hear the water running in the bathroom, the blue sterile light of the fluorescent globe shining through the crack of the door, which lay slightly ajar. He could vaguely see the form of a woman through the frosted glass of the shower screen. He gazed at her for a minute or two and turned his head, suddenly aware that he probably shouldn't.

He sat bolt upright. Shit, where was he?

Rubbing his eyes, he remembered being in the alley... Blood... And Aya pulling him off his kill.

She brought him to the motel, and they talked into the night and he slept. Now he remembered. And he knew he had to go back to the manor and face Sam and Liz.

He groaned at the painful memory and shook his head. They had to work it out. And they had to deal with Katrin. Katrin had to die a true death before she found a way to kill them all.

Zac pulled on his shirt, his resolve piecing itself back together.

It was time to grow the hell up.

The warm water streamed down Aya's face as she closed her eyes, letting it wash her thoughts away.

She'd let Zac get too close and let her control wane. After all that'd happened to her, she was incapable of loving anyone. She couldn't hurt him like that after Liz, whether she felt drawn to him or not. He didn't deserve it. Two thousand years of revenge had not changed her mind yet. She had to block off her sensitivity to other's emotions before she did something she would regret.

Turning off the water, she heard him move about in the next room and steeled herself for the charade she'd have to play. It was twice now that she'd compelled Zac and she hoped it was the last.

Wrapping herself in a towel, she stepped from the shower and caught sight of him dressing through the crack in the bathroom door. Thankfully, his back was to her and didn't notice her gaze.

She dressed and abruptly opened the door. Towelling her hair dry, she picked up the car keys from the dresser.

"Ready to go," she asked, tossing the damp towel back into the bathroom.

Zac turned at the sudden movement and glanced away. She caught the flush in his cheeks and was confused. Was he embarrassed? He nodded and they made their way out to the car.

"Aya... I don't know what to say," he began.

"Don't say anything. You called me. I'm making sure it wasn't for nothing. I do have a vested interest in doing away with Katrin, so don't worry about it."

He frowned. "Just doing your duty."

"If you want to see it that way."

"Sure," he said sullenly, getting into the driver's seat.

Starting the engine, Zac glanced sideways at Aya as she climbed into the passenger side and put on her sunglasses.

She was the most complicated person he had ever met, and it frustrated him to no end. Secretly, he was glad she cared enough that she came for him. He still felt the need to stalk human blood, but when she was with him, he could control it and he didn't understand why. Shaking his head, he reversed out of the lot and turned onto the adjoining interstate.

That he was drawn to her was no great secret to him. Why, was the real question. She infuriated the hell out of him, even more since the previous night at the motel. He thought back over their conversation but could see nothing unusual about it. She'd convinced him to return to the manor and he'd slept the same dreamless sleep he'd had for decades.

If, by some miracle, they could kill Katrin once and for all, he wondered what she would do then. Would she stay with them for a while or go straight to the next hunt?

"Can I ask you a question?" Neither of them had spoken for the last four hours they'd been driving.

"Yes," she replied, still gazing through the windshield at the road ahead.

"What will you do after this? I mean, if we deal with Katrin."

She was silent for a while. "I don't know."

Zac glanced at her and focused back on the road. "When you hunt a witch, do you kill them?"

"Not always."

"Why?"

"I save them when I can," she said matter-of-factly.

"But why, if they're already corrupt?"

"I wasn't always this monster," she snapped. "And neither were you. Surely, you can still feel an affinity with mortal life. That is reason enough."

Suddenly, he felt foolish. The vampire in him was speaking, not the human. She had two thousand years of control and understanding, and he felt insignificant in comparison. A strained silence followed and they didn't speak again for some time.

They pulled into a gas station around dusk. Aya sat on the hood of the car staring into the distance as he pulled the hose from the pump and began to fill the tank.

"What are you looking at?" he asked.

She didn't answer straight away. "I'm not looking at anything. I'm listening and right now you're making too much noise."

"What are you listening for?" he asked, ignoring the warning tone in her voice.

"Bad things stalk us, Zac. Things only I can hear coming." She was annoyed.

He raised an eyebrow at her, even though her back was to him. He didn't understand how she could say everything but give no information.

As if sensing his annoyance, she turned and looked at him up and down over the top of her sunglasses. He put the nozzle back into the pump more forcefully than necessary and went to pay for the gas.

Aya was back in the passenger seat when he returned. Slamming the door closed, he turned to her. "Well?"

"Well, what?" She scowled in reaction to his curtness.

"Did you hear anything?"

"No." It was a statement designed to end the conversation.

Zac leaned his head back against the seat and exhaled. "You have to give me something, Aya. Do you realise how frustrating you are? It's all I can do..."

She turned to him, pulling off her sunglasses, her eyes cold and angry. "What do you want from me, Zac?"

"Anything," he exclaimed, his voice rising. "You never explain yourself. Our lives are on the line and you never give me the full story. How can I protect them if I don't know what I'm fighting? How can I protect—" He stopped, unable to say what he really meant. He wanted to protect her just as much as any one of the others. As much as his brother, who was more dear to him than his own life. *What was happening to me?*

Her eyes narrowed in warning. "Be careful what you say next, Zac."

He drew in a sharp breath and struggled to keep his mouth shut. Beautiful women would be the death of him, not some psycho witch from beyond the grave.

"I don't want you to leave," he whispered finally, not daring to look at her.

"I'm not going anywhere," she conceded, the anger dropping from her voice.

"Not yet," he muttered, turning the key in the ignition.

CHAPTER 15

Zac cringed at the relief that flooded Sam's face when he slunk through the door behind Aya. He'd snapped his brother's neck, but he was still glad he'd come back. He was reluctant to speak to Sam and Liz. He knew exactly what they'd say. Every single word.

Aya grabbed his hand when he hesitated in the doorway of the parlour, pulling him into the room. Sam stood and shook his head when he laid eyes on his older brother, his gaze flickering briefly to Aya, who smiled wryly and left the room.

"Why did you run, Zac?" he asked gently.

"I snapped your neck, Sam."

He sighed. "Yeah, I was there."

"Do you understand the meaning of ironic?" Zac snorted.

"Stop it, Zac," Sam said, trying to hold himself

back. When he was human, his neck had been snapped—that was how he'd died.

"What do you want me to say?"

"Sorry would be a good start."

Zac's gaze shifted to Liz. "Sorry about what?"

"Don't even go there," Liz said exasperated.

"You started it, Liz, but this was never about you," Zac said with no emotion.

"Then what was it about?" Sam directed his brother's attention back to him.

"The same thing it's been about for the last one hundred and whatever years, Sam. You trying to prove that somewhere in here," he thumped his hand on his heart, "there's a good guy wanting to get out. When will you just stop and let me be?"

"We grew up together, Zac. We are as close as two brothers can get. Yeah, we're different, but I know you better than you seem to know yourself. You're so much better than this. Fighting...*war*. It's not all there is."

"Don't you think I've spent every single day trying to find something else?" he spat. "She told me it was the only thing I was good at and I believed her. I still believe her."

"Who told you this?" Sam asked, already suspecting the answer.

"Victoria." He ignored the confused look on Liz's face.

Sam shook his head, not believing that Zac had kept this to himself for so long. He'd hardly ever spoken to him about his first few months as a vampire. The extent to which Victoria must have manipulated his brother scared him.

"Now do you understand?" Zac asked.

"I won't give up on you, Zac." Sam shook his head. "You never gave up on me when it mattered the most. So, don't think I'm going to start now, or ever."

Zac glanced from him to Liz, surprised that they had forgiven him so quickly. "You know I'm..."

"Sorry?" she asked.

"Even if I can't say it, you know I am." He looked away.

She began to speak, but Zac cut her off, "I know. Believe me, I know all about it. And if you don't mind, I'd like to be alone with the liquor cabinet."

Sam nodded and motioned for Liz to follow him out of the room.

Thankfully, they left without another word. Zac had, had enough heart to heart to last the rest of the decade. He felt foolish and pathetic, two things that should never be associated with him in his own opinion. Taking out an unopened bottle of whiskey, he drank a quarter of it in one shot.

Groaning in frustration, he picked up his bowie knife from the mantle and sat on the couch. Standard issue to the Confederate Infantry during the Civil War, this knife had followed him in life and death. It had cut open the wrist of the woman who had made him. The knife that had drew the blood that'd made him a vampire.

Placing his hand on the antique coffee table, splaying his fingers, he stabbed the knife in-between his index and middle finger. Then middle and ring fingers, ring and little, thumb and index. It was a game he used to play to make his fellow soldiers uneasy. One he never lost and one that never failed in gaining their respect. If that respect was garnered through fear, then all the better. Each war he'd been in, the knives got longer and sharper, the men bigger and rougher.

The knife stabbed through the centre of his hand, pinning him to the table. Grimacing at the sudden pain, he refused to make a sound, blood pooling from around the blade. He wanted to feel something real and this pain was as real as it was going to get.

Pulling the knife free, blood gushed onto the coffee table. Running his thumb across his open hand, the wound began to close as it healed itself.

"So, you're into self-mutilation now?" That annoying voice came from behind him. Aya. Always there to make a smart-ass comment.

"Don't presume you know anything about me," he snarled, standing to glare at her.

"Likewise." Aya raised her hands, eyeing the knife. He knew it would be gone in under one second flat if she thought it were a threat. He sat back down and stabbed the knife into the tabletop, facing away from her.

"Keep your head screwed on, Zac," she said without any inflection.

He turned to retort, but she'd already gone. Shaking his head, he sunk back down into his melancholy.

Somewhere he'd lost his way. Why had they come back here in the first place? To pretend that they were human again?

Deep down he knew Sam wanted him to find something in himself that wasn't about fighting and killing. Victoria had once told him that it was the only thing he was good at...and perhaps it was.

<hr>

Liz sighed as her fifth call to Alex went straight to voicemail. It looked like she would have to go the direct route.

She felt guilty neglecting him the last few days, especially after he'd been attacked, but everything had blown up in her face after she'd kissed Zac. Sam's broken neck and having to send Aya off to pick up the pieces. She now felt she owed the two-thousand-year-old vampire and that couldn't be good...but something told her Aya had done it as much for herself as for them. She could see her and Zac finding themselves together someday, even if they couldn't.

She had spent the last few days with Sam, working out what had happened while they waited for news from Aya. Sorting out what it meant for them. It seemed that love did prevail, at least this time. Liz would never let herself waver again.

Hovering on the sidewalk, she watched Alex work in the garden. What the hell would she say? 'You were being attacked by a crazy vampire controlled by a two-thousand-year-old witch while I was off cheating on my vampire boyfriend?' She shook her head and set off across the grass before she could change her mind. Alex deserved the whole sordid truth.

He caught sight of her as she approached and glared. "Hell, Liz. Can't you take a hint?" He rolled his eyes, beginning to walk away from her, but she was in front of him a little too fast to be normal, blocking his way.

"Can I just explain? Then you can decide what you want to do," she pleaded. "If you never want to speak to me again, then I will respect it."

He groaned and sat on the grass by the bandstand. "Don't sugarcoat it, Liz. If I have to sit here and listen, you need to tell me everything. I was attacked by a vampire and saved by two more. It wasn't pretty."

"I know," she said. "All-in."

They sat on the grass, Liz thinking for a moment, trying to piece it all together in the simplest way to describe everything that had happened in the last year. Taking a deep breath, she began.

"I didn't know what Sam and Zac were before it happened a year ago. I just thought they were two rich brothers who had moved to town just like everyone else. Not until the day I changed the route I usually took when I went for a run." She paused, quietly gauging Alex's emotions. "The details are still sketchy. I don't think I'll ever remember everything that happened that day. I do remember being attacked, but nothing about who it was. There was a lot of blood, that I know. Theirs or mine, I have no idea. When I woke up, Sam was holding me."

When she stopped, Alex reached out and held her hand, sensing that she needed this gesture at least. He was still looking off into the distance, scowling.

Squeezing his warm hand, she continued, "He thought I was dead. I *was* dead. The way he held onto me... He was horrified and relieved all at the same time when he realised I was alive. We've been together since. Sam and Zac, they helped me through it all."

"Did you find out who did it?" Alex whispered.

"I don't know," she replied. "I know for sure it wasn't the brothers. I trust them completely. They tried to find the vampire who attacked me but couldn't find any trace of them. I've come to accept the fact that I'll probably never know."

"What about Aya?"

"Aya," Liz said with a sigh. "Well, that's more complicated."

Alex frowned, rubbing his temples with his calloused hands. "I'm all ears."

"A few weeks ago, a vampire came to town and got

into a fight with Zac. Zac killed him, but managed to get on the bad side of an ancient and powerful witch named Katrin in the process. Gabby helped him cast a summoning spell she found for help, to call a vampire known as the Witch Hunter. At the time we didn't know who that was. We had nothing else to go on and it seemed like a better option than just letting Katrin kill him. Aya hid her true self from us for ages, gauging our intentions, but she came when she was called and decided she wanted to help. Katrin is after her as well."

"Why?"

"I don't know. She's secretive, but I would guess it has something to do with being referred to as a Witch Hunter." Liz sighed heavily. "That's pretty much where we are now. Trying to deal with Katrin before she can kill us."

She watched his features change as he thought through everything she had said. He looked angry, confused, and strangely enough, relieved.

"You know this is... Well, it's crazy," he finally said.

"I'm sorry," she whispered. "I was trying to protect you. I thought the less you knew, the safer you'd be."

"But you've been lying to me," he said. "It's not just a little white lie. This is the motherload, Liz."

"I'll do anything it takes," she pleaded. "*Anything.*"

"Well," he said after a minute, "you and Gabby are my oldest friends. I can understand why you wouldn't tell me, but it doesn't make it hurt any less."

"I know."

"You have to promise not to keep anything from me anymore. I can handle it, Liz. I'm not a mess now, am I?"

"You are surprisingly calm," Liz said carefully.

He shrugged. "When life hands you lemons…"

"Oh, Alex!" Liz flung her arms around his neck, hugging him just a little too hard.

"I don't know what I can do," he said, extracting himself from her hug. "But you owe me. *Big*. No more secrets."

"Thank you, Alex. This means a lot to all of us. A lot to me."

He sighed, rubbing his eyes. "Let's just work on it, okay?"

Gabby sat cross-legged on her lounge room floor, the grimoire in her lap, her face screwed up in concentration.

Groaning dramatically, she put the book aside and drew her knees up, resting her head on her arms. She was getting absolutely nowhere. She was a pathetic excuse for a witch.

She'd felt different all her life but had never understood that feeling she got whenever her powers were trying to come out and be embraced. She still couldn't fathom what she was; being on her own was difficult and having vampires as friends went against everything the grimoire had taught her. But she wouldn't turn away from her friends and all things took time, right?

It didn't stop her from getting frustrated, though.

Gabby began wondering if she should try to contact her grandmother. She hadn't seen or spoken to her for years, not since she was ten. That's when she'd disappeared.

Her grandfather was a less than pleasant man, severe and old-fashioned and extremely set in his ways. He'd passed a few years ago, but Gabby remembered that he'd threatened to have his wife committed to an asylum, but before it could go any farther, she'd up and left rather than stay with her husband a moment longer.

Since awakening as a witch, Gabby always felt the reason behind it was because she was a witch and even her own family was afraid of her...simply because they didn't understand.

She'd found the grimoire a year and a half ago, hidden in the attic. That was the day she was moving out and into her apartment across town. She'd gone through all her old boxes, the ones everyone had—stuffed full of childhood toys, high school yearbooks, and other mementos—but there was one hidden at the back, one that didn't fit.

When she'd opened it, she found the most curious things inside. On the top was the grimoire and under that, wrapped up in a deep purple quilt, was an ornate knife with a bone handle, a silver bowl, and several jars of dried herbs.

She took the box without mentioning it to her parents and began to visit the old cemetery, trying to understand what she was. It wasn't long before she realised the strange things she'd been feeling all her life was the earth trying to speak to her.

It'd been over a week since Aya had entrusted her with finding what kept Katrin's soul attached to the living, and for the life of her, she couldn't work it out.

She'd spent hours poring over the grimoire, but she couldn't understand most of it. Many pages were written in an old, strange language. The nights she'd spent communing with the earth, searching its energy for anything that seemed out of place, but came up empty time and time again. Truthfully, she didn't know enough to understand what she was looking for.

Sighing, Gabby put the grimoire aside and climbed into bed, exhausted. Tomorrow was another day and she would try again. She had to, even though she knew she would come up empty-handed.

Soon, she was fast asleep, her mind wandering into different dreams—of her grandmother, the story she'd read about Aya, and her search through the grimoire, the pages blending into one huge blur.

As her dream settled, she found herself in the old cemetery, sitting cross-legged in the middle of a circle of power as if she had been in the midst of meditation. The night was gloomy around her, the wind wailing with a brewing storm. The only light that pierced the darkness was the flickering candles that surrounded her.

Gabby froze as she saw a woman emerge from the darkness. She approached calmly, her hands clasped in front, her expression cold and unwavering. She wore a white dress made of long white folds of silk that hung low over her shoulders and draped to the ground. It cinched at the hips by a low golden belt. Long auburn hair spilled over her shoulders that lay still, even as a strong breeze buffeted the cemetery.

How Gabby knew that this woman was Katrin was beyond her. The witch stood at the edge of the circle, her expression closed as she assessed her. Then she stepped harmlessly across the circle and through the line that kept others out. Her gaze flickered to the grimoire on the ground and her covetous look didn't escape Gabby.

"I'd hoped that you were one of mine." Katrin rested an ethereal hand on Gabby's shoulder. "But you're Ismena's. Not to worry."

Gabby was too surprised to say anything and when Katrin reached out and placed a hand over her eyes, she froze.

Katrin murmured under her breath, then said audibly, "Your eyes will be one with mine. What you see and hear will be mine."

Gabby gasped as she woke with a start. Confused,

she blinked hard a few times before she realised she was at home in bed, and it was three a.m.

The dream slipped from her mind just as quickly. An odd feeling told her to try to remember before it was gone, but nothing came to mind. The only thing that she could think about as she fell back to sleep was that she would be wrecked at work tomorrow.

Several days had passed since Aya had returned to the manor with Zac in tow and she'd avoided him for several days. Apart from walking in on him and that knife, she'd evaded him and his annoying questions. She grimaced remembering his blood all over the table. The sound of it had pierced through her head, splitting it open.

For two thousand years she had learned to deal with people, read their emotions, decipher the meanings to their words, decode their motives, untangle their wicked webs of deceit, but she had no idea how to deal with the insinuated meaning in Zac's words he spoke as they drove to the manor.

I don't want you to leave.

It was the first time she'd felt so protective of someone and it was an alien feeling. No one wanted her to stay once they knew even the smallest sliver of truth about her, and she gladly compelled away their memory of her. These vampires knew nothing but the barest facts and still…

Her greatest secrets would remain buried. *They had to.*

The impenetrable wall she'd built around herself had always served her well. All that kept her going was the purpose she'd set herself to last her eternity. *Revenge.* There was no room for anything else; so to save Zac from her, she made him forget their kiss. It was for his own good.

But those words…

Maybe compulsion wasn't enough this time. She shook her head and pushed those thoughts away. It would do her no good to dwell when there were bigger threats lingering.

She finally had an opportunity to end Katrin once and for all—her first and possibly only opportunity—but it all relied on Gabby.

Aya lingered in the parlour, her plan growing in her mind. The brothers were gone somewhere she didn't really care about. Brotherly bonding to pull Zac back on the wagon no doubt.

They needed a plan. Enough time had passed in which Katrin could put together whatever grand scheme she had up her sleeve and she needed something to at least counter whatever was coming. She'd been distracted by one particular brother's issues far too much.

That's why Aya had sought out Gabby and asked her to come to the manor.

The young witch had access to immense power, but it was still beyond her reach. If Aya could help her learn, she was confident they had a chance of prevailing. Gabby just needed a push in the right direction.

She was ready and waiting when the front door opened. Gabby joined her in the parlour, looking pale and drawn.

Aya looked her over. "You look ravishing this morning."

"I'm exhausted," the witch said. "I've barely been sleeping."

"And?" The vampire waited.

"You really think I've got what it takes to face Katrin?"

Aya raised her eyebrows. "You need to stop with all that self-depreciating business," she told her, "it's getting old."

Gabby sighed and set her grimoire down on the coffee table. "Have you dealt with spirits before?"

"Yes, but not the spirit of a witch this powerful," she admitted.

Gabby sighed again, her stress obvious. "I'm so lost."

Aya frowned. "Give me the grimoire. I can read the older entries."

"You can read that?" Gabby asked, raising her eyebrows. "I don't even know what language it is."

"I'm older than it is. I've been around long enough to learn a lot of different languages," she replied, flipping through the pages. Coming to rest on the spell that'd summoned her, she groaned. "This one we can do without."

Gabby grabbed Aya's arm as went to tear the offending page out.

"Don't," the witch pleaded. "It's all I have of my grams. Don't destroy it."

"We need to get rid of it, Gabby. As it is now, it's just a call. With the right inflection, it could become a summoning."

"No one will take the grimoire," she said. "It's safe with me."

"Fine, but don't say I didn't warn you." *Tearing out the page would hurt something fierce, anyway.* She continued to flick through pages, stopping when something caught her interest.

"Nothing?" Gabby asked, when Aya handed the grimoire back.

"I don't know." She sighed dramatically. "There's no one in your family you can talk to? Other witches?"

"No," the young witch said with a shrug. "My parents have no power, at least none they know they have. There's my grandmother, but..."

"I would advise you think about contacting her," Aya said, giving her a little nudge with her words.

"I'm not even sure where she's living," Gabby protested. "Or if she's still alive."

"Well, you better get a clue." Aya raised an eyebrow at her. "She might be the only one who can help you find what's in there." She jabbed a finger at Gabby's heart. "Otherwise, dying might be the best solution for all of us."

It was late afternoon when the brothers finally came home. Aya was in the garden, sitting on the stone bench, staring at the sky. She assumed they'd been doing some brotherly vampire bonding thing. *Stay away from my girlfriend and stop eating people* type of exercises. Building bridges so they could get over it already.

"How was your AA meeting," she asked as she heard them come up behind her. She didn't have to turn to know that Zac was glaring at her. It was the first time they'd spoken since the knife incident.

The brothers weren't fast enough to catch the movement to their left, but Aya was up from the bench and in front of Zac in a millisecond, grasping a stake that'd been thrown at him.

And it was thrown back just as fast, a thud sounding as it found its mark.

She growled in annoyance as an unknown vampire came from the garden behind, stake in hand, lunging for Sam. But Aya was there again, grabbing the male vampire's wrist, stopping him dead in his tracks.

She sighed, beyond exasperated. "You people never learn." She squeezed her hand around the assailant's wrist, a crack echoing across the garden, and the stake dropped to the ground.

The vampire grimaced, but kept coming, obviously on a kamikaze mission. There was no way he'd survive her.

Aya grabbed his hair before he could duck and drove his head into the ground so hard there was a loud crack as his skull shattered. She held his head in place as blood pooled beneath them. If she moved it even slightly, the vampire's brains would spill out of his broken skull and he would be as good as dead. Her eyes were chillingly opalescent as the scent of blood filled the garden and she hissed deep in her throat.

"When you get to the other side, tell that *bitch* Katrin that she'll have to try harder than that to best me." She let her grip slacken and the vampire's eyes glazed over as his brains slid out of his broken skull.

She turned to the brothers, who stood in the same spot with shocked expressions. Only a minute had passed, but it was more than enough to get the job done. Her eyes refusing to clear, she sneered, "Do that piece of shit a favour and stake him."

"Your eyes..." Zac whispered. "What...?"

Aya grinned. "I'm a new kind of monster, vampire. One of a kind. Limited edition."

"But you are a vampire?" Sam asked, picking up the stake.

"Unfortunately." She rolled her eyes, the colour shifting back to their regular icy blue.

"Then why are your eyes white?"

"Consider me an albino. Cataracts from old age. Storm from *X-Men*," she replied sarcastically.

Zac raised his eyebrows. "You learn quick for someone who's been out of it for decades."

"Adapt and survive...or die. I don't know about you, but I'm a survivor." She pushed past him, going back inside.

Sam ran after her. "Aya, wait."

"Katrin is making her move...*finally*," she said, not waiting to hear what he had to say. "Whatever she's going to try will happen very soon."

"She's testing our defences," Zac said, coming up behind his brother.

"Aww, there's the captain we all know and love," she said mockingly.

"Give it a rest. It could also be a diversion. Sam, I suggest you check in on Liz and Gabby. I will have a look around the grounds."

"I would be more worried about Gabby," Aya said. "Going after Liz would be pointless. And besides, there's no one else here."

"How do you know?"

"Why do you still have to ask?"

Sam grimaced. "I'm going to check on her."

"I'm coming with you," Zac said.

Sam held his hand up. "No, stay here. It might be exactly what Katrin wants you to do. I won't be long. I'll call once I know more."

Zac looked to Aya, but she just shrugged and went inside.

"Fine," he said reluctantly. "Call me the second you know anything."

"I will," Sam reassured him, then disappeared around the side of the house.

While they waited for news from Sam, Zac convinced Aya to help him bury the desiccated vampires in the yard. Between them both, it didn't take long to dig holes deep enough to conceal them for a very long time. Graves were something Zac had become familiar with over the years.

"Why are your eyes white, really?" he asked when Aya made it clear she wasn't going to speak to him.

She sighed loudly. "Because they are."

"Why won't you tell me anything about yourself?"

"There's nothing you'd want to know. I'm a vampire. Plain and simple. Why are your eyes green and mine blue? Because that's the way we were made. *The end.*"

"You've heard more things about me in the last few days than Sam has heard in his entire life." Annoyed at her evasion, he tossed his shovel aside and wiped his dirty hands on his jeans.

She leaned on her shovel and glared. "I never once asked you to divulge your secrets."

"Yeah, you practically beat them out of me, Aya," he scoffed, remembering the night they'd spent at the motel. He wasn't quite himself then, coming down from the disgusting high of stalking human blood. "You can walk into any human house without being invited, the sun doesn't bother you in the slightest, your eyes are white, and you seem to know where the hell I am before I even get there. Who the hell are you, Aya? You're like a ghost."

"I don't owe you anything, Zac. Least of all an explanation."

"Of course, you don't." He ran his hands through his hair in frustration.

"Don't worry about me when you've got your own problems to deal with."

He flinched at her sharp tone. "Thanks for reminding me, Aya. Real smooth."

She sighed heavily and sat on the bench. "It's always been about control, Zac. You may be good at killing, but it's not all of who you are."

"You don't need to tell me that," he said as he sat beside her. He didn't really want to hear it, but assumed he was going to anyway.

"It's about control for all of us. Some choose to harness it; some choose to relinquish it. It is the intent that separates good from evil," she said, looking at the sky. "Why do you hold on to your humanity?"

Zac shrugged, remaining silent.

"It's for Sam's sake, isn't it?" She peered out the corner of her eye, judging his reaction.

He was scowling, looking at his hands. Finally, he said, "I don't want to be this monster, but I can't help myself."

"You have to do it for yourself. You might think you're doing Sam a favour, but you're not. If you don't want it, then you're making it harder than you need to. You *can* help yourself." He was still looking at his hands, wringing them as she spoke. "Tell me, what would you have done after the Civil War?"

"I don't know." He would have continued in the Army, perhaps. Joined the new United States. Maybe as a Confederate they would have taken him and put him on trial instead. It wasn't something he was at liberty to think about once he'd turned. That life was gone.

Aya turned to look at him. "That's the best answer anyone could ever hope for."

He was confused. "What do you mean?"

She shrugged. "If you don't know, then you could do anything."

Zac sat for a moment, trying to process the notion. His life had been taken away from him, but he still had a say as to what he did next. He'd always believed Victoria had taken all his choices and left him to be the only person he knew how to be—a monster. But maybe he could be more than that...if only he knew how.

He hesitantly reached out to touch her hand that rested on the back of the bench, Aya eyeing him warily as he did. She edged back ever so slightly, so slightly that only his vampire eyes could see the gesture. Her expression was blank as they stared at each other until her eyes unfocused and her body became rigid.

"Zac..." she said with a sharp note of panic. Then, she was gone.

Zac stared for a moment, dumbfounded.

She'd disappeared. Not like she'd done before, where she'd moved too fast for him to stop, but she'd completely vanished.

Regardless, he got up from the bench and searched the house, calling her name. Stopping in the study, he roared and sent the papers that littered the desk flying, his face in his hands.

They'd been so stupid. Katrin was coming for *Aya*, she didn't want him anymore. Her voice was one of surprise and panic, like she didn't understand what was happening...and he was powerless to stop it.

Aya had vanished.

Gabby stomped up the six flights of stairs to her apartment.

It sat on top of a small complex of twelve, in a leafy street surrounded by enormous family homes and smaller cottages that dated back to pre-Civil War days. A horror of 1970s architecture in an otherwise beautiful street.

She was a mere six blocks from the town centre, and seven blocks from the office where she worked. The view stretched for miles, but there wasn't really anything to see other than the surrounding houses, forest, and bayou. Despite all of this, she loved her place. What she didn't love, was the six flights of stairs.

Her mind was in turmoil over her conversation with Aya. She'd come straight home from the manor, wanting to be alone, extremely frustrated with herself. How could she find her grandmother? Who knew where she was and if she was even still alive?

How was she going to find someone that didn't want to be found?

The long blue drapes in the living room were pulled open, letting the late afternoon light into the apartment. She put her bag on the kitchen bench, with the grimoire beside it, and went through to the bedroom via the bathroom.

Her place had an odd layout. The bathroom connected to the kitchen on one side and through to a small walk-through closet, before emerging into the bedroom. The kitchen and lounge were all in one.

Pulling off her sweater and hanging it in the closet, Gabby stilled as she heard a dull thud. Her attention was drawn back through to the kitchen. It could've been her neighbour banging about across the way, but it'd sounded like it'd come from inside her apartment. Shaking her head, she dismissed the notion, positive she'd locked the door behind her.

Walking back through the bathroom, Gabby stopped to splash icy water on her face. Gazing at her reflection for a moment, she sighed. What did Aya expect her to do? She wasn't powerful. Hell, she couldn't even scry or control anything wilder than a gentle breeze.

Peering at herself in the mirror, she blinked when she saw her image waiver. Rubbing her eyes, she frowned when it did it again. *What the...?*

Her head snapped toward the kitchen as she heard the same thumping sound through the door.

Panicking, she pressed her ear against the wood and listened.

This time she was positive it'd come from her apartment. Someone was in here with her.

Looking around the bathroom, she couldn't find anything she could use as a weapon. The only option was a can of hairspray. She grabbed it anyway because it was better than nothing.

Gabby took a deep breath and edged the door open a crack and peered through. The kitchen was empty, her bag still on the bench.

She edged herself through the door, her heart beating so fiercely it was a wonder it didn't give her away. If it'd been a vampire in here, it would have, but first she would have to invite one in. It had to be a human.

The kitchen was empty, so she discarded the hairspray and eased the largest knife from the block as silently as she could. Aiming it in front of her, she edged along the wall to the lounge. Leaning around the corner, she gasped as she saw an ominous figure leap out of the window. The drapes billowed inward, the wind outside picking up.

Running forward, Gabby leaned out of the window. It was a three-story drop and the guy had just jumped. When she looked for him below, no one was there. He'd vanished.

"Shit," she cursed and ran back toward the kitchen. *The grimoire!*

Knocking her bag onto the floor in her haste, she groaned, tears sliding down her face. It was gone. Panicked, she paced back and forth. What should she do? Who'd taken it? Even as she asked herself, she already knew the answer to that question. Katrin was behind this. There was no one else.

Suddenly, there was a splitting pain behind her eyes that made her cry out. Doubling over, she grasped the edge of the kitchen counter, gasping for breath. Her head felt like it was literally tearing open.

She sank to the floor, realising someone had been spying on her. The ache in her head was a dead giveaway.

No, that wasn't quite right. Gabby had been used *as* the spy. The only reason they would go for the grimoire was because of her conversation with Aya. There would be nothing special about hers that distinguished it from another witch's other than...

The summoning spell.

Her reflection! It was the clue that made her believe she'd been used as Katrin's looking glass. Even if she was wrong, there was no harm in using her energy to dispel herself.

Holding her head in her hands, she drew her knees close and began to chant.

The pain still tore through her skull, but she kept going. She assumed Katrin was trying to erase her memory. As the last word left her lips, all the air was pulled from her body and she gasped, trying to draw in new oxygen as spots pricked her vision.

Gabby's eyes snapped open as she came to. She was lying on her side on the kitchen floor, shivering. The lounge room windows were still open and her bag was on the floor.

She'd passed out after all.

Rubbing her eyes and sitting up slowly, she felt much better. The spell was gone. Groaning, she realised what she'd allowed to happen.

She'd been used as a spy and now the grimoire was gone.

Gabby jumped when there was a sharp knock at the door. Dragging herself up, she looked through the peephole and her shoulders sagged in relief. She burst into tears as she threw open the door.

"Sam!" Gabby cried in relief as he stepped inside. "Someone was here, I…"

"It's all right," he said, embracing her. "Are you okay?"

"Y-yes," she stammered.

"What happened?"

"Katrin cast a spell on me in my sleep. She was using me to spy," she sobbed.

"Was?" he asked carefully.

"She's not here anymore. I-I took care of it."

Frowning, he walked through the apartment, checking every corner. Finally, he looked out the open window to the street below. Closing it behind him, he sighed.

"Sam..." Gabby began, "I was with Aya today."

There was a brief pause before he grabbed her shoulders. "What did you say, Gabby? What does Katrin know?"

"The summoning spell," she replied. "They took the grimoire."

<hr>

"What do you mean her grimoire was stolen?" Zac yelled into his cell. He paced back and forth as Sam tried to calm him down on the other end. They were on their way back to the manor. Sam and that goddamn witch, Gabby. "How the hell did they get in?"

"Gabby said it was a human man. She was in her apartment at the time. No vampires are invited in besides me and Liz. He had to be compelled by someone."

"Of course, he was," Zac spat.

"He jumped out the window before she could do anything. There was nothing there when she looked out, so—"

"*Hell*," he groaned. "Someone was waiting for him, it's a three-story drop."

"Katrin." Sam sounded like he'd finally got everything that'd happened the last few weeks.

"Duh. You know Aya's gone, right? They stole the

grimoire and used the summoning spell against her."

"What?"

"*You heard me.*"

"We're almost there, brother. Calm down and we'll discuss this when we get there, all right?"

Zac grunted and hung up without answering. Stopping his restless pacing, he sat on the sofa across from the fireplace and got up again. He went into the study, then back into the yard. Unable to sit still, he hurled one of the shovels across the yard and over the fence, roaring in frustration. He was back in the parlour in a second, downing a bottle of vodka. He knew he had to calm down or it would be bad news for everyone. Problem was, he didn't want to.

When he finally sensed movement outside, he sighed. What had taken them so long? Glaring at the doorway as everyone filed in, he began pacing again, agitated. Liz and Alex sat on the couch and placed Gabby in between them. They knew he was unpredictable after his disappearance and he resented the precautionary methods they were taking.

Sam came up beside him and placed a hand on his shoulder, stopping his momentum and asked, "What happened?"

"She disappeared into thin air. *Like magic*," Zac spat, throwing his hands into the air in exasperation.

It wasn't until she'd gone that he realised he was falling for her. As irritating as she was, he wanted her. All the amplified emotions he'd been feeling, while trying to be a good human for Sam, had compounded into this...this tangle of... He couldn't say the word, let alone think it.

All Zac knew was that he had to go after Aya no matter how hopeless the situation was.

"We should have destroyed the spell once she revealed herself to us," he added. "We were *stupid*."

"They might try to use her as bait for you," Gabby mumbled. "She was the easier mark what with the summoning spell."

Zac turned on her, glaring. "Don't you understand, Gabby? Katrin wanted Aya from the first moment she realised she was with us. She disregarded me a long time ago. Do you remember Alistair? He was here looking for *her*. Aya is good as dead thanks to you."

Gabby's expression fell.

"It's not anyone's fault." Sam placed a restraining hand on Zac's shoulder. "It's unfortunate, but we can do what we can to find her. It might not be too late."

"Is there any way you can use your power to find out where she is?" Alex asked, speaking up for the first time.

"I don't have the kind of power it takes to track her, let alone to summon her back. I'd have to scry, and I've never got it to work before."

"Then we need to find someone who does," Sam said, glancing at Liz as Zac fell into a chair.

"I have to go find my grams," Gabby said. "She is a witch. She'll know what to do."

"Gabby, you haven't heard from your grandmother in ten years," Liz said gently.

"I know," she murmured. "But she left me the grimoire. I have to find her. It's meant to be. I know it is."

"Then we'll help you," Alex said. "Whatever you need."

Gabby glanced at Liz. "I need to confront my parents. Liz, I don't know how they will take me being a witch. Can you come with me? In case I need you to..." She stopped, not wanting to say it out loud.

"Why not just compel the information out of them?" Zac said through clenched teeth, his head in his hands.

"They're my parents, Zac. If there's a chance they could accept me, then I'll take it. Stop being so goddamn heartless."

"I'll go with you," Liz said. "Of course."

"Why are you still here? Clocks ticking," Zac said exasperated.

Gabby edged away from him and made for the front door, followed closely by Alex and Liz. Sam hovered over Zac's shoulder, giving him a look that he'd become all too familiar with over the past few weeks. A look that said he was waiting for him to snap...again.

It frustrated Zac to no end that he couldn't do anything but wait. Wait for a feeble little witch to go get help. What could he do? Go find another witch who might help? That could take forever and there was no guarantee he could convince a vampire's mortal enemy to help locate and free the infamous Witch Hunter. For a creature that had all the time in the universe, he suddenly couldn't get enough of it.

"Zac, I know you want to go after her, but you just have to wait," Sam said, pre-empting what he was going to say. His little brother had become good at reading his mind as of late.

"I know." Zac held his head in his hands and sighed. "There's no trail for us to follow, Sam. She disappeared into thin air. She could be on the other side of the world for all we know."

"We've got to trust Gabby, Zac. I know it's hard, but we have to sit back and let her do her thing," Sam murmured, anything he felt about the situation carefully hidden in his voice. He knew as well as Zac did that there wouldn't be another witch who would be willing to help them.

"I can't just sit here while they do God knows what to her." Zac stood and began to pace again, his rage simmering beneath the surface.

"Zac, do you..." Sam started, concern creasing his brow as he put two and two together. "Are you in—"

"Sam," he interrupted, glaring at his brother. "We just need to find her."

"Zac—"

"Shut it, Sam. We got her into this mess. Now we've got to get her out."

CHAPTER 18

One moment, Aya was talking with Zac in the garden, and the next, she was on her knees, gasping for breath in complete darkness. A circle of flame erupted around her with a whooshing sound, heat radiating on her face.

Her eyes widened as a familiar, stocky, male stepped through the circle. He was dressed head to toe in black, his short, dusky blonde hair cropped close to his scalp, broad shoulders held proudly.

It'd been three hundred years since she had seen the vampire who stood before her and her blood ran cold. They'd finally caught up with her.

"Caius?"

"Hello, dear one. I'm glad you could make it." He smiled lopsidedly.

"Looks like I didn't have a choice," she said, noticing the three witches who stood outside the circle.

Before he could answer, she lunged for him, fangs

bared. To his amusement, she was brought to her knees before she could lay a finger on him. A sharp pain tore through her head like something was trying to claw its way out. Grasping her temples, it was all she could do to remain focused.

"Traitors," she spat at the witches, grimacing through the pain.

"They're useful, your family's pets," Caius mused, watching her tortured expression as she tried to calm the storm that raged inside. "They know how to keep your kind under control."

"Murderous bastard," she hissed at him.

"In that regard we are more alike than you'll ever come to admit."

"We may both be vampires, Caius, but I'll never be like you."

"Oh, but that's where you're wrong. You're not a true vampire, dear one. My brother should never have created you."

"When I free myself and kill your pathetic witches, I will tear you to shreds. And this time, I won't put the pieces back together," she snarled, kneeling in the dirt.

"Wow," he said with a laugh, "I forgot how spirited you are."

"*You killed my family.*"

"I can't possibly take all the credit for that," he said. "My brothers enjoyed it as much as I."

She glared up at him, trying to fight through the

splitting ache in her head. "Why did you do it, Caius? Was it because she ordered you to?"

"You killed half my family, so it's only fair. Tit for tat and all."

"Well, here I am, Caius. Fight me with honour. Isn't that what you Romans believe in?"

He walked around her, sizing her up before sighing. Killing her mustn't be on Katrin's agenda just yet.

"It wasn't part of our bargain, you know," he said, his guard dropping slightly. "To do her dirty work. To hunt you."

"Then why do it? Why not just let it go?"

He snorted. "You want me to let it go? After you killed my brothers and sister? You would continue your revenge on us regardless. And we will still hunt you, no matter if Katrin wants us to or not."

She didn't reply, waiting to hear what he would say next.

"All's fair in love and war, dear one." He grasped her face, fingers digging into her skin, and kissed her cheek.

Aya shook her head free from his hand. "Remember that time I snapped your neck and locked you in that house you weren't invited into?" she sneered at him. "It was the highlight of the century watching you tear yourself apart."

"You see," he pointed at her, "this is why I miss you. Your creativity." Stepping forward, he grabbed the back of her shirt and dragged her through the edge of the circle. The flame flickered out, plunging them into darkness. The witches followed, their power still focused on subduing her.

For the first time Aya glimpsed her surroundings. There were several rundown buildings around the yard. No doubt from some kind of factory that hadn't seen operation in a very long time. Night had fallen entirely, the darkness complete around them, the stars twinkling brightly. There was no light pollution flooding the sky, which meant they were away from human habitation. But where exactly that was, she had no idea.

Caius opened a steel door in the side of a large building and took no care when he threw her inside. She rolled in the dirt, coming to rest against the far wall, cracking her head against hard metal. The outside door slammed shut with a boom that echoed through the dreary room.

Standing the moment she felt the witches' power lapse, she threw herself at the door with all her strength, but it didn't budge. The thud of her body colliding with steel echoed around her. Trying again, she came to the same conclusion. The door had to be spelled by those witches, there was no other explanation. When she got out of here, they would pay dearly for consorting with the enemy.

Aya cursed, her head thumping against the door. The only way she could have been summoned here was if someone had stolen Gabby's grimoire. She'd warned her only the day before to destroy the pages. It was no secret that all of them were being watched, but to what extent? Had Katrin cursed Gabby to use her as a spy? *Probably.* Aya hoped she was smart enough to work it out.

Looking around for another weakness, she noticed the walls were smooth, so she couldn't climb to the ceiling. The air had an old smell of grain about it, so she assumed it was a kind of grain silo. That would explain the smooth interior and lack of exits.

She sat in the middle of the room and sighed. Caius was keeping her alive, which surprised her, since they'd had no problem with trying to kill her all that time ago. Which only meant they wanted her for the same reason they'd imprisoned her the first time. And going by past experience, they couldn't get anything out of her even if she wanted to tell them.

Turning at the grating sound that signalled that the outside door was opening, Caius strode into the silo, a dark look of malice written on his features. Taking any opportunity she could, she lunged for the vampire, but was on her knees as pain ripped through her head. The witches were behind him, crippling her into submission.

Looking up, she realised he was carrying chains and some large steel meat hooks. This wasn't going to be pleasant.

Caius grabbed the back of her shirt and dragged

her to the far side of the silo where some steel rings had been welded to the wall. He attached the chains to them while the witches stood between her and the door. Then he approached her, dragging the chains through the dirt. The meat hooks were a part of the chain itself, attached to either end. She screamed in rage as he pierced one through her wrist in a single fluid movement, blood gushing from the wound onto the ground. He did the same to the other as he laughed at her discomfort. Pulling the chain, he hoisted her up, her feet barely touching the ground. She moaned in agony as the hooks dragged on her wrists, blood pouring down her arms, soaking her clothes.

"I have been waiting for this day for a very long time." He stroked her face with the back of his hand. "It's a shame my brothers couldn't be here for the occasion."

Bending down, he drove another hook into either ankle, securing her to the floor. Pulling hard on the chains, Caius tore her wounds open, the steel keeping them open and bleeding, unable to heal. He intended to drain as much of her blood as he could, take her strength until she withered into eternal unconsciousness. Only feeding would bring her back from that kind of death.

Standing back, Caius gestured for the three witches to come forward. They formed a triangle around her and began to chant. As she felt their power build up around her, she realised that they were trying to break her, crack her mind open and bring her to insanity. Aya fought against the chains, but she knew there was no escaping, not while the witches watched over her.

Zac, Sam, where are you?

Did she really want them to come? If they could find her, they would walk into a bloodbath. No, it was safer to assume she was alone in this.

Groaning, she felt the witches claw at the edges of her being, preparing her for when her life began to drain away with her blood.

It was so lonely here in the forest. With nothing but my own rambling thoughts to keep me company. All I had been doing lately was thinking. So much thinking. It was becoming dangerous—I was questioning myself...my motives, my being. So much had happened in the last two thousand years. Maybe one too many narrow escapes had put these doubts into me.

Aya's head snapped up and she snarled at the witches, "Get out of my head!"

Caius was standing off in the shadows, watching her suffer. The sound of his satisfied laughter reached her and she pulled against the chains defiantly, tearing her wounds open further.

There was no escaping. She was tightly restrained, but she grasped onto what little control she could.

They wouldn't break her. They couldn't break her.

"The sooner she gets what she wants, the sooner we will be free of her," Caius said. "Stop fighting."

"It's a lot more than a mere link, isn't it? She's

forced you into servitude, hasn't she?" Aya prodded. "That's the part she left out, wasn't it?"

"It's none if your business, witch," he snarled, striking her across the face and splitting her lip.

Drawing a sharp breath between her teeth, she didn't let up. "She tricked you into making the ultimate sacrifice so she could use you...all of you. And it was all for *nothing*."

"Silence!" Caius' roar echoed around them.

"You'll never get what you want from me. I'm the last and you'll never know."

With an inhuman swiftness, he was directly in front of her, eyes black and fangs bared. Grasping her around the neck with his pale hands, he began choking the life from her, his anger finally besting his control. Aya felt her airway beginning to collapse under the force of his grasp, but her gaze never left his, showing her complete defiance.

"She wants her alive, sir." The soft voice of the witch to her right broke through the tense silence.

Caius took a few deep breaths and let her go, the chains that held her aloft rattled.

"You will never break me, Caius," Aya growled, her voice rasping.

He smirked, his eyes glittering in the semi-darkness. "Unfortunately for you, you won't have a choice in the matter."

CHAPTER 19

Gabby's parents lived in the same house they'd bought when they first got married. Over the years it had changed little. It was a typical Southern American home. Two-stories, clad in cream weatherboards, a wide porch that stretched across the entire front, and a double garage. She grew up here as an only child amongst happy memories.

The only thing that marred it was when she was ten, when her beloved grams had disappeared. Everyone said she was crazy and did all they could to find her so they could get her the help she needed. But Gabby had never believed any of the things her family told her.

Liz and Alex hovered behind her on the porch, content to wait outside while she spoke to her parents. They'd already invited Liz in some time ago and she was ready in case she was needed.

Letting herself in with her key, Gabby called out to her parents, who were in the living room.

"Gabrielle," her mother called, coming out into the hall. "This is a nice surprise. We weren't expecting you."

Gabby's mom was probably the nicest lady anyone would ever be likely to meet. She was more than happy to help her only daughter if she needed it, whether it be help with school projects or more grown-up problems like getting stubborn stains out of her clothes. Her mom was fair and on first glance, Gabby didn't look that much like her at all. Her dark colouring came from her dad, who was half Spanish on his mother's side. His mother being her grandmother, the one she so desperately wanted to find.

"I know, Mom," Gabby said, wondering how she could broach the subject.

"I would've made you something nice for dinner," she said with a smile, offering just as Gabby knew she would.

"That's okay. Where's Dad? I want to ask you something." Best sit them down first.

"Is everything okay, honey?"

"Yeah," she replied, walking into the living room where she heard her dad moving about.

"Gabrielle!" he said as she walked in.

"Hey, Dad," she said, sitting down on the familiar

leather armchair beside the matching sofa which her parents now sat on. They looked at her expectantly, wanting to know what she had paid them this impromptu visit for. "I want to ask you about Grams," she said carefully.

Her mother stared at her in shock, obviously under the impression that it was all swept under the rug and no one would ever ask about it again. "Why do you want to know about her?"

Gabby looked to her father and then back to her mother, gauging their reactions. They were against the clock. Who knew how much time Aya had, if she had any left at all? She had to have the courage to do what was needed.

"I want to find her. I need to speak with her."

"Gabrielle," her father said in his familiar stern voice. He'd used this tone with her frequently when she'd been in trouble for something or other when she was a child. But he hadn't used it since she'd finished high school.

It was perfectly reasonable that she would want to speak with her grandmother one day, so why was it such a hassle, regardless of her reasons?

"Dad," she said, "it's important. Please, if you know where she might be—"

"No," he said. "It's best that you stay away. She's not quite...right."

"Not quite right?" she scoffed, offended. "What's that supposed to mean?"

"Gabrielle…" He frowned, clutching her mother's hand. "Your grams, well, she was sick. She claimed she could do things that weren't…ordinary."

"Yes, I know," she exclaimed, exasperated. She was ten, not stupid. Certainly old enough to catch on to what was happening. "Did you ever stop to think that she was telling you the truth?" Gabby saw the hesitation in her father's eyes and knew he'd seen proof of it. He'd had to. "You knew exactly what she was, didn't you?"

"I'm sorry, Gabrielle, but we still agree with your grandfather," her father said, the lie clear in his voice. "The best place for her was at the hospital."

"How can you say that?" she exclaimed. "Even after what you saw?"

"Gabrielle, please," her mother whispered, ever so subtly wanting to quell the situation, to stop a scandal plaguing the town with them at the centre of the gossip. "We didn't see anything. Your grandmother was sick. We tried to get her some help, but she wouldn't listen."

"No, Mom. It's *you* who wouldn't listen. Even when you saw it with your own eyes." Tears were threatening to spill over as she pointed to the candles on the mantle angrily, willing them to light. "Then how do you explain this?"

As the wicks burst into flame, apparently of their own accord, and her parents recoiled with shocked gasps. Gabby was too angry and disappointed to see the denial that was so clear. They would send her away now, too, wouldn't they?

"Gabrielle," her father said, glancing at her warily.

"I'm just like her. I'm a witch. Are you going to have me committed? Do you think I'm crazy?" She saw the fear in their eyes and imagined it was the same one that had plagued their features when they realised the truth about her grandmother.

It broke her heart. Her parents shouldn't be afraid of their daughter. They attempted to put her grandmother away when she was a little over ten years old for the exact same reason—because they wouldn't accept what was right in front of their own eyes. She wished she could take it all back. She wanted to think her parents were above all of this, but then again, everyone thought that about their parents until they proved themselves otherwise. And they had just proven they weren't above anything.

"Liz?' she called, a tear running down her cheek.

Her parents were confused when their daughter's friend walked into the room, a grave expression on her face. "Are you sure?"

"Yes." She nodded, her voice a whisper, before she could change her mind.

With a nod, Liz turned and said, "Mr. and Mrs. Cohen? I'm very sorry, but I'm going to have to ask you to forget everything that happened tonight." The two adults gazed into her blue eyes vacantly as she compelled their memories away. "When we go, all you will remember is that you had a nice dinner and a pleasant evening watching television together. You will forget all about Gabby being a witch and about her questions. Do you understand?"

They nodded indifferently, eyes unblinking.

"Good. Now, don't move until we've gone." Liz took Gabby's arm and steered her toward the front door where Alex was waiting on the porch. When it closed behind them, she heard the faint sounds of her parents moving about inside, the television turning on.

Alex wrapped his arms around Gabby and let her sob into his shirt, Liz hugging her from behind. It took a few minutes before she could pull herself together, pushing her disappointment to one side, but not forgetting it.

"What do we do now?" She sniffed, wiping away her tears with the back of her hand.

"We go back to the manor and look for her ourselves," Liz stated kindly. "Whatever we need to do."

Alex smiled. "Whatever we need to do."

Once they arrived back at the manor, Liz pulled them into Sam's bedroom. She opened his laptop and gave it to Alex. The best place to look for Gabby's grandmother was online. They had access to genealogy websites, phone books, and Google. And if that failed, perhaps it could help in other witchy ways.

"Vampires have the internet?" Alex raised his eyebrows.

"Sam likes Wikipedia." Liz shrugged. "They might have been born in the eighteen-hundreds, but they do keep with the times, you know."

"I doubt she would be in the phone book." Gabby scowled when she saw what Alex had pulled up on the screen. "She hid from my grandfather for years before he died. It seems too simple."

"There might be a chance she listed it after," Alex said, placing a reassuring hand on her arm. "You never know."

"We should try everything, even the obvious," Liz said while Alex brought up the online version of the phone book. "Perhaps she's looking for you too and hoped you would find her one day."

"There is only one Sophia Cohen in the whole United States in the phone book," Alex said, peering at the laptop screen. "Mobile, Alabama."

"That's only two-and-a-half hours away," Liz said. "Are you going to call her?"

"It's worth a try, I guess," Gabby muttered.

Signs and omens seemed to be popping up into her life more often now that her power was growing. Sometimes it was like the universe was trying to steer her in the right direction, as if she were connected to it somehow.

She'd call and then she'd know.

Pulling out her cell, she punched in the number and hit call. Her hands shook a little as it took a moment for it to connect and start ringing. As each tone came, her stomach twisted and her heart beat hard against her chest. Forgetting Liz could hear those kinds of things these days, she jumped as her friend's hand rested on her shoulder.

"Hello?" a female voice asked.

Gabby couldn't speak, the words died in her throat the second she heard her grandmother's voice. There was no doubt it was her. She knew it. Every part of her knew it.

It was a few seconds before the voice on the other end said, "Gabrielle?"

"Hello," she managed to say.

"I knew I would hear from you one day." Sophia sounded relieved, like she'd been waiting a while longer than she thought she would.

"Grams," she began hesitantly, "I know it's been a while and I'm sorry to call you like this out of the blue, but I didn't know what else to do."

There was a moment of silence. "You better tell me about it."

"I'm in trouble," she said haltingly. "We're mixed up in something big. It has to do with the founding witches. With Katrin... She's taken our grimoire and I don't—"

"The Betrayer?" Sophia was horrified.

"Who?"

"Well, my dear," she replied,, "I'd say it's an impressive deal of trouble."

"Can I come see you?" She hoped she would say yes. *Please say yes.*

"Yes, come right away." Her voice became serious. "Gabrielle, tell no one. Do you understand? Tell no one where you are going. I can help you, but we must keep this from her."

Gabby was relieved. "I understand. Two friends already know, but I trust them with more than my life."

"Elizabeth and Alex." Sophia sounded perfectly calm.

"How did..." She'd stopped being amazed at the things she could do a while ago, but being able to see whom she was with in a telephone conversation? That was a new one, but perhaps it was foresight.

Sophia continued, "There will be time for explanations later, dear. Please come as soon as you can."

As Gabby scribbled down the address her grams had given her on a piece of paper, she explained that she'd would be there in a few hours. "I need to go right now," Gabby said to her friends, who were looking on, eager to hear what had happened.

"Don't you mean we?" Liz smiled.

"I can't ask you to come, you know that," she told them. She'd asked them to do so much already.

Alex hugged her. "Gabby, we've been friends for almost ten years. I'm not letting you go alone."

"And I'm coming, too!" Liz pulled Gabby to her feet. "Let's commandeer Zac's car before he notices." When Alex coughed and raised his eyebrows, she said, "It's much better than your truck. Sorry, Alex." She stilled.

It always weirded Gabby out when Liz stopped and listened to something. She looked like a statue and always had to check to see if she was still breathing.

A moment later her friend declared, "Right, they're not here. Let's go!"

By the time they reached the first signs that they'd arrived in Mobile, it was almost eleven p.m. The night was clear and bright, the moon almost full again.

The town centre was typical of the South. Manicured lawns, immaculate streets, quaint little teahouses and cafés, little topiaries and flowerbeds lined the main thoroughfare, along with a few locals out enjoying the warm evening.

Sophia lived on the opposite side of town in a small house with a wild garden out the front. Greenery covered everything but the path to the door and the porch. Gabby instantly liked it. It seemed like a place a witch would live.

Liz and Alex followed her to the front door, and she knocked.

The door opened an instant later and Gabby laid eyes on her grandmother for the first time in ten years. Her face bore a few more wrinkles than she remembered, but it was her grams. Caramel-coloured skin, warm chestnut eyes, and silver-streaked hair, just as she had remembered. Before Sophia could speak, she stepped over the threshold and hugged her tightly.

"Gabrielle, dear." She sounded surprised but relieved all at the same time. "It's good to see you. My, how you've grown."

"Grams," she said, suddenly becoming her ten-year-old self again.

"I'm sorry dear," her grandmother said glancing to Liz and Alex, who hovered in the background. "But your vampire friend must wait outside. I cannot invite her in."

"It's okay, Gabby. I understand." Liz smiled. "Mrs. Cohen, if you don't mind, Alex and I will wait for you on the porch."

Sophia smiled and nodded. "Of course, but we may be some time. Perhaps you may like to go get some rest. It is rather late."

"That's okay," Alex said. "We'd rather wait, if it's all the same to you."

She smiled and shook her head, looking to her granddaughter who stood beside her. "You have some loyal friends, Gabrielle. Human *and* vampire."

"I know," she replied. "I would do the same for them."

Sophia gave her a look that said that she expected as much. After all, their family had a history of befriending all kinds of supernaturals. She'd learned as much from reading the grimoire.

"Come," Sophia said, closing the door behind them, "we have a lot to talk about."

For the second time that night, Alex and Liz waited for their friend outside. When they said as much to Sophia, that they didn't mind one bit, they really were telling the truth. Both of them would do whatever they needed to help get Aya and the grimoire back. She'd helped both of them in different ways.

She saved Alex from Katrin's rogue vampire, and she'd helped Liz by bringing Zac back...and telling her a few home truths that, in hindsight, she really needed to hear.

Alex sat on the bench under one of the front windows and said, "Well, at least it's a nice night to sit outside."

"Yeah," Liz said, gazing at the stars above. If only Alex could see what she could.

"Do you think Mrs. Cohen will be able to help?" he asked.

Liz shrugged. "I don't know. Gabby seems to think so, and she's never given us a reason to doubt her."

"I just hope she can help her locate Aya." It wasn't any secret that he liked the vampire, even if she intimidated him now that he knew that she was over two thousand years old. His life seemed insignificant in relation to hers.

"I hope she can find her for Zac's sake," Liz said as much to herself as to Alex.

"Zac's not my favourite person in the world, you know."

"Yeah, I know."

"He's never been nice to me and I've just come to accept it. And I shouldn't," Alex said. "I feel myself wanting to keep him away from Aya. Someone like that doesn't deserve her. If it wasn't for Zac, none of this would've happened. This whole situation is majorly screwed up."

"He loves her, Alex." Liz sighed. She wasn't blind. His reaction to her disappearance was as much evidence as she needed to convince her. "He might not see it yet or have accepted it, but he does."

"It doesn't excuse him."

"I know," she said. "He's got a lot of issues. Some of which he hasn't even told Sam about. How he was turned... It was really screwed up, Alex. He should have died in 1865. Instead, he was forced to become a vampire. According to Sam, he wasn't like this at all when he was human. He was a good guy."

"Sounds like being a vampire screwed with his head," Alex said.

"That's not the half of it," she said with a grimace. "Aya may be the best thing that's ever happened to him."

"As long as he wakes up and sees it."

Gabby looked around her grandmother's living room.

She decided she liked the mismatched furniture and crochet pillows, but as she sat on the sofa, she felt a sudden pang of shyness. She was about to talk to her long-lost grandmother about things she'd kept secret from all but a handful of people. It was surreal and that was saying something, considering the mess she was in.

"Making friends with vampires?" Sophia asked.

"Yes, Grams," she replied as if she were a child again.

"Are you sure that's wise?"

"Maybe, maybe not, but they're decent people. They've helped me as much as I've helped them."

Sophia chuckled and said, "It's okay, Gabrielle. Our family has been friends with several vampires over the years. They're not all evil creatures and certainly not all of them wanted to be changed in the first place."

"My thoughts exactly," Gabby said, relieved she wasn't going to get a reprimand. "What vampires are you talking about?"

"Well," her grandmother began, "they're all long stories, but the same one keeps cropping up, helping our family from time to time. She assisted my grandmother, your great-great grandmother, before I was born. And back in the Middle Ages..."

Gabby knew she was likely referring to Aya. She'd been in Ashburton before she went to sleep.

Before she went on, Gabby had to ask the question that had been bothering her for a very long time. "Grams, why did you leave?"

Sophia sighed, as if she'd been waiting for her to ask. "I was frightened when Edward found out what I'd been hiding. I'd kept the largest piece of myself secret from him, knowing he wouldn't understand. Your grandfather was a difficult man, Gabrielle. He was set in his ways and only believed in things that were tangible. You and I know the world doesn't work that way, but there was no convincing him otherwise. Despite his faults, I loved him, but it was best for all of us that I left. My only regret is that I had to leave you to find your gift on your own."

"I know," Gabby murmured. "I just wanted to hear it from you."

Sophia smiled at her granddaughter. "Give me a

moment," she began as she walked over to the overflowing bookcase. "Ah, here it is." She plucked a book from the shelf and returned to the sofa.

"Wait," Gabby said as Sofia handed it to her. It was a grimoire. "I thought our grimoire was the only one in our family. What's this?"

"This," Sophia said, sitting back down, "is *my* grimoire."

"Yours? You wrote this one? All of it?" she asked, excited.

"Yes. It is all of my accumulated knowledge and I have just the thing that will help us bring the other grimoire home." She flipped through pages that were much whiter and crisper than the pages that Gabby was used to looking at. "Ah...here we go."

Sophia turned the grimoire around and pointed to a page. Gabby began to read, but realised it was in the same language as a lot of the pages in her own grimoire.

"I-I can't read this," she said, her cheeks flushing.

Sophia smiled and pushed the grimoire closer to her. "Its witch-speak, dear."

"You mean you can read it?"

"And you can't?"

Gabby shook her head. "No, only the ones in English."

"You can read it if you try. You're a witch," Sophia said it like it was the simplest thing in the world.

"Aya could read it, but I assumed it was because she's old."

"Aya?"

"That's why I've come, Grams. Katrin took her and... I don't know how to find her."

"This woman..." Sophia began. "She could read the grimoire?"

"Yeah, but I don't understand how she could have if it's only meant for us. She's a vampire. Witches who've turned loose all their powers."

"Ah, I see. Then she must be one of the stars," her grandmother concluded. "It's no wonder Katrin took her."

Gabby was beginning to realise just how much she had to learn. "What do you mean, one of the stars?"

"In our stories, there are the ones known as the stars, the beginning of the witches. If your friend still has her abilities after being made a vampire, then she must be a star. There is no other explanation," she explained. "If that's the case, then she is in much more danger than you think."

"How...? What...?"

Sophia smiled. "I think it would be reasonable if a star was turned into a vampire, it would still shine a little."

Gabby blinked. "What can we do?"

"First, we need to call the grimoire home. Second, you need to realise your true potential." Sophia reached over and took her granddaughter's hands in hers. "Read the page again. You cannot have practiced magic and not know this language. It's in your blood, Gabrielle."

Had she been speaking this language unknowingly all along? When she'd performed the spell that'd called Aya?

Tenderly taking the grimoire, she looked again and read the words as they appeared, emboldened by the presence of another witch. The ink seemed to shift around, like it was trying to pry itself away from the page. As she read, she realised it was an incantation. The farther she went down the page, the more power she felt building inside of her, but regardless of her sudden wariness, she kept going. Sophia had asked her to read this page for a reason.

As the magic built, Gabby realised she was calling forth her power, the power that'd been born inside of her. Understanding exploded within her as her magic filled her veins.

When Gabby read the last word, she looked up to the smiling face of her grandmother and said, "*Thank you.*"

Sophia seemed pleased. "It's my pleasure, dear. We should've done that a long time ago. Now, you are who you were meant to be."

"It was an unbinding, wasn't it?"

"Yes, but in this case, it was used to wake what couldn't naturally. You just needed a little prod," she explained. "Now, if you're up for it, let's call our grimoire home where it belongs."

Gabby laughed, feeling better than she had for a long time. "Oh, I'm up for it."

She positioned herself on the other side of the coffee table, pulling up a footstool. As they linked hands, she felt her grams' power for the first time and it was *epic*. Sophia was an extremely powerful witch and it seemed to run in the family...or it could've just been the adrenaline. Gabby now felt like she could do just about anything.

"Follow my lead," Sophia said and began a simple incantation. After the first time through, Gabby picked up on the words and joined in, their voices echoing eerily around the living room.

The incantation was woven with words that called back what was bound to the two witches by blood. It was theirs and theirs alone. No one else had a right to possess the grimoire, not even another witch. They infused their call with the longing of an age, the trials of their ancestors, their own stories echoing through the wave of power that seemed to warm the surrounding room like the sun was beating down on their shoulders.

Gabby felt the building power within her flow down her arms and into their linked hands, merging with her grams'. It wasn't long before the air between them glowed with a point of golden light. Sophia spoke the incantation more forcefully and squeezed Gabby's hands.

It was working.

Just when Gabby couldn't bear the flow of power anymore, the point of light flared brightly and they were plunged into darkness, the electric lights flickering off for a moment. When they came back on, she gasped. The grimoire sat on the coffee table.

She dropped her grams' hands and grabbed it, holding it close. It felt warm, like it'd been left in the sun.

"Incredible," she cried.

Sophia nodded. "You're a rare witch, Gabrielle. Be careful how you choose to use your gift."

Gabby understood fully now what it was to be a witch. How easy it was to be corrupted. The power she now felt was intoxicating and would take her down dark roads if she let it. "We have to go back," she said, suddenly. "I don't know how much time we have left to help Aya."

"Then go," Sophia said, nodding toward the door. "There's much at stake. We'll have time together."

"But Grams," Gabby said, her eyes wide, "aren't you coming with us?"

"No, dear. I can imagine the reception I would receive from your parents," she said. "My place is here. This is your time." Gabby went to open her mouth to protest further, but she was interrupted.

"To save the star, you must look deep inside

yourself, child. You'll find what you're looking for there."

They hugged tightly for what felt like an age, but Gabby soon pulled herself away, knowing that Aya's fate was still in her hands. She had to go back to Ashburton and find out where the vampire had been taken. Her fate depended on everything.

After leaving Sophia's, they went straight back to the manor. It'd been more than a day since Gabby and Alex had slept. Liz could go without sleep for a few days if needed, so she was still bright, doing the honour of driving them home so they could doze on the way.

Sam was waiting for them when they pulled up front. "Nice to see Zac's car is back in one piece."

"Our pleasure!" Liz chirped as Alex and Gabby dragged themselves inside.

He shook his head and followed them into the parlour where Zac was waiting, still as agitated as when they'd left.

Gabby placed several things on the coffee table—the grimoire, several folded maps, and an atlas, one of the United States and one of the entire Earth. Beside them, she carefully placed a crystal pendant with a long silver chain.

"How are you?" Sam asked, making Zac almost explode at the delay.

"I'm okay." She smiled as Alex and Liz sat beside her. "Better than okay, actually."

"Can you find her or not?" Zac interrupted.

Gabby nodded, ignoring his impatience. "I need something of Aya's so I can scry for her. I should be strong enough now to get a read on her." And she desperately hoped that Aya was alive, otherwise it could only mean one thing. If she couldn't find her, then it would be likely that Aya was dead.

"Aya doesn't have anything," Sam said, remembering the day she moved into the manor, the same day they found out who she was. "She only has her clothes."

Gabby frowned. "I don't know if that'll work."

"I'll see what I can find." Zac was already halfway out of the room.

Opening the door to the room that had become Aya's, he felt like a trespasser, even though this'd been his when he was human. As they had thought, the room was bare, apart from some clothes in the closet and dresser. He pulled the pillows from the bed and saw a red, leather-bound book hidden underneath.

It was his father's copy of Shakespeare's *Julius Caesar*. There was a slip of paper in the pages like she had been reading it. Flipping through the pages, he scowled, knowing she'd taken it without him knowing. Irritated, he snapped the book shut. He'd repeatedly asked her not to go into the study, but she had ignored him. It would be ironic if this insignificant defiance was the thing that helped them find her.

Returning to the parlour, he noticed Sam's frown as he saw the book in his hands. He knew who it belonged to. "This is all she had," he said. "It was our father's, but she's been reading it. Will it work?"

"I'm not sure," Gabby said, raising an eyebrow. "Give it here." She took the red, leather-bound book in her hands and closed her eyes. "Yes. This will do."

Zac groaned. Of course, it would.

"Why the two maps?" Sam asked as Gabby spread out the map of the United States.

"I'm starting small," she said. "If nothing comes up on this, then we go bigger. She was summoned, so she could be anywhere."

Gabby closed her eyes and held the book in one hand and the crystal in the other. The pendant swung back and forth across the map for almost a minute before it shot to a location and stuck there as if it were magnetised.

She heaved a sigh of relief. Wherever she was, Aya was still alive.

They all peered at the map, seeing where it'd landed. It was in the middle of nowhere, but reassuringly close and still in the US.

"It's too vague," Gabby said, reaching for the atlas.

Laying it open at a page that showed Memphis and the surrounding area, she let the pendant swing again. This time it landed on a more distinct location.

"She's in *Tennessee*?" Zac exclaimed like it was the most horrifying place in the world.

"Technically, it's Mississippi," Alex said, looking at the map. "Off route 61."

"Well, let's go."

"Wait," Alex said as he got out his cell. "Let me look it up. See what you're walking into."

Zac sighed and sat down again.

"It looks like a factory or a silo of some kind," Alex said after a moment. "It's not marked, but it's on the satellite image." He gave the cell to Zac, who handed it to Sam.

"It could be abandoned," Sam said, grateful for the technology.

"Could be," Alex said. "It's the perfect place for—"

"Right," Zac declared, cutting him off. "Glinda, you're with Sam and me. C'mon."

"Wait," Liz began to protest.

Zac sat her back down. "We're walking into a fight, Liz, not a Sunday picnic."

Sam kissed her. "He's right. It's safer here. Leave this to us. We'll be okay, I promise."

Alex nodded his agreement. "I'll stay here with you. They can let us know the moment they're on their way back."

Zac was already gone, having pulled Gabby out the

front door with him. Sam followed, glad that Alex was there to keep Liz company. There was no way that he'd willingly let her come along when there was a chance that none of them might come back. If he lost her... Well, then he'd know how Zac felt.

CHAPTER 21

Memphis was an eight-hour drive across state lines and to Zac, it felt like the other side of the world.

As soon as Gabby pulled up a map on her cell, they got into the car and were on the highway. The sooner they left, the sooner they got there.

Zac hardly said a word to Gabby, still angry that she'd allowed the grimoire to be taken, but he hardly gave it more than a brief thought. He was too focused on Aya. If she'd been hurt, or worse, dead, he didn't know what he'd do. It was partially his fault that she was in this mess. After all, he'd been the one to convince Gabby to summon her in the first place, alerting Katrin to her whereabouts.

Now he had to do something to fix it. After what'd happened at the massacre, he'd done what he could to help Sam, but it wasn't enough. It'd never be enough for his brother, but he could at least attempt to get Aya out of this, whatever condition she was in.

"What do you propose we do once we get there?" Sam asked, breaking the silence, his eyes on the road.

"There would have to be witches and vampires there," Gabby said. "I think we should just grab her and go."

Sam glanced to Zac, who sat in the passenger seat beside him. He had said nothing since they got into the car. "What do you think, Zac?"

He was looking out into the gloomy night as it flashed past, seemingly deep in thought. Sighing, he said, "First we case the joint—buildings, entrances, exits. Gabby should sense out any witches and vampires who might be hidden by their magic and what their locations are. Keep an eye out for any traps, magical or otherwise. Determine where Aya is being held. Only then can we devise a plan."

"Well, there you have it," Sam said wryly.

"What if they catch us?" Gabby asked.

"If there's anything hostile, *kill it*," Zac said, looking back out the window. There wasn't much they could do until they got there, and he settled down for the long haul.

Gabby had been awake for a long time, having been through a great deal since leaving the manor the day before. When she fell asleep, the brothers left her, content to wake her once they'd arrived.

It was past midnight before they reached the site of the factory.

They left the car off the side of the main road, hidden behind some trees and walked the rest of the way, keeping off the service lane. The chain-link fence that'd once surrounded the property had half fallen, so they had no issue trying to get Gabby in.

Once they reached the edges of the yard, the surrounding plant life thinned, exposing them more than Zac liked. Circling round the property they found a rise close to the main entrance and he made them crawl on their stomachs so they could peer over the edge. From here they had a good view of the factory, which turned out to be the site of an abandoned grain silo and storage yards.

Train tracks still ran through the remains of buildings that, at one time, would've stored an impressive deal of grain for export.

In the centre was a large yard. It was open and clear, except for a few old shipping containers to the left side, flanking a half fallen warehouse. The roof was badly rusted, most of the sheet metal hanging by a thread or missing entirely.

To the right, at the opposite side of the yard, was the silo. Its roof was linked to the warehouse by some kind of walkway and chutes that'd once fed grain into waiting trucks and train cars. Old foundations of other buildings remained around the rear of the property, having been knocked down haphazardly by age, weather, and vandals.

At the outside edge of the warehouse was another service lane, where two shiny black Jeeps were parked side by side. Someone had left them there in preparation for a quick getaway.

Because the warehouse was only partially standing, Zac could see through to the rear inside wall where a room still appeared to be intact, a green metal door closed over its entrance. There was no other exit other than gaps where windows once were. He assumed there was another exit on the other side, and this was where they'd set up shop.

Zac passed this information to Sam and Gabby. "There's movement somewhere, but I can't tell who or what it is."

"There's witches down there," Gabby whispered. "Two or three, I think. The silo is spelled. It's a good bet that that's where Aya is being held."

"Can you disable the spell?" Sam whispered back.

She was silent for a moment. "No." She shook her head. "We have to either knock the witches out or kill them to break it."

"Then we kill them," Zac stated.

"I can't kill another witch, Zac," Gabby protested.

"What do you think Aya would do?" he retorted. "They're obviously corrupted and well past saving. Do the world a favour."

"Are there any vampires?" Sam asked, pulling her attention off his brother.

"One," Gabby said. "In the warehouse."

"Where are the witches?" Zac asked.

"Behind the silo." She squinted at the yard below. "There's a faint barrier around the entire yard. If we cross—"

"Let's go." He grabbed Gabby's arm and pulled her down the rise and into the yard.

As if on cue, three female witches came out into the open to meet them.

The light breeze around them picked up and Zac glanced at Gabby who said, "They're controlling the wind."

The three witches advanced on them, the wind swirling fast, the dust from the yard creating a miniature tornado. Gabby had to take control of the wind or it would overwhelm them.

Zac and Sam flanked her as she let her earth sense wash over the yard. They wouldn't be able to do much to help her, but their presence reassured her...at least a little.

Immediately, she felt the power of the three witches combined into two spells. The one controlling the wind and the other sealing the silo.

The tornado whipping around them was designed to detain. For what or who, Gabby wasn't sure. There was only one vampire here. Unless the vampire was as old as Aya, or Katrin was being summoned. Either way, she had to overpower the witches and fast.

Gabby felt her magic flow from her even before she meant to release it. As the tornado sped up, she knew it was too much, but couldn't do anything to stop it. Her intent had been unleashed and it had to run its course.

The witch's fear echoed through her open earth sense, making her bones ache. *They were afraid of me.*

Crying out in pain, Gabby felt their life forces rip away into the tornado and they swirled around her, shrieking as they disintegrated.

Suddenly, the wind dropped, the trash and plant life that'd been picked up fell abruptly. They were left standing in a clearing, surrounded by a barrier of chaos. The brothers glanced at her, equal parts shocked and afraid—even Zac, who she assumed would've been delighted at the scene.

Gabby stared at the place the witches had been standing, her body numb. She knew the pain that'd ripped through her was her power tearing them apart. There was nothing left of them to say they'd ever been there in the first place.

Gabby fell to her knees with a strangled cry. She was more powerful than the three of them combined... and that terrified her.

The vampire emerged the moment the witches disintegrated.

Cursing, Zac swung around to find a male vampire standing directly behind them. Ducking just in time to miss being punched in the face, he kicked the vampire's legs from under him, pulling out a stake he'd hidden in the back of his jeans.

The vampire kicked, throwing Zac off balance, and flipped to his feet. His fist slammed into Zac's ribs and sent him hurtling across the yard, the stake falling harmlessly to the ground.

The vampire turned on Sam as he advanced, sizing up his opponent.

Zac scrambled to his feet, knowing they had to end this fast, otherwise their trip would've been all for nothing.

Sam made a grab for the fallen stake and aimed it directly at the vampire's heart.

Fortunately, Zac had the same idea and lunged from behind, grasping the vampire around the neck, the motion disorienting him for a split-second. It was more than enough time to get the job done.

Sam drove the stake into the vampire's heart at the same moment Zac snapped his neck. The body fell to the ground with a thud as Zac dusted off his hands.

"Can't be too careful," he declared when Sam raised his eyebrows. The corpse began to desiccate as they moved off toward the silo.

"That was way too easy," Sam said, looking around the now silent yard.

"Gabby," Zac called, frowning.

Gabby came up behind them and pointed to the door. "The spell is gone. Aya is in there. I can sense her."

"I don't like it," Zac said, agreeing with Sam's observation. "Let's get her and get the hell out of here."

Before they could try the door, a loud gasp drew their attention back to the yard. Looking back, Sam cursed as the vampire they'd just killed stirred. He sat up and wrenched the stake from his chest, tossing it to the side. Muscled arms reached up and twisted his head, correcting the haphazardly fused bones with an audible crack.

"That feels better," he snarled, looking up at the three of them. "Now...who wants to die first?"

"How the hell did he come back to life?" Sam muttered in shock as he pulled Gabby behind him.

"I'm one of the first," the vampire spat as he rose. "I can't be killed by the likes of you."

Sam balked and held his arm out to keep Gabby behind him.

A founding vampire?

Zac hissed. They had to distract him long enough so they could find Aya and get the hell out of there.

Gabby pushed past Sam in a moment of bravery and stood in front of them, her eyes narrowed in challenge.

The vampire laughed at her and held out his arms. "If you wish, little witch." But the malicious smile wiped right off his face when he fell to the ground, roaring in pain.

"Go!" Gabby yelled at the brothers. "I can't hold him for long!"

Zac grabbed Sam's arm and pulled him toward the silo.

<hr>

Aya didn't know how long she'd been hanging in the silo, her blood slowly draining from the wounds in her wrists and ankles.

She felt it trickle down her arms, staining her clothes, sticking her shirt to her skin. She'd become used to the smell hours ago, around the part where she'd lost track of time. If she lost enough blood, she would desiccate and then she could sleep. Sleep seemed like bliss compared to the delirium that was setting in.

She was vaguely aware of a dark form standing in front of her. She lifted her head an inch and blinked, trying to clear her vision. Everything was blurred, nothing was making sense. She wasn't sure if anyone was there. She drew a ragged breath as she heard her name, but no one alive knew her true name. Not even... She forgot who. Wasn't she helping someone?

The figure was still hovering in front of her,

whispering her name, calling out to her through the darkness. Then she saw his face, shimmering skin, and blue eyes. Her brother! How she had longed to see her brother again.

"I couldn't save you," she muttered through the haze, a tear sliding down her cheek. "I'm sorry... brother..."

He hesitated and she didn't understand. Her brother was dead, wasn't he? The figure reached up and wiped her tears away with a stroke of a thumb. Suddenly, she dropped to the ground, the chains that held her giving way. The figure grasped her around the waist, supporting her limp body as she slumped over their shoulder.

It's not your bother, it's not your brother... It's a hallucination. If that were true, it could only mean it was Caius come to hurt her again. Then she realised there was two of them, the other one had let her down. If she didn't attack now, she wouldn't have any hope of escape.

Ignoring the searing pain in her wrists and ankles, she lunged for the nearest form, the chains dragging through the dirt. Before her fists could connect, she was pulled up short. Falling backward, she screamed with pain as her arms were wrenched over her head.

She heard someone yell and she was on her feet in a flash, lunging for the source of the sound. Arms wrapped around her from behind, pinning her arms to her sides. Struggling, she lacked the strength to free herself.

Crying out in fury, she felt the chains wrap around her. She wouldn't be imprisoned again, not by anyone. Thrashing, she tried to break her bonds, but couldn't move. Her wrists felt like they were on fire, the hooks dragging against torn flesh.

The more she struggled, the quicker she weakened, finally falling to the ground with a mournful cry. Her legs curled to the side, the hooks still protruding from either ankle and from her wrists behind her back. Taking heaving breaths, her head hung exhausted, tangled black hair falling about her face. *Whatever you're going to do to me, bring it on.*

She felt hands on her face, tilting her head up. She shook her head to knock them away, but they held firm. Blinking hard, she tried to focus on the face before her. Through the heavy fog clouding her mind, she realised someone was speaking to her.

"Aya, it's okay," the voice said. "It's Zac and Sam. We've come to get you out of here." There was a hard impact to the air and the face looked toward the source.

"Shit," the other figure said. "Gabby's losing her hold on the vampire. We don't have much time."

She knew something bad was happening, but she didn't care. It would be so easy to close her eyes and let the darkness take her again, but the hands pulled her face back up.

"Aya, please. We need you. *Come back.*"

She blinked hard, grimacing, her vision clearing slightly, "Zac?"

"Yes," the voice said relieved. "*Yes.* Can I let you go now?" She nodded and the chains loosened. "You look like hell, Aya."

"Very perceptive, Mr. Degaud," she muttered. The chains had fallen away, but the hooks were still embedded. Grimacing, she reached down and pulled the annoying pieces of steel from her ankles, blood now free to gush unhindered.

"Let me do that." He pulled her close, bracing her with one hand while the other traced the length of her arm. She hissed through her teeth as he slid the meat hooks from her wrists one at a time. Her blood was everywhere, but the wounds began to heal enough to stop the flow. Collapsing back into Zac's arms, she exhaled, gazing up into his eyes, her fingers tracing the edge of his jaw. He'd come for her... *No. They'd* come for her. She let her hand drop limply, squeezing her eyes closed.

"You've lost a lot of blood. You need to feed," he said, his brow creased in concern.

She shook her head. "No."

"It's okay, Aya. I want you to." Zac pulled her closer.

"The vampire is still outside," Sam said. "Gabby won't be able to keep it up for much longer."

"Gabby?" Aya said vaguely like she was trying to remember who she was.

"Yes, Gabby."

Her eyes widened and she snarled, "Caius."

Before Zac could ask any questions, Aya grabbed the hair at the back of his head and wrenched him to the side, exposing his neck. He gasped in surprise at the sudden pain as she sunk her fangs in and drank. When she was done, she pushed him to the ground, wiping her mouth with the back of her hand. She was across the room and outside before they could react.

<hr>

Aya was a little impressed. When she emerged from the silo, she saw Gabby mere inches from Caius' most fearsome vampire face. All fangs and black eyes. She was staring him down, holding him in place with her will, moments from death. So, she'd finally found her true powers.

Walking up to her, Aya placed her hand on Gabby's shoulder and Caius' simultaneously, breaking the spell. As he stumbled forward, the force in her outstretched arm brought him to a stop. Gabby gasped, blinking wildly, and scrambled backward. Sam was there, grabbing her around the waist and hauling her to a safe distance.

Aya held Caius' shoulders, pushing against him as he reached up and grasped hers in return. They were face to face, their foreheads touching.

"You will never win against me, witch," he

threatened, the grunt in his voice betraying the fact that he was using all his strength to hold her back.

"That's where you're wrong, Caius," she snarled in return. "I have skills you've never seen."

"You'll never get the chance to use them."

Aya shifted her weight slightly, ramming her shoulder into his stomach. He'd been pushing against her so hard, that the forward motion sent him flying across the yard behind her. She heard the bang as he collided with the side of the silo and her mouth twisted into a satisfied grin.

Caius scrambled to his feet with a snarl and rushed her, knocking her off her feet with the force of the blow. Twisting to the side, she rolled out of the way of Caius' boot, narrowly missing a blow to her ribs. Rising behind him, she punched his spine, aiming to snap it, but he twisted at the last second. She cried out in pain as his elbow came back to meet her jaw, which made an audible crunch as it shattered.

Turning, Caius' hands grasped empty air. Aya was on his back, an arm around his neck, her hand on his face. She wrenched with all her strength, trying to snap his spine, but he threw her over his shoulder. Landing heavily, her eyes widened as Caius' bulky form loomed over her.

They were evenly matched in strength and skill and could be here for hours at this rate.

Grabbing her around the neck with one hand, Caius picked her up off the ground and let out a deep rumbling laugh. A look of triumph was plastered across his face as he squeezed, cutting off her air supply. Instinctively, she clawed at his hand, trying to free herself.

In the corner of her vision, she saw Sam and Zac approach in Caius' blind spot.

"Stay back!" she yelled at the brothers, holding her palm out.

"Once I'm done with you, they're next," Caius rasped, his breath hot against her ear. "It won't be much of a challenge, but they will beg me to kill them all the same."

She felt a familiar twist of rage build inside her and closed her eyes as she called for it. Reaching up, she grasped Caius' wrist, a familiar burning sensation traveling up her arms like thousands of electric shocks. Opening her eyes, a blue glow surrounded them, popping and fizzing, making the air thick with the tangy scent of burning copper. Caius' eyes widened in surprise as the blue energy traveled down her arms and crawled over his forearm.

Aya had never felt her power stronger than this, but the biting taste for revenge was overwhelming. This man, this vampire, had been responsible for her family's death and her torture and imprisonment. He would die like the others...at the mercy of her rage.

Caius gasped in pain and dropped her as the fire traveled down his arm. She fell to her knees for a moment before getting up, using the upward force to slam both her palms into his gut, pushing the air from his lungs. He doubled over, clutching his stomach. For a split-second he was disorientated, and it was all it took for Aya to plunge her hand into his chest.

Clutching his still beating heart in her right hand, she clasped his shoulder with her left, her lips to his ear. "This is for my family," she whispered and poured all her rage into him.

He gasped and clawed at her hand, but he was already turning grey, his skin withering, crackling with the strange electricity. Only when his heart finally collapsed in on itself, the ash falling through her fingers, did she push him off her onto the ground. Staring down at his corpse, she felt nothing. The burning rage had left her, and she was empty.

Aya was vaguely aware of Gabby and the brothers hovering at the edge of her vision. Now she would have to explain herself. They weren't meant to see what she could do...ever. It'd been two thousand years since she used this part of herself...

She suddenly felt all the feeling bleed from her limbs and it was only adrenalin that was keeping her on her feet. She closed her eyes and wished them away.

There was a comforting hand on her arm. "Aya." It was Zac. Of course, it was him.

Looking up at him, she saw the expression of awe written on his face, but Sam and Gabby were afraid. At least they were smart. Zac should be afraid of her. She wondered if she should compel him again. Compel them all to forget how she'd killed Caius, but she doubted it would work now. She was done.

When she didn't respond, Zac put his arm around her waist and guided her away from the yard to his car that was parked toward the road. As she was put in the back, the seat belt was fastened for her. Gabby sat beside her and clasped her hand, and the brothers took the front.

Gazing blankly out of the window into the night, she managed to whisper, "Thank you."

CHAPTER 22

The early morning air was heavy against Aya's skin as she sat in the garden.

The manor grounds hadn't been worked in a long time. They were wild and green, full of flowers that tended themselves shaded by the long branches of whispering willows. Usually, she would just enjoy being here, but today her thoughts were troubled.

It'd been several days since the brothers and Gabby had freed her from the silo. Several days since she had killed Caius. She'd come one step closer to what she'd pledged to do, but in doing so, she'd done the one thing she shouldn't have. She'd drunk Zac's blood.

She looked up as Sam sat down beside her and wondered what question he was going to ask first. The air was silent around the manor which meant Zac had gone somewhere else. She didn't want to deal with his questions today.

Taking in her faraway look, Sam asked the

predictable-Sam-question, "How are you doing?"

"After all the time he's spent hunting me, you'd think I'd be glad he's dead, but I don't feel anything."

She felt his apprehension as he asked the next burning question. "In the silo, you thought Zac was your brother?"

"It was a hallucination," she replied curtly.

"What happened to him?"

"He was slaughtered in his sleep," she spat. "Do you want a play-by-play?"

"No, I'm sorry. It's just... you're a hard person to read, Aya." He sighed, fidgeting with the hem of his shirt. "Who was Caius exactly?"

"He was one of the first vampires. One of the family called the Romans," Aya said matter-of-factly.

"And how old are they, these Romans?"

"Not much older than I," she replied. "Maybe a year or two, I'm not sure."

"Why are they called the Romans? Where did they come from?"

Aya sighed at the barrage of questions. They would ask them eventually. Best to get it out of the way. Besides, she'd rather talk to Sam about this. He was much more understanding than Zac and at least he would stop pressing when he knew he couldn't get any further.

"They were part of the Roman armies that invaded Britain around 43AD. I know little about their human lives other than one was a high-ranking officer, others foot soldiers and lower-ranking officers. I suppose they all wanted what most humans want."

"And what's that?"

"Power. Immortality."

Sam nodded. "And what did you do to Caius? To kill him?"

"I stole his light," she said, referring to the story in Gabby's grimoire, reluctant to explain further.

"Aya, I don't understand. It was magic, wasn't it?" he asked, almost desperate for answers.

"Sam, that's the one thing I cannot explain to you. I am indebted to you for coming to free me, but this...? This, I cannot give you."

He stared at her for a moment and decided not to push her further. They sat in silence for a while and it was almost companionable, the two of them enjoying the wildness of the garden. It reminded her of many things, but she closed her thoughts off to the memories. She'd been to many places, done many things, and punished many people—none of which bore another thought, at least not today.

"You've changed him, you know," Sam said carefully, breaking the silence. "Zac. He's different around you."

"How so?" She frowned. This was one of those things she didn't want to talk about.

"He cares about something other than himself." He laughed weakly, shaking his head.

Aya grunted, pulling her knees up to her chin,

feeling uneasy about what Sam hinted at. Zac had been through enough without this. One day she would have to leave, and he would be back at square one, even she had enough heart not to do that to him.

"Aya," Sam said, picking up on her uneasiness, "its a good thing."

"If you say so," she whispered, not believing him.

Zac had never been to Gabby's apartment before. It sat on the top floor of a complex of twelve similar places, six flights of stairs, and no elevator. She must love the view because the climb would've been a deal breaker.

They sat on the floor in the lounge, a silver bowl between them, the grimoire off to the side. Gabby was chanting under her breath, eyes closed, a faraway look etched on her dark features.

Zac's thoughts were more troubled than usual. Aya was amazing. What she'd done to Caius...that was something else. So much more than a regular vampire was capable of. What was she? Perhaps when this was all over, she would give him some answers.

And he had to find a way to tell her how he felt. If he told her, then maybe...maybe she might stay.

Now Gabby had access to all her magic, she was determined to try just about anything to get Katrin of their backs, and Zac was glad she was finally on the same page. The lingering threat was wearing thin, especially after everything that'd happened at the silo. They mightn't be so lucky the next time.

Focusing back on Gabby, Zac concentrated on the spell she was casting. She'd found an incantation in the grimoire she hadn't been able to read until now. A spell for knowledge. It would reveal the path to the thing that they most desired, and that was to bring an end to Katrin.

The spell was the only reason Gabby had finally invited Zac into her apartment. They shared a personal connection over their desire to end Katrin and it meant a better strike rate. All of Gabby's previous attempts at finding what anchored the founding witch's spirit to life had led to nothing, and at this point, they were willing to try just about anything.

Gabby had been muttering her incantation under her breath for ages and Zac was positive it wasn't working. She seemed different after what she'd done at the silo. Her increased power was blindingly obvious with the way she obliterated those witches. He'd never seen a witch do such a thing and he was glad that she was on their side, but it didn't help them right now. Nothing was happening.

Just as Zac was about to complain that she was taking too long, he felt the spell cloud his thoughts.

Gabby smiled in relief. "I can see a way forward, but I need to speak to Aya."

When she mentioned Aya, Zac's expression slackened and his eyes went blank. Gabby waved her hand across his line of vision, but he didn't react. It took a moment before he came back from wherever it was he went. Blinking as Gabby came back into focus, he realised she'd been shaking him. He groaned, holding his head in his hands.

"Zac, what is it?" she asked, concern in her voice.

"She compelled me!" he roared, knocking the bowl across the room. It clattered to the floor loudly, its contents spilling everywhere. Gabby scrambled backward, suddenly aware she was in the same room as an angry vampire.

"Who?" she whispered, afraid of provoking him.

"Aya!" He was on his feet, pacing back and forth, thinking about what he would do. He was so intent on his thoughts, he forgot Gabby was in the room. He roared again and left the apartment in a whirlwind of fury, leaving Gabby shaking on the floor.

***

Aya liked to sit in the study. She knew it irritated Zac, but he'd stopped asking her not to ages ago. It felt comforting, especially after her earlier conversation with Sam. She spun the globe in the corner, running her finger along the surface, waiting to see where it would land once it came to a stop.

Katrin wouldn't try anything right away, not after she'd killed another of her so-called children.

Her finger landed on France. She'd been in France

before coming to America.

She could hear the telltale hum that announced Zac had come home. He was in the doorway looking at her.

"Hello," she said. Not turning around, she spun the globe again. When he didn't answer straight away, she knew he was angry.

"I was just with Gabby," he said, restraining the anger in his voice.

"Were you now?" She smiled. Her finger landed in the middle of the Atlantic Ocean.

"I helped her cast a spell." He was cracking.

"And what kind of spell did she cast?" The globe spun again.

"A knowledge spell." The tone in his voice unsettled her.

"Be. More. Specific." She disregarded the globe, allowing it to spin freely.

"A spell to find the knowledge to obtain what one desires the most." He was right behind her now, his gaze burning into her back.

Aya tensed. "And what happened?"

"Gabby learned a way to stop Katrin. She needs to speak to you."

Turning her head slightly, she asked, "And what did you learn?"

He grabbed her shoulder and turned her abruptly, pushing her back against the wall. Her expression darkened in warning, but Zac ignored it.

"I remember everything," he snarled, holding her in place across her chest with his arm.

Aya's eyes misted over into shimmering pearls and she pushed him across the room. He collided with the opposite wall, his shoulder leaving a hole in the plaster. He fell to the floor with a grunt.

"If you remember everything, then you know it was all for your own good," she spat.

Zac was back on his feet in a second. "After everything that's happened, how could you compel me?"

"I saved your life, Zac."

"Only from the werewolves."

Aya closed her eyes, trying to control her anger. "I also saved you from me. You saw what happened to them when I lost control. You saw what I did to Caius."

The anger faded from his face into one of surprise. "I don't believe you."

"Then you're a fool. You've only seen the smallest part of me. The smallest part of the monster I truly am. No one could love a walking horror such as I."

Zac was dumbfounded. "After everything we've been through. After the wolves, the motel, the way you looked at me in the silo—"

"Stop it," she hissed.

"You're two thousand years old, Aya," he went on. "I'll never know every part of you, but I know the ones that matter."

She pushed him back against the wall. "*You know nothing!*"

"You can compel the memories from me, Aya, but you can't compel away my feelings," he said evenly.

"Get out!"

"Aya, please," he whispered.

She stared at him with a wild look in her eyes. "*Leave.*"

Zac pushed her back against the wall and kissed her passionately, pressing his body into hers. His left hand pulled her hips against him and his right held her face to his, fingers wound in her hair. And she kissed him back just as deeply and she knew he was lost...maybe she was as well. He was hers, body and soul.

Suddenly, she pulled away and pushed him back, a look of dismay on her face.

"Aya..."

"Don't," she whispered, looking toward the floor. "There's so much you don't understand, Zac. So many things I can't tell you. So many reasons why this can't be."

He took a step toward her and she held him back with her arm. "Please."

"*Aya,*" he whispered huskily.

She could feel the tears welling in her eyes. "Please don't make me do this."

"Do what?"

She was gone so fast, it was as if it had never

happened at all.

Gabby was about to knock on the front door of the manor when it burst open, her fist poised mid-air. Aya stood in front of her, glaring as she dropped her hand awkwardly. She guessed she was too late.

"Aya," she began. "I was coming to see you before… I got here as fast as I could."

"If you're talking about the knowledge spell, I found out about that." Aya rolled her eyes, pushing her backward off the porch and into the yard.

"I'm s-sorry," she stammered. "I didn't know it would work the way it did. I had no idea—"

"I hear you need to speak with me," Aya interrupted.

Whatever Aya had compelled from Zac, Gabby knew she'd better leave it alone.

"Yes, I have an idea. The spell revealed a loophole to Katrin's anchor, the spell holding her spirit," she began.

Aya pressed her finger to her lips to silence her. Understanding that other ears were listening, Gabby nodded. The vampire grabbed her arm roughly, guiding her down the driveway and across the yard. They walked right down to the lake, stopping at the shoreline.

It was an abnormally cold day, the wind rippling

the surface into waves that lapped the rocks at the water's edge. The noise seemed sufficient in covering their conversation to a point.

Once she was certain they were alone, Aya turned to Gabby. "There's a lot I'd like to tell you, Gabby, but I can't. For now, you'll just have to trust me."

Gabby nodded. "I'm sure it will all make sense one day, but for now, as long as we can banish Katrin, then I'm satisfied."

"Good." Aya was pleased. "What did the spell reveal to you?"

"Katrin is channeling some serious power in keeping her spirit attached to life. A power that is very much like... Well, I'm not quite sure how to explain it. It feels like death." Gabby didn't quite understand. "Like a negative energy."

"Negative," Aya mused.

"In science positive cancels out the negative, so I'm hoping that counts as the same for magic."

Aya's brow furrowed as she thought over this. "What do you suppose the positive would be?"

"The positive is you, Aya. That's what the spell revealed to me. You're the key, but I don't know what that means exactly. I was hoping you might know."

Aya was silent for a while. "That may be a problem. What you're asking...well, it may call upon abilities I've lost. Abilities that no longer exist in this world."

"Were you a witch...you know, before?" Gabby asked hesitantly.

Aya frowned. "Not exactly. I had a lot of things in common with your kind, though." She said this with a finality that dissuaded Gabby from asking more, but she continued, "When I was changed, many things were taken from me. Abilities that were second nature disappeared and were replaced with vampire traits."

"But the spell wouldn't have revealed you to me if it weren't possible. Would it?"

"I assume so." Aya was lost in thought for a long time, her blue eyes focused on a faraway point across the lake. Finally, she turned. "I can only do this with you, Gabby. You complete the parts of me that were stolen. Together we have the power to destroy Katrin once and for all. Yes, I think it will work."

Stolen. Gabby now realised Aya had been turned against her will. The realisation made her understand a lot of things about the vampire. Why she was the way she was. She suspected her drive for punishing witches came from a need for revenge, to set things right.

"What was stolen," she murmured. "You had abilities like mine? Like a witch? My grams called you one of the stars."

"You're a rare witch, Gabby." Aya didn't answer her question. "You've unlocked your potential but have yet to see the limits of what you can do."

"How can you tell?" she asked.

"I can feel it."

"Really?"

"I knew who you were the first moment I saw you,"

she said. "I could tell exactly which line you were descended from and how strong you were. And before you ask, it's not Katrin."

"*Thank God.* Who then?" Gabby wanted to know more than anything.

"Ismena," Aya said, looking out across the lake, fixing her gaze on a point far into the distance.

Gabby felt a familiar stirring inside her. "Did you know her?"

"Not well." She turned back to her and smiled. "She was a dear friend of my mother. She was one of the five founding witches. All humans. Katrin betrayed the other four in her lust for power. Before the others realised she had corrupted, she'd already created the first vampires. By then it was too late. It was all they could do to save their own lives, let alone anyone else's. They disappeared after that. I never saw any of them again, but I suspect they would've tried to end me if they knew my fate."

Gabby didn't know what to say. "What makes you think we can succeed where four founding witches couldn't?"

Aya sighed. "They didn't have me."

Gabby didn't know what she meant and wasn't sure she wanted an explanation. Aya had known the founding witches—the witches who were the beginning of her kind, the beginning of magic. How had they come into their power? Were they given it or born to it? She was unsure if she was ready to know the origins of power when she could hardly control her own.

Aya glanced at her, sensing her uneasiness. Gabby still felt remorse over the three witches in Memphis… how easy it'd been. Things just kept getting even more complicated the deeper she got into this mess.

"I would have killed them, you know," Aya said, sensing her thoughts. "They were in league with the founding vampires, and not to mention Katrin herself. They'd given themselves over to evil. They were corrupted."

"I know," Gabby whispered. "But it doesn't make it any easier."

Aya shook her head. "It never does."

They were silent for a time, their thoughts running off in their own directions.

"I think I know what to do now," Aya said uncertainly, breaking the stillness. "I can do most of it, but we have to join minds so I can lend your powers. Don't worry. I used to do it with my brother when we were children. It's easy, but you will feel a little tired when I draw on your power."

Aya had a brother?

"Okay." Gabby nodded.

"I know it's not much to go on," Aya said, "but I don't see any other option. It's our first and only chance. I don't know what'll happen if we fail."

Gabby hoped her trust in Aya would be enough to see them through. "Then we better win."

CHAPTER 23

Aya and Gabby worked out a plan as they sat by the lake. As simple as it sounded, it was actually quite complicated.

Once they executed it, Aya would be totally and utterly revealed to Gabby, everything she'd hidden from the world for thousands of years. If she was being honest with herself, that was more terrifying to her than facing Katrin.

Aya stood with her back to the room, staring into the cold fireplace, hyperaware of the irritating buzz of Zac in the room behind, not able to bring herself to look at him. Everyone was at the manor, even Alex, despite him not being able to help. His show of support was strangely comforting, and she was thankful. For a human, he had a great deal of courage.

"We need to go to an in-between place." Gabby was explaining their plan as simply as she could. The others were on a need-to-know basis only. "It's the space that exists between life and death. Limbo. There, we will be able to sense what's keeping Katrin's spirit anchored to life. If it's what we suspect, then we can try to destroy it."

"And where does Aya come into it?" Sam asked.

She felt everyone's gaze fall heavily on her back. Turning, she said, "You saw what I can do. It will be an advantage."

Aya considered asking Zac if she could drink some of his strange blood again. Curiously, it had strengthened her other abilities and she was sure that it was the only reason she had summoned enough power to destroy Caius. Then she remembered their argument, Zac declaring himself to her. Disregarding the thought, she knew that he'd ask more of her than she was willing to give if she dared ask. Besides, it was too personal a thing to share with another vampire and he would undoubtedly take it the wrong way. Knowing Gabby was there with her, she was reassured they had more than enough power to get the job done.

"No magic can penetrate the veil," Gabby said, "but matter can. Anyone can just walk into the between place while we have the doorway open. That's why we need you all to keep watch."

"You just want us to sit there and wait?" Zac sounded exasperated. "What are you going to do in there?"

"It's witch business, Zac. I don't have to tell you

anything," Gabby said. "We just need our backs watched. Can you do that?"

He grunted in response.

"When are you going to do this?" Sam steered to conversation away from the inevitable bickering.

"Tonight," Gabby said. "At the old cemetery."

"That's not much time to prepare," Liz said with concern.

The witch simply shrugged. "No time like the present."

Night had already fallen, but they'd all assembled at the cemetery—four vampires and one witch. Sam, Zac, and Liz had positioned themselves around the clearing at the centre of the cemetery, watching the forest. Aya stood next to Gabby as she chanted under her breath, summoning the doorway that led to the place between life and death. Limbo.

It was an eerie sensation when the mist crept into the clearing, the surrounding air still warm from the day's humidity. Gabby felt the change in her spirit, felt herself slip into the place between life and death. Her eyes widened in surprise when she felt the depth of Aya's power as they joined minds. She had had no idea, even after witnessing it in Memphis. She was something else. No wonder witches feared her coming.

"We need to detect where her anchor is," Aya said

after she had gathered her thoughts. "Let me know if you can feel anything. No matter how small."

Before she could cast her mind out, Katrin was before them, her expression total darkness. Gabby staggered back, almost severing her link to Aya. How had she known they'd be here? Had she expected it? If this truly was the place where her spirit lived, she would undoubtedly know when anybody set foot in it.

"Do you really think you can end me, Aeriaya?" Katrin scoffed. "You and your pitiful little witch?"

"Yes," she replied, "I do."

"I control this place," the witch snarled. "*You have no power here.*"

Gabby glanced sidelong at Aya. Was that her true name? As her thoughts swirled, the grey mist swelled around them, the emptiness melting into another place. Katrin was creating a vision in the void, and Gabby could feel the power pulsing in the close air, reverberating in her bones. The founder was more powerful than she'd ever thought possible.

The vision swirled around them, morphing the mist into a glade of deep green, speckled with a carpet of white flowers. A house was nestled at one end, the trees of the surrounding forest tall and ancient, sheltering arms reaching into the sunlight. Through Aya, she understood it was a protected place of power. A place of light and love...until blood began to drip from the trees. It wept from under the front door of the house, from the windows, through the walls, its sickly copper tang filling the surrounding air.

"Stop it!" Aya shouted at Katrin as her eyes misted into two white orbs, her hands clawing at her black hair.

"It was your fault," the founder sneered as the vision changed again.

They stood in the middle of a bedroom dominated by an enormous bed. Gabby's heart thudded in her chest, Aya's fear echoing through their link. The room was full of blood. It was splattered over the walls and pooled on the floor. Gabby knew if she stepped forward, she would see bodies on the bed.

"They killed them! You ordered them to!" Aya cried, tears streaming down her face. "They tore them apart, my brother, you—"

"*You killed my son*," Katrin said, drawing her toward the bed. "Then you killed two more of my children. *It was your fault.*"

"He was a vampire!" she cried, trying to avert her face. "He was a monster!"

"No," Katrin said with a sneer, "you are the monster, Aeriaya. Look at what you've become. Look at what you forced onto your family."

Gabby, who was linked so thoroughly to Aya, gasped in horror as she saw the remains of a man and woman on the bed. They'd been torn to shreds and placed back together by some sick sociopath. Their unearthly silver hair was tinged red by their mingled blood, the pallor of their skin marred by their brutal death, their lifeless hands linked.

Gabby knew these people were Aya's mother and father and her heart shattered.

Aya roared in pain, her hands over her eyes to block the horrible sight. "It's time to die, Katrin. I won't let you get away with this! You've no right to call yourself witch. I'm taking it back!"

Katrin laughed at her, secure in her knowledge that she was the all-powerful witch who cheated life and death.

It was then that Gabby felt Aya draw on her power. She'd asked for her complete trust. The link couldn't be severed now, even if she tried. All she could do was watch as the vision cleared around them, dissolving back into the grey mist of the void.

Katrin's expression faded into one of utter shock. She mustn't have expected her vision to dissolve so easily, but Gabby was too fixated on Aya to notice. She was changing.

Her hair seemed to shimmer with strands of shining silver and her skin danced with tendrils of colour as if she was made of pearl. She was becoming like her parents. Silver hair and translucent skin.

Katrin was visibly afraid as she stood face to face with the creature Aya had become.

"No," Katrin gasped in disbelief. "How did you...? You can't. The Celestines are dead."

"Goodbye, Katrin," Aya declared. "You'll face your

judgment from the true founders. You'll answer for the eradication of my kind and the evil you spread in this world. I am honoured to be the one who delivers you to them."

Gabby shielded her eyes as a pure white light gathered around Aya's form. The power emanating from her was overwhelming and she was vaguely aware that Katrin was begging, her voice becoming more desperate as the light grew. The anchor holding her spirit was being severed, the power Gabby had sensed earlier dissolving.

The drain on her was extreme as she wavered on her feet, desperate to hold on, her trust now completely in Aya.

Through the link, Gabby could see the entire universe—stars, galaxies, planets, and the threads that bound them all together.

Aya really was one of them, just like her grams had said.

And just as suddenly as the vampire had changed, Katrin was gone. The power she'd sensed, the anchor, was completely gone. Whatever Aya had done, it'd worked.

Abruptly, they were back in limbo, just the two of them. All traces of the house and the mist had fallen away.

Aya stood before her, her hair black and skin death pale, but she carried an echo of her past. The creature she'd become was buried again, but not gone.

"Aya," she whispered, clutching the vampire's forearms to steady herself, "I don't understand who you are."

"I'm the last of my kind, Gabby. A horrible, incomplete hybrid," Aya said with a note of sadness that was so deep, it made tears fall from the witch's eyes.

Gabby would probably never fully understand the woman who stood before her, but she'd learned much that made most of what she knew make complete sense. Her peaceful existence had been torn from her in the most brutal way possible, turned by the creature who killed her family and destroyed her home. It was no wonder that she'd sought vengeance on those abusing their gifts.

"I... We all came from you, your family...didn't we?" she asked, not quite believing the people Aya had come from had given the first witches their power.

"This is important, Gabby," Aya said. "You must keep this a secret. It's not for others to know. What I am, what you've come from, this is a secret that must be learned. If you were to tell anyone...something horrible will happen."

"Like what?" she asked, a note of fear in her voice.

"I don't know. I've never known anyone foolish enough to try. That is enough warning in itself."

As the edges of the forest reappeared, she nodded feebly. It was done. They had won, but she'd learned a deadly secret in the process.

Exhausted, Gabby sank to her knees. She couldn't fathom any of it. At least, not right now.

A gust of wind blew her unruly hair into her eyes and she scraped it away from her face, but something black and twisted rushed past. She gasped as she saw a dark shadow flying around them. It had the form of a person, emanating a dark malice that penetrated deep into her bones. She knew that it was trying to get back into reality, back into the forest where her friends were. But her power was spent...she couldn't do anything to help them.

"Stay down," Aya cried, standing over her. "It's not over yet."

•

Aya stood over Gabby and raised her hands to fend off the shadow, but now that she had returned her power to Gabby, they were equal. A stalemate. Regardless, she tried to fend it off, but her fingers slid through its inky blackness. It had to remain in limbo. She kept trying desperately, aware their reality was coming back into focus, the presence of the three vampires waiting for them pressing on her senses.

Abruptly, the wind dropped, and the shadow thing wailed out into the forest. It collided with Zac, disappearing into his body. Gasping in shock, he fell to the ground and began to convulse. Sam dropped to his knees beside him, holding his shoulders down, calling for Aya.

Liz fell to her knees beside them, grasping Zac's shaking hand. "He's dying, his skin is turning grey!"

Aya dropped into a crouch beside them, placing her palm on Zac's forehead. "She's cursed him. Katrin has cursed him."

It was Katrin's last-ditch effort to hurt her, to not die without a fight. She knew Zac was Aya's weak spot, that she would do anything for him.

Anything…

The only thing that would save him from the curse was her blood. Would she really do anything, knowing the consequences for doing so? Her blood…

Yes. Yes, she would.

Leaning close, she brushed Zac's messy hair from his forehead and whispered, "Please let me save you, Zac."

She bit the vein in her wrist open and went to place it at his mouth, but Liz grabbed her arm, wrenching her away.

"What are you doing? Your blood will only make it faster," she cried.

That's right, she'd lied and told Sam her blood was poison to vampires.

Aya pulled her arm free and glared at the vampire who Zac had once loved. "My blood is the only thing that will save him now," she growled. "Do you want him to die?"

Liz edged away, her eyes wide, and shook her head.

Turning back toward Zac, Aya leaned in close and whispered, "Please let me do this for you. *Trust me, Zac.*"

His eyes were wide as he shook his head. She couldn't bear to force him to drink her blood after they'd all been turned against their will. He would have to choose to live on his own.

He was a dark grey now, his body almost desiccated. Time was running out, and fast. All she had left was the truth, and she hoped it was enough.

Her blue eyes were full of sorrow as they pierced his dying muddy green and she whispered, "I love you, Zac. Please let me save you." Stroking his face, she kissed him softly on the lips, her tears dripping down onto his cheeks. "Don't make me go on without you."

When she offered her wrist again, he took it and drank until his convulsions stilled. Colour began creeping back into his skin as her blood purged the curse from his body.

Sam relaxed his grip and looked sidelong at Aya, but she couldn't look at any of them. Such an admission tore her apart and her blood... She was alarmed at what Zac might see once he recovered.

She stood and backed toward the line of trees, her knees shaking. The loss of blood had drained her physically after her transformation, and the emotions flying about the clearing were overwhelming. It was all she could do to keep her focus.

Liz was back at Zac's side, stroking his hair from his eyes, her hand against his forehead and Aya felt a stab of jealousy. His skin was almost back to normal, the curse disappearing as her blood circulated. Zac was out cold, his breathing so slight it was a miracle his heart was still beating.

"Thank you," Sam murmured, looking up at her.

Aya shivered with exhaustion and wavered. "He will sleep awhile," she said detached. "When he wakes, he will be well."

Sam nodded his acknowledgment. His eyes focused on a point behind her, widening in surprise, and she knew that she had made a fatal mistake.

The last thing Aya saw was a hand bursting through her chest, clutching her heart.

Oh no, not again... Not now...

Then there was nothing.

Sam and Liz stared in shock as Aya fell to the ground, her eyes wide and vacant, a gaping hole through her chest.

But she couldn't die, she just couldn't!

Liz grasped Gabby's hand. She was still exhausted from the fight with Katrin, her skin deathly pale.

Sam hissed and stood over Zac's unconscious body, glaring up at Aya's murderer.

He was shorter than Sam by a head, with deathly

pale skin, close-cropped dark brown hair, and a hard face. A long scar from forehead to jaw marred his otherwise good looks. He had blood up to his elbow, a heavy hand still clutching Aya's heart. He threw it to the ground beside him like trash and a sly smile curved his lips. "So, the witch made some friends. *How quaint.*"

Sam growled deep in his throat in warning to the vampire who stood before them. "And who the hell are you?"

The man bared his fangs, eyes turning black. "I am Arturius. *I was her maker.*"

Arturius stood inside the tree line watching the group of vampires.

Their witch was calling forth the void where Katrin's soul dwelt.

He stood and watched the events unfold, his presence hidden by magic. As long as he didn't move from the tree line, he would be undetected and the final piece of their plan would come to fruition.

Katrin wanted Aeriaya dead and Arturius would deliver the final blow. He was here at her request, but he would have done it anyway. It was his mistake to fix, after all.

Aeriaya was just as he remembered. It'd been hundreds of years since he had laid eyes on her and he could scarcely remember the circumstances, but he would never forget that day he'd sat with her in that dungeon. His lips on hers, her soft translucent skin under his hard, calloused hands. He would never forget the moment he held her head in his hands and snapped her delicate neck.

After so much time, it was hard to separate the lies from the truths. There was never any hope for him. As soon as he set foot in Britannia, it had disappeared forever.

As Aeriaya vanished into the void with the witch, he remembered the blood between his fingers and grimaced. He had ripped her brother to pieces at Katrin's command. He had no choice. That's when he realised that he could never escape. Katrin had trapped them all, lured with the promise of power.

It wasn't long before he felt a pull at the edges of his mind. He felt disoriented for a moment, then the clarity hit him like a ton of bricks. Gasping, he clutched his head. For the first time in two thousand years, he felt free. Aeriaya had done it, as he knew she would. Even he knew that this time was different.

As the void slipped away, Arturius watched as Katrin's curse wailed out into the night and collided with the man who'd killed Alistair. Now he would wait and see what Aeriaya would do.

Sneering as she knelt over the vampire whispering how much she loved him, he rolled his eyes as she gave him her blood. *Stupid woman.* He'd thought better of her. Vampirism had turned her into something cold and heartless, so how could she justify that this was the right thing to do? Even if she loved him, it would give everything away.

Aeriaya stumbled back toward the tree line where he stood hidden. He didn't have to do it anymore. Katrin was gone and the compulsion had evaporated along with her. But he would never forget his dead brothers and his poor, dear sister. Men he had known in life and death, brothers in both.

He hadn't loved her for a long time.

So he'd do it anyway.

For himself more than them.

He didn't love her anymore.

He didn't.

As Arturius stepped out into the clearing, he caught the gaze of the younger male vampire, whose eyes widened in surprise.

He didn't hesitate.

Plunging his hand into Aeriaya's chest from behind, his hand grasped her heart and pushed it straight through into the humid night air. She would see her death, just as his brothers had.

He wrenched his hand away and let her fall, her blood dripping from his fingers onto the ground. It stained his arm up to the elbow, her cold heart still clutched in his palm.

"So, the witch made some friends. *How quaint.*" He threw her heart to the ground, a sly smile on his lips.

The vampire growled deep in his throat, standing over his fallen friend. "And who the hell are you?"

Arturius bared his fangs, feeling his eyes swirl into darkness. "I am Arturius. *I was her maker.*"

A Sneak Peek...

Lake District, United Kingdom
Autumn, 43AD

Aeriaya was the last daughter of the stars to walk the Earth.

The last of the race known as the Celestines. She was twenty-five of what the humans called years, and she alone held the weight of an impossible responsibility on her shoulders. She was to be the last caretaker of the Earth.

Sunlight filtered through the dense canopy of the forest, casting its dappled fingers through the deep green grass below. It was an abnormally warm day. The earth was still damp from the morning mist, thousands of tiny dewdrops clinging to moss-covered trees.

Aeriaya wandered through the wood, her long pale fingers playing through the light, savouring the small points of warmth. Coming to a clearing, she smiled, her long silver hair blowing across her face in the sudden breeze. The sun had coaxed the little field to come alive with small, white flowers. Pulling her hair back into place, she walked out into the sunlight, gathering as many of the blossoms as she could carry. She knew her mother would love them.

Glimpsing a figure approaching, she shook her head. She wasn't meant to be out walking today, but she needed the peace of the forest...if only for an hour or two.

Smiling, she turned, expecting to see her brother emerge from the forest. He had a habit of following her and playing tricks when she least expected it. But it wasn't him.

She gasped as she caught sight of a menacing figure lingering in the tree line, their form shadowed by the surrounding forest. Dropping the flowers in surprise, she took a hesitant step back. He was covered head to foot in heavy black linen and leather clothing, not an inch of skin showing. A large hood hung low over his eyes, shielding his face from the sunlight.

Aeriaya took a few steps back, fear creeping into her heart, knowing she wouldn't be able to escape even if she ran.

A satisfied smirk pulled at the man's lips as he watched her back away.

How did he get here? He shouldn't have been able to find the clearing, let alone get into the forest. She should've sensed his approach, but even now it was as if she were alone. He was not one of them, nor was he human. He was...dead?

Aeriaya stood frozen in fear, unable to tear her gaze away from him. Something was terribly wrong.

Before she could react, the man lunged forwards, faster than she thought possible, and grasped her around the waist, flinging her over his shoulder. Looking within herself, she sought the coil of power that was the centre of her being. Her parents always taught her to use it for good—that to kill and destroy was wrong—but surely this time was different.

She let her power wash over her, but nothing happened. It sputtered and died, leaving her empty.

"No!" she cried, beating her fists against the man's shoulder. *It couldn't be.* "No!"

Letting out a blood-curdling scream, she beat her fists harder against his back, trying to free herself, but his grip was like iron. He was so strong, her fists and raking fingernails had no effect on him. Even when she tried to bite and kick, he continued to run.

The forest grew dark as he took her farther away from her home, the air colder and more desolate. She pleaded with the man to let her go, but he wouldn't respond, instead he ran faster, never seeming to tire.

She didn't know how much time had passed, but before long, she was dropped like a stone onto a hard floor. Taking heaving gulps, she looked around, her eyes searching for a glimmer of hope, but she found none.

She was in a dark stone room, surrounded by four men and one woman, and she couldn't sense their presence, either. They were dead, just like the man who'd taken her.

Panic overtook her and she scrambled backwards, crashing into something hard. Looking up, she gasped as she realised she'd collided with the man's legs. Jerking away in horror, a satisfied smirk pulled at his lips as he laughed down at her.

There was a scraping sound as a heavy wooden door opened and a woman walked into the room. It closed behind her with a dull thud that echoed off the walls.

Looking around for the first time, Aeriaya realised that the stone room wasn't just any room. Earth was all around her...she could feel it through the walls. She was in a dungeon.

The woman paused just inside the doorway for a moment, a look of triumph plastered on her face. She was tall and slim, with fiery auburn hair that fell in waves over her shoulders. Aeriaya knew she wasn't like the others as her heart beat steady in her chest.

Aeriaya regarded her warily as the woman walked forwards. This woman was very much alive and very much a witch. This was all so very wrong. Just by looking at her, Aeriaya could tell the witch had created the dead creatures who stood around her.

"Well done, Regulus." The woman caressed the man's face with a delicate hand. The man who had taken her from the forest. "*Very well done.*"

"Who are you?" Aeriaya's musical voice sounded

misplaced in their dark surroundings. "What do you want?"

"Oh, forgive me," the woman exclaimed. "Let me introduce you to my family. Regulus you have already met on such intimate terms. This is my lovely daughter, Octavia. And my sons, Marcus, Titus, Caius, and Arturius. And I...? I am Katrin."

She knew that name. She was one of the Five. The power she'd been granted had been corrupted.

"What have you done?" Aeriaya whispered, still cowering on the floor.

Katrin laughed. "They're dead. They're vampires. The creatures of myth brought alive by my will. Bound to the night, slaves to blood." She gestured to the six vampires, who moved forwards.

One of the men grabbed her roughly around the waist and hauled her up, holding her lithe form in place. One by one, the vampires came forwards and dragged her head to the side, sinking their fangs into the soft skin of her neck. They took her blood without a care for her.

She tried to fight at first, but each burning tear into her flesh made her limbs heavier.

Why were they doing this to her? She'd never done anything to hurt anyone. Was she to die?

Once they'd all drank, they let her go, and the cell door slammed closed. Alone in the darkness, she sunk to the floor and sobbed, her tears and blood dripping onto the hard, dirt floor.

Aeriaya didn't know how long she was in the cell before someone came. Darkness and fear were her only companions until she heard footsteps approaching.

Scrambling back as far as she could, she curled herself into a ball against the wall. Her neck stung and dried blood flaked off her pale skin and stained her dress.

As the door scraped open, she held her hand over her eyes at the sudden light that filled the cell. One of the vampires stood just inside, holding a flaming torch which he put into the holder on the wall.

She watched him with frightened eyes. There would be no choice for her in what happened next. Her power was gone. Whatever Katrin had done, she had given the means to Regulus to take it away. She was completely at their mercy.

The vampire crouched down, gazing at her, his expression almost sad. She knew he was one of the human people who called themselves Romans. He had that look about him—broad shoulders, dark curly hair cropped close to the scalp, deep-set brown eyes. A long, white, puckered scar began above his right eye and ended below his cheekbone, marring his face. Ugly.

"Are you ill?" His rough voice was a surprise, just as

much as his concern was. When she didn't answer he said, "I'm sorry. I don't want to hurt you."

"But you did," she whispered, tears spilling down her face.

"I'm sorry..." He frowned. "But you must understand. I cannot go against the others so openly."

She was confused. Was he really sorry? Would he try to help her? She had to escape this place. Her family had to be warned about the witch and what she'd created. She hadn't been granted this gift to use it in such a way.

"I cannot be here," she said.

The vampire frowned and looked at his hands. Reaching out towards her, he went to grasp her hand that clutched around her knees, but she jerked back, afraid of his touch.

"What is your name?" he asked, letting his hand fall away. She didn't answer, staring at him with unearthly blue eyes. He looked at her a moment, unsure of how to proceed. Finally, he said, "I am Arturius. I must go before I am missed, but I will return."

Standing, he regarded her once more before turning and leaving, the door closing and the heavy bolt driving home with a thud. He left the torch behind, the smoke spiralling upwards towards a grate in the ceiling high above. One small kindness so she didn't have to endure the darkness.

Arturius came to see her many times over the coming weeks. He brought food he'd stolen, but he'd eat nothing, content to watch her sate her hunger.

In all that time, she heard nothing of the outside world. Nothing of her family or why she'd been taken. She was at the mercy of the witch and her Roman vampires.

They came to visit her as well, but it was only to take more of her blood. For what reason, she didn't know.

The young Roman, Arturius, told her much about his life before he came to Briton. He told her stories about his family back in Rome, how he became a soldier in the Legion and how he'd come to be here on the other side of the ocean. The ocean, he said, was as beautiful as it was deadly. Blue, sparkling water as far as the eye could see, its surface choppy with waves, the bow of their great ship dipping in and out as they travelled, giant ocean fish racing them and leaping from the water.

He was a commander before he met Katrin. He told men what to do. He was a fearsome leader, respected and admired. He'd fought many battles defending Rome, the realm of goodness and light, learning and science. The day that Katrin had made them into vampires was the day he realised that the world he knew was a lie. There were no gods. No god would do this to him, he said. Not even all the gods in the underworld would sink that low.

And Aeriaya felt sorry for him. Katrin had betrayed them too, had she not? She'd coerced them into servitude, linking them to her through what Arturius called magic. While all of them had come willingly, they had been tricked into their own prison. Their free will was taken. If Katrin willed it, they had to see it through.

"That," he said, "is why I cannot free you. I want to, so badly. But I cannot." He sat beside her, his back resting against the wall, his arm touching hers. Taking her delicate hand in his, he ran a thumb across her knuckles.

"I would do anything for you," he whispered, letting his lips brush against her cheek.

She shivered and glanced away, suddenly shy where she had become so comfortable with him. Arturius had shared so much of himself with her and she had told him nothing, yet he still gave.

He traced a finger along her jaw, turning her face back towards him. His brown eyes searched hers for a moment before he leaned forward, pressing his lips against hers. She drew a sharp breath as he pulled her close, a powerful hand caressing her waist. Taking the opportunity, Arturius slid his tongue into her mouth. It was a sensation she'd never felt before. She felt herself kissing him back, sliding her tongue against his, feeling him.

Finally, he pulled away, burying his face into the crook of her neck. She jerked back slightly as his lips brushed her torn skin, but he didn't bite down as she thought he would. Instead, he let out a contented sigh.

"She wants to know the secret to your power," he murmured in her ear, kissing the corner of her jaw. "The power of your kind."

No, she could never tell him any of her family's secrets. It didn't work that way; she couldn't tell. Something horrible would happen, something that she didn't understand, but something horrible, nonetheless.

"All you need to do is tell Katrin what she wants to know, then you can go home." Arturius sat on the dirt floor and pulled her against his chest, stroking her silver hair. "I will take you myself so you are safe."

She sobbed into his shirt, shaking her head. Why couldn't they understand? She couldn't. Even if she wanted to, even if it meant her own life.

"Please," he pleaded. "They couldn't learn anything from your blood."

She was confused. Her blood? What did that have to do with anything? The Romans were just tormenting her, drinking her blood to sate themselves. Driving her to give up what she could not.

"Your blood gives us dreams," Arturius whispered as he measured her expression. "They thought to learn what they wanted that way. They hoped... That way, you wouldn't have a choice."

When she didn't speak, he sighed, resting his forehead against hers. "I can't stop her," he said. "She offered your release to your family in exchange for the same information, but they denied her."

Aeriaya froze. Her family had betrayed her? Her parents were strong, they could tell Katrin what she wanted to know. Why hadn't they come to free her, despite the witch's offer? There were too few of them left to leave her to die. Why hadn't they sent someone to rescue her?

"Please, you must, or I don't know what she'll do to you." Arturius grasped her hands in his almost desperately. "Please, my love."

She stiffened in his grasp. *Love?* What did she know of love?

"I cannot," she whispered. "Even if I wanted to betray them, I couldn't. It's impossible."

"What do you mean?" he asked.

"I am bound. I cannot," she stated.

Arturius frowned, trying to mask the anger that'd begun to creep into his features. If they couldn't get the information they needed from her, then what was her fate? Death?

She began to panic, her heart thudding in her chest. Arturius reached out to calm her.

"Come, my love," he beckoned. Falling against him, she gasped as he forced his wrist to her mouth. She gagged at the coppery taste of his blood, but there was so much of it she was forced to swallow several times.

"There, there," he crooned, stroking her silver hair with his other hand. "This will only hurt a moment, my love."

Her eyes widened with panic as he took her head in his large paw-like hands, blood dripping from her chin. Suddenly, he twisted and the last sound she heard was the snap as he broke her neck.

The Return is OUT NOW!

OTHER BOOKS IN

THE WITCH HUNTER SAGA

series is complete!

Enter a world full of supernatural creatures, ancient curses and love that stretches over hundreds and thousands of years. You've never seen vampires and witches like this before...

The Witch Hunter #1

The Return #2

The Shadow's Son #3

The Awakening #4

Young Blood #4.5

The Unhallowed #5

The Keeping Place #6

ABOUT NICOLE

Nicole R. Taylor is an Australian Urban Fantasy author.

She lives in the western suburbs of Melbourne dreaming up nail biting stories featuring sassy witches, duplicitous vampires, hunky shapeshifters, and devious monsters.

She likes chocolate, cat memes, and video games.

When she's not writing, she likes to think of what she's writing next.

Follow Nicole Online:

Website: nicolertaylorwrites.com
Facebook: facebook.com/nrtaylorwrites
Newsletter: nicolertaylorwrites.com/newsletter

Want more novels just like this one? Check out Nicole's other series:

AUSTRALIAN SUPERNATURAL - In the harsh and unforgiving Australian Outback lies the tiny opal mining town of Solace. A witch runs the general store, a vampire cuts and polishes opal, the mechanic is a werewolf, a fae is the local layabout, and an elemental works the mine. But what's hidden underneath the baked earth is the most dangerous thing of all.

THE ARONDIGHT CODEX - An ancient war with demons. A lost sword with the power to end it all. And a woman with purple hair is the world's only hope.

THE CAMELOT ARCHIVE - Set in the same alternate Arthurian world seen in **The Arondight Codex...** Deadly secrets. Murder and revenge. The end of the world is nye and Camelot is the last bastion of hope.

THE WITCH HUNTER SAGA - Vampires and witches collide in this thrilling Urban Fantasy adventure. You've never met vampires quite like these...

THE CRESCENT WITCH CHRONICLES - Witches, shapeshifters, and ancient myth collide in this colourful Irish flavoured series! Come on an adventure fraught with danger and forbidden romance... and the ultimate battle to save magic before it's gone forever.

THE DARKLAND DRUIDS - A woman with no living relatives travels from Australia to the other side of the world to find out the truth of who she is...only to land in the middle of a prophecy of destruction. Druids, witches, fae, and shapeshifters abound in this thrilling magical adventure!

Find out more at: NicoleRTaylorWrites.com

See what titles are FREE at: Nicole's Free Reads